## Daniel Margeson

Jackie,

I appreciate the kindness
you bring to the office.
I hope you enjoy this
book!

Dn M

# The Life of Death

A Novel

Daniel Margeson

ISBN-13: 978-0692991749

# Prologue

*Summer, 1997*

The ache Lucas Braun felt throughout his body was getting worse. Though he hadn't moved in several hours, his legs burned as if he'd spent the day walking. No matter how he twisted or turned, he could not stretch enough to rid himself of the knot in his lower back. To make matters worse, the batteries for Lucas's portable compact disc player died three hours earlier.

He was a prisoner, trapped in the back seat of the family sedan with nothing but his mind to entertain him. His father and mother, sitting in the two front seats, were navigating through the dark in the midst of a thunderstorm. The rain pounding on the front windshield, which was startling twenty minutes earlier, was now nothing more than background noise to Lucas.

He needed something to ease his mind of boredom. Fourteen hours in the car in a single day was a lot to ask of someone, and Lucas wasn't prepared. He only had three states worth of material to occupy his mind. In Illinois, he thought of his pending freshman year of high school, which was due to begin in just a few weeks. The worn map of the school rested beside him. Lucas had memorized his routes weeks earlier and reviewed them once more during the trip. Finding his classes wouldn't be the problem. But there was one thing the map wouldn't help him find, friends.

Lucas could be described as a forgettable. The other kids didn't gravitate towards him, and he was far too shy to initiate anything himself. The loneliness was harsh for Lucas, but he was grateful to be off the radar of the class bullies. Some kids had it much worse than he did, or so that's what he told himself. But even the kids who were picked on had friends.

Once the family sedan crossed the Iowa border, Lucas's thoughts shifted from making friends to getting a girlfriend, an even more improbable daydream. He hoped a girl would miraculously approach him and all his five-foot-one-inch frame had to offer. If anyone were to do it, it would be Rachel. She was friendly, always offering a smile when they crossed paths in the hallways. But she was already dating a sophomore who was on the football team. Lucas doubted she would break up with an older football player to pursue a relationship with him.

Then came Nebraska. Lucas thought about what he would do with his life. He would be starting high school in just a matter of weeks. After that, he would be off to figure out his place in the world. His father was a manager at the local supermarket, and his mother was a nurse. Neither occupation appealed to him. He thought maybe he'd eventually go into business, but he wasn't exactly sure what it meant to go into business. What do people in business do all day? Lucas recalled seeing movies of men and women dressed in suits and sitting in conference rooms for meetings. Why does it seem like they have so many meetings? What could they be meeting about every day? The idea of having that much to talk about in business intimidated Lucas, but he was fond of thinking of inclusion. It would be difficult to be forgotten by the people you sit with in meetings each day.

With school, girls, and the future covered, Lucas was left in Colorado with a blank mind. He'd hoped they'd be stopping soon to rest for the night. He'd be able to pick up some batteries for his compact disc player and regather his thoughts for the rest of Colorado, then Utah, and finally, Arizona. It was his family's first vacation. His mother and father both worked long and irregular hours, making it difficult to organize time off together. When they did find time off together, they were often too tired to consider traveling across the country. Lucas overheard his mother and father conversing in the kitchen one evening when they thought he was working on homework in his room. "Frank, we've got to take a family vacation. Lucas is our only child, and he's starting high school this year. We'll be lucky if he even wants to be around us during his remaining teenage years and after those are up, he'll be in college and out of the house," his mother said.

Though Frank was tired and wanted nothing more than to spend his free time at home with his family, he agreed with Mary. The two had been so busy working and raising Lucas that they let the years get away. It seemed like it was just yesterday when they were bringing their newborn home from the hospital, and now they were already talking about him moving out of the house.

It saddened Lucas to think his parents were concerned about him not wanting to be around them during his adolescence. He loved them and was grateful for everything they sacrificed for him. If it weren't for them, he would have no one in his life to eat pizza with, watch movies with on Friday nights, or talk to about video games, though he sensed they weren't as enthused about video gaming as he was.

Lucas wanted to tell them that they didn't have to take the vacation for him. He would be perfectly happy staying at home with them. But he also yearned to explore the world, and visiting the Grand Canyon was on his bucket list. There was so much history in those rocks, some nearly seventy million years old. According to his science book, seventy million years ago was about the time of a mass extinction which marked the end of Cretaceous period.

*What would life be like today if it weren't for an asteroid causing mass extinction to life as the world knew it all of those years ago? Would I even be here today if it weren't for that asteroid? Was the tragedy of that era the miracle of my era?*

The sound of the rain on the windshield of the family sedan was getting louder. Lucas sensed the tension in his parents as they journeyed through the storm. His mom had a map in her lap as she leaned forward, looking for a road sign indicating lodging was near-by. His father, shoulders up and neck stretched forward to bring his eyes closer to the windshield, drove anxiously with a grip on the steering wheel that was tighter than the hold of an alligator's jaw on its prey. There were three things about driving which gave Frank Braun anxiety: being in unfamiliar surroundings, driving at night, and driving in the rain. He was maneuvering through all three nightmares on this night in a search for a hotel.

The tension Lucas sensed in his parents made him more aware of his surroundings. He too was now peering through the window, hoping to find a hotel. He tried to look through his passenger window, but it was too dark. The storm knocked out the electricity in the area, and street lights which should have been lighting the highway were all off.

He positioned himself in the middle of the car to look between his parent's shoulders and through the front windshield, hoping the light from the headlights would be enough for him to find an indication of a hotel. It seemed as if the wind was blowing the rain straight at them, making it nearly impossible to see. Lucas was impressed his father was able to see enough to keep the car on the road.

Lucas looked harder, squinting his eyes to help him concentrate on seeing clearly.

*What was that?*

It was then that he heard the horrifying shriek let out by his mother. "Frank watch out!" Mary said, reaching both hands out to brace against the front of the car.

Lucas looked up, struggling to see through the rain, and sensed a change of direction when his right shoulder slammed into the door with the car now spinning in circles, completely out of control from Frank's instinctive sharp turn to the left. With the adrenaline rushing through Lucas's body, he didn't feel the throb he should have felt in his head from the blow it took when it hit the top of the car as it flipped end over end off of the road and down a ravine. But the car gained speed as it tumbled down the ravine, and after the third blow to Lucas's head, everything went black.

# Chapter 1

*Summer, 2017*

The Meadows, a newly developed subdivision located thirty miles southwest of Chicago, was a peaceful neighborhood where every lawn was green, every flower bed was in bloom, and the laughs and shouts of children running from house to house filled the air. After a day working as a pharmaceutical sales representative for Cure-iosity Pharmaceuticals, Lucas walked through the subdivision on a crisp summer evening. With each house Lucas passed, he couldn't help but fantasize about what it would be like to be one of the families living in these homes. Not so much that he envied the style of the newly constructed 3,500 square foot homes, as his tastes were more traditional and much smaller. It was the idea of what it would be like to be inside those walls which made him envious. The idea of coming home to a family every night and being amongst people who loved him, people who he didn't have to hold anything back from.

Years earlier, his realtor took him through a half of a dozen neighborhoods similar to this one during Lucas's search for a new home.

"I know the houses may seem big, but a man like you likely won't be on the market for much longer, just like these houses," she encouraged.

Lucas was of average height with an athletic build and had thick brown hair, which complemented his dark brown eyes. The boy who went unnoticed during his school years turned into the man everyone noticed when he walked into a room. If his female coworkers were not trying to seduce him themselves, they were attempting to set him up with their friends.

In spite of this and in spite of his yearning to find a wife and settle down, Lucas found himself empty-handed when it came to love. He had an important job to do which couldn't be compromised, and it was that job that brought him to the Meadows this evening.

A breeze softly grazed Lucas's skin as he looked up to see he had arrived at his destination, 2419 Ambassadors Lane. Instinctively, he reached into the front pocket of his denim jeans to make sure he still had the serum. He knew he had it, but a nervous mind can enforce doubt amongst the most-sure of people. The solid wood door had a dark brown stain applied to it and featured an arched stained-glass window.

He raised his fist and nervously pounded on the door, but there was barely a thud as the solid oak soaked in the sound waves like a sponge. Lucas waited anxiously with each passing second.

*Was my knock loud enough? Is it too soon to try the doorbell, instead?*

Just as Lucas reached for the doorbell, the large door opened, slowly. The man behind the door peaked his head around, looking as if he was unsure if someone would actually be standing at his doorstep. With a confused look, the man said, "Hello?", emphasizing the end of the word to make the statement sound like a question.

"Hi," Lucas began anxiously, "I'm Lucas Braun. I was taking a tour of the neighborhood and immediately fell in love with it. When I came to your place, I noticed the Chicago Cubs flag hanging from your porch. This is going to sound odd, but I'm wondering if I could trade you my tickets for the game this Saturday in exchange for fifteen minutes of your time to learn more about the neighborhood?"

The man paused for a moment, appearing to be contemplating if the stranger at his doorstep could be trusted. From a quick observation, Lucas looked a lot like the man; thin, average height, and dressed in dark denim jeans and a t-shirt. The only difference was the man had a touch of gray creeping into his hair color and was about ten to fifteen years his senior.

His guard fell as he replied, "You know, I actually have the game on the T.V. right now. It's in the first inning. Want to come in and have a drink?"

Lucas nodded as he stepped into the entrance. Early in life, he learned people are much more likely to trust people who look and act similar to themselves. Showing interest in the area, being a Cubs fan, wearing the blue jeans and t-shirt uniform, Lucas couldn't have played the part more perfectly.

"I'm Tom Dempsy," said the man as he reached out to shake Lucas's hand.

"Lucas Braun," he replied as he shook Tom's hand, being sure not to grip harder than Tom in an effort to make himself appear less threatening.

"The wife and girls are out tonight, shopping for back to school clothes. I used to go with them. But as the girls got older, they expressed a desire for these nights to be nights only for the girls. That way they can talk about boys and the latest fashion without fear of me overhearing anything they don't want me to be hearing."

"Ahh and now you're left to take in an evening of baseball," Lucas said as he followed Tom into the living room.

"Precisely," Tom agreed, turning to smile at Lucas.

"It's an exciting year," Tom continued, "I think we've got a good shot at winning it all this season. So, tell me a little about yourself, Lucas. Family? Work?"

Tom handed Lucas a beer before taking a seat in the recliner. Lucas took the beer and his position on the loveseat.

"I'm currently single, still searching for Mrs. Braun, and I work as a sales rep for Cure-iosity Pharmaceuticals. Each morning I bike to the train station and board a train for downtown Chicago. I spend my days attempting to explain to physicians why our drugs are more effective and safer than the competition's."

Tom took a drink of his beer and replied, "My brother-in-law carries the bag too. He deals more with headache medication, though. Between you and me, I'm not sure if it works."

Lucas smiled and took a sip of his beer. It was an IPA made by a local brewer. Lucas didn't care for IPAs, but this brewer made a better beer than most. As he took a moment to take in his surroundings, one thing became apparent, the place was spotless. From what he could tell, everything was in its place, and nothing was out of its place. A perfect balance.

*Unfortunately for Tom and his family, one critical piece of this home will be out of place when I leave here tonight.*

Wanting to keep the encounter as peaceful as possible, Lucas asked, "Tom, were you expecting company? There isn't a speck of dust to be found in your house."

Tom smiled and replied, "No, not tonight. A cleaning service comes in once every two weeks to tidy up. It looks to me like they were just here today." He paused and looked at his half empty beer before rising from his chair. "I'm only halfway through my second beer, and I've broken my seal. I'm going to hit the restroom. I'll give you my take on the Meadows when I get back, and hopefully, we will see the Cubs score some runs."

Tom walked down the hall and into the room on the right to use the restroom, providing a perfect opportunity for Lucas to take action. He reached into his pocket and pulled out the serum. On the bottle in tiny print read, *For immediate impact inject or consume the entire contents of the bottle. For future impact consume less. Diagnosis – Stroke.*

*Simple enough, he thought.*

Lucas had used this formula before and had experimented with the doses over the years. He knew half of a bottle would need six hours to take effect, giving Tom enough time to see his family one last time. Although he tried not to think too much about the people on his list, Lucas couldn't help but feel sad in thinking about the pain which would soon be inflicted on Tom's family. That was the worst part, thinking about the families left behind. It was bad enough he had to take someone, often before they were ready. But the pain was quick for them. For the families though, the pain might never go away. He hated that Tom's name had shown up on his list, and he hated it was his responsibility to act upon the list. But there was nothing Lucas could do to stop it or fix it. Tom's name was on the list, and he had to go.

The sound of water running through pipes broke Lucas's train of thought. It was the toilet flushing. It will only be a few seconds before Tom comes out of the bathroom. He bolted from his seat as his opportunity for a peaceful execution was quickly slipping through his fingers.

*I hope he's a thorough hand washer.*

He opened the cap of the serum bottle and swiftly made his way towards the end table where Tom's IPA rested. It was then when he heard doorknob down the hall begin to turn.

*Shit. Tom doesn't wash his hands.*

Lucas quickly turned the serum bottle upside down and accidentally poured three-fourths of the serum into the beer bottle.

Tom stepped out of the bathroom and saw Lucas standing near the end table.

"You have a lovely family," Lucas said when he saw the surprise in Tom's eyes. He grabbed a small picture of Tom and his family which featured them standing in front of a small lake. Lucas slid the serum bottle back into his left pocket and out of Tom's sight before Tom got closer.

"I am very fortunate," replied Tom as returned to his chair to take a seat. Lucas set the picture on the end table and returned his spot on the loveseat.

"I met Janice back in college. She was a biology major at the time, and I had a class with her my first semester. She was so beautiful and smart. Every guy in the class was in awe of her, but I don't even think she noticed. She has always underestimated how beautiful she is and the effect she has on men.

Janice never missed a class. I know this because I never missed that class either. Before each class, I thought maybe this class would be the one where we bump into each other, and she smiles at me while I say some lame joke, initiating our magical journey together. When she entered the room, it seemed as if the world would just pause for a moment until she got to her seat."

Tom's eyes were glowing as he looked towards the wall, reflecting on the memories he had of when he first met his wife. Although Lucas was sad for Tom, knowing he wouldn't be making future memories with his wife, he felt a sense of joy in knowing Tom did at least have the opportunity to leave a memorable impression on loved ones.

"The first semester passed, and I never spoke to her. I never asked if she had a boyfriend or if she wanted to grab a smoothie. I thought I blew it. Then in the spring semester, fortune was in my favor. I was sitting in the middle row of a half-empty classroom as students made their way into Dr. Barne's pre-calc class. I wasn't ever much of a math person, but I had to check off the prerequisite as part of my curriculum before continuing towards my psychology degree. As I was reaching into my backpack to retrieve my notepad and pencil, Janice came into the classroom and took the seat right next to me. Before I could speak, she said, Look. I don't want to put up with another semester of playing shy. After class, we are going to grab a coffee. Then you are going to walk me to my next class and ask me for my number. Later this evening you are going to call and ask to take me to dinner and a movie this Friday night."

Lucas looked back at Tom in admiration He wished he could have a story like that, a love story. Though Tom was only moments from his death, Lucas was envious of him.

"Aww come on! You call that a pitch? I could have thrown that!" Tom screamed at the television as he watched the Cubs starting pitcher give up a grand slam to the opposing team. He looked at Lucas and shrugged his shoulders. "Well, bottoms up."

Tom drank the rest of his beer as Lucas watched each gulp empty the liquid into his throat. His job here was finished. Lucas poured three-fourths of the serum into the bottle, giving Tom about five more minutes before he would encounter a life-ending stroke.

"So, Lucas. What can I tell you about the neighborhood?" Tom continued, utterly oblivious to what just transpired.

Lucas thought for a moment. He couldn't think of a witty lie or story to tell about why he wanted to move into the Meadows, and as he looked at Tom's warm and welcoming green eyes, he realized he didn't care to lie to this man any longer.

"Before we get to that, can I ask you a question?"

Tom replied, with a hint of anticipation, "Sure."

Lucas briefly paused, looking at the floor as he came up with the words. But there were no words. There wasn't an easy way to put it. He just wanted it out there, and finally, he did just that by asking, "Do you believe in the Grim Reaper?"

The look of curiosity and anticipation on Tom's face quickly changed to confusion and concern as he replied, "Honestly I've never thought much about the matter." His initial warm and inviting tone had now turned cold and direct.

Lucas looked back at Tom and saw confusion in his eyes. He considered the opportunity before him, the opportunity to be completely honest with another human being for the next five minutes. Afterward, Tom would be gone, and Lucas would be back to his life full of secrets.

"For most of my life, I have never been able to truly be honest with people. I want to be closer to people, but I spend most of my time avoiding becoming too close to anyone. My lifestyle doesn't allow it. I have frequent absences which I cannot explain to people. Nights like tonight, for example."

Lucas saw that his last words appeared to have struck a nerve with Tom and could imagine how Tom must feel now after inviting him inside. But Lucas could see that Tom was very skilled in hiding his emotions and watched as Tom pulled his cell phone out of his pocket and looked at it with concern before saying, "You know Lucas, I think we might have to do this another time. I just received an email from one of my patients, and there is a matter which requires my attention."

Lucas didn't budge, showing no emotion on his face as he thought back to his vacation twenty years earlier, the one which eventually led to him being here, in Tom's living room.

Lucas sensed his silence and persistent eye contact was making Tom uncomfortable.

*I better get on with my story if I want someone alive to listen.*

"When I was young I dreamed I could be you. Not you in particular, but someone like you. I would graduate college, meet the love of my life, have a family, teach my children how to throw a baseball, and one day have grandchildren to spoil. Unfortunately, things didn't work out as planned," Lucas said with a hard, cold face.

Tom rose from his chair. His voice cracked as he said, "I'm sorry, but I'm not sure where you are going with your story. I wish I had more time, but I need to take care of this patient."

Lucas was in no hurry to return to his empty home, pausing before slowly saying, "I can assure you that I have no intention of staying much longer. There is nothing more I need from here."

"Nothing more?" Tom replied, now sounding more agitated. "What did you take when I was in the restroom? Money? Jewelry? I don't care. Just leave."

"I didn't take anything. I just initiated the process. Whether or not I leave or stay, it doesn't matter. Just like it doesn't matter whether or not I want this to happen. I like you. You seem like a genuinely nice man, and I wish your name didn't come up. I wish you didn't have to meet me for a very long time. Unfortunately, I don't have control over when people meet me. "

"Don't have control over when people meet you?" Tom repeated back to Lucas.

Lucas could see he was confusing Tom. "Earlier I asked you if you believe in the Grim Reaper. Whether or not you believe is irrelevant. It would be easier to explain if you did, but people often don't believe things which are right in front of their eyes."

"Are you suggesting that you are the Grim Reaper? The myth who walks around in a cloak and carries a scythe?" Tom asked. He remained standing and tense, appearing ready to attack in the event Lucas made a sudden movement.

Lucas let out a sigh as he nodded to answer Tom's question. "For the point of being quick, that is what I am saying. I am here tonight because your name came up on my list. It is time for you to move on. In about 1 minute you feel a sharp pain in your head, and it will bring you to the floor. You have kissed your wife goodnight for the last time. You have played with your children for the last time. You have eaten your last meal and watched your last Cubs game. When your family returns home, they will find you laying on the floor, dead. When the autopsy report comes in, your family will be informed that you suffered a stroke. I'm sorry. The timing of these things is always bad. I wish there were something I could do."

Tom gave Lucas an incredulous look and said, "That's it. I'm calling the police. We are done here."

As Tom began to dial the number for the police, Lucas rose from his seat and walked towards the trash can.

"Hey! Where are you going? Sit back do……"

Before Tom could finish his sentence, he winced in pain, raising his free hand towards his head to apply pressure. The phone fell from his hand to the floor, followed by Tom a few seconds later. Lucas tossed his beer bottle in the trash and walked towards the door. Before leaving, he pulled a piece of paper with a blood red embroidery from his pocket and looked through a list of names it displayed. He found the name Tom Dempsy and crossed it off.

# Chapter 2

Lucas gave the waiting room at the local hospital a quick scan, observing the characteristics of the three patients who were waiting to be seen. One, a middle-aged man in slacks and a button-up shirt, was scanning his phone, likely checking email from work.

Sitting a few seats to the left of the man was an elderly woman, waiting patiently in her chair with her hands clutched tightly to the purse resting on her lap. Lucas took a moment to admire her. He visited over thirty doctor offices a week, and it was rare when he saw a person just sit and wait for a long period of time without turning to their smartphone.

The third person in the waiting room was a younger lady, likely in her early twenties, who appeared to have caught a bad cold. She was curled in a ball in her chair as she sniffled with a handful of tissues in one hand and a bottle of water in the other.

Lucas opted to veer as far as he could from the contagious looking patient as he approached the receptionist.

"Good Morning Rebecca!" Lucas said as he greeted her a smile.

Rebecca had been the receptionist in the primary care group for the past four years. She was approaching forty years old, divorced, and had two children. Jonathan, her oldest, was fifteen and had been the main source of Rebecca's anxiety over the last couple of years. Samuel, her youngest, was eight years old and a straight-A student.

Lucas happened to be working a sales call at the office on Rebecca's first day. She was given little training and was struggling to learn the computer system. She also learned there was a department meeting beginning at noon for which she was supposed to have lunch ready. It was 11:35 in the morning when Lucas walked in, and he could tell she was ready to bolt.

"Good morning, ma'am. First day?"

Rebecca was so frazzled that she didn't even look up to see who it was. She didn't care. She just needed someone to talk to.

"Yes. I can't get the scheduler to work for me, two people have come in without appointments, demanding to see a doctor immediately, I was apparently supposed to have a lunch ordered for a department meeting which starts in fifteen minutes, and the only reason I'm here is that a few months ago my husband decided he'd rather spend time with his receptionist than me."

As Rebecca looked at Lucas with tears rolling down her cheeks, he could see that she was embarrassed, realizing she just confided in a complete stranger. Her eyes assessed the room and fixated on the door.

"Well," Lucas said with a slight pause, "You won't believe what happened on my way here." He lifted his arms, revealing two large paper bags. "I stumbled across a couple of bags of sandwiches and salads from the deli down the street. There is no way I can eat them all. I've been coming here long enough to know a thing or two about the scheduler, and for the record, your ex-husband is a damn fool for leaving those bright eyes behind."

Pharmaceutical Sales 101 – birds of a feather flock together. Physicians were more likely to say yes when stress was low and the staff was happy. Lucas called on this hospital every other Monday, and the place was hopping with enthusiasm on those days. The entire staff enjoyed talking to him, and he always brought sandwiches from their favorite deli, all while his quarterly bonuses continued to soar.

"Hey there, Lucas! How's Chicago's most eligible bachelor doing today?" Rebecca asked with a wink as she greeted Lucas.

Lucas's cheeks turned red as he grinned. Comments like that were not uncommon to Lucas, but he always struggled with the how to handle and respond to them. He had his mother's brown eyes and his father's big smile, which revealed his pearly white teeth. His build was slender and his stress relieving bicycle rides and runs have left him with an athletic tone. Single women wanted to be with him, and married women wanted to set up their single friends with him, but all Lucas wanted to do was stay off people's radars.

Without acknowledging Rebecca's flirtatious hints, he looked at her eyes as she leaned forward, seemingly inviting Lucas to look down her low-cut shirt. He didn't break eye contact and said, "How was Jonathan's soccer game?"

"Oh, great you know, a bunch of boys running back and forth across a field and kicking a ball into each other's heads," Rebecca said with a touch of sarcasm.

She wasn't thrilled with the idea of Jonathan playing soccer. The recent articles about kids causing brain damage unto themselves from using their heads to hit a ball had worried her. There was no way she would allow him to play football. That only left golf and soccer. She would have been ecstatic if Jonathan chose golf, but he was reluctant to join.

"Mom, if you make me play golf, you'll be sorry later when you don't have any grandchildren," he would protest.

Rebecca bit her tongue and met him in the middle of football and golf with soccer.

"Don't worry too much about it," Lucas said to Rebecca, aware of her concerns. "The damage done on the soccer field isn't nearly as bad as the damage which could be done if he felt he was secluded and left out. You're doing the right thing."

Lucas could relate to the feeling of being alone. He spent most of his days feeling like an outcast. He had no close friends to come over for a barbeque or no significant other to spend a weekend getaway with. He did not even have living relatives to spend time with during the holidays.

In times when it seemed like too much to bear, he asked himself why he continued living in this manner. But then he reflected on the terms of the agreement. Reaping was the only real option he had if he hoped to one day live a normal life.

After a slight pause, Lucas said, "Is Dr. Gupta in today? I have some samples of our new allergy spray to drop off, and I think he might be interested in hearing about the progress of our newest pain medications."

Rebecca held her smile as he let out a faint sigh. "Yes, he just finished up with a patient. Go on back to his office."

Lucas smiled, and he stepped through the door and into the familiar scenery of a hospital. The offices at this hospital were typical of most hospitals. The floors were covered with the stick-on tiles, the walls were pale white, and the doors were made of a manufactured material, which was made to look like wood, but was hollow underneath.

The cold air smelt of hand sanitizer and there wasn't a spec of natural light coming into this part of the building. To this day, Lucas still pondered what conversations were had when architects designed these buildings. This was supposed to be a place where people go to feel better, but the longer he stayed in the dim artificial lighting, the worst he felt.

The door to Dr. Gupta's office was closed, as usual. Most doctors kept their doors open, but he preferred to keep his closed. He didn't care for small talk, and with his door closed, people were less likely to stop in to ask him how his weekend was or what his plans were for the evening. Not that they would be very likely to do so anyway. Dr. Gupta wasn't the type to keep many friends. It was more important for him to display superiority and prestige than empathy. That being said, he was one of the smartest physicians on Lucas's call list, an opinion which he never planned to share with Dr. Gupta.

Lucas knocked on the hollow door and waited for a response.

"Can't I ever get a break around here? Who is it?" Dr. Gupta shouted from his room.

"Dr. Gupta, it's Lucas Braun. May I come in?"

Lucas had been working with Dr. Gupta, the area's largest prescriber of allergy medication, for nearly five years. Most sales reps would give up their entire call list in exchange for just fifteen minutes of Dr. Gupta's time.

He never prescribed Cure-iosity's brands to his patients before Lucas began visiting him. The reps before him quit trying. In every quarterly business review, their sales director would bring up Dr. Gupta as a target who they needed to convert, and the sales representatives would reply that he's a dead end.

After a few quarters, the sales director for the area went to visit Dr. Gupta. The door didn't open for him, either. He stopped mentioning Dr. Gupta's name at the reviews with his reps, but his Regional Vice President didn't stop taking notice. He decided to realign the region, and he assigned Steve, the district manager for the area, to Dr. Gupta and informed him he had six months to win the physician over.

Steve walked away from the conversation thinking he had six months to find a new job. He thought of himself as being the best of his group. If he couldn't get Dr. Gupta to begin prescribing his company's medications, then no one in his group would. He went down his list. Jason and Stacey were his best, but they both had already spent six months trying to convert Dr. Gupta. Sean, Liz, Terri, and Justin were average reps at best and likely couldn't get the win in just six months.

He then came across Lucas's name. At the time Lucas was a mid-tier rep, similar to Sean Liz and Terri, but something about him was different from the others. In this field, Steve had encountered a lot of people putting on a show. He was never able to really know anyone, mostly because the people didn't really know themselves. But Lucas had always appeared to be genuine. He wasn't trying to tell the best joke, was never flirting with the female reps, was never wearing designer clothes or shoes, and was never talking about his place on the lake. When Steve talked to him, Lucas always asked about his life and family, and never broke eye contact.

Steve wasn't sure if it would work when he sent an after-hours email to his team with the latest physician call list. On the top, it clearly indicated that Lucas Braun would be calling on Dr. Gupta.

Lucas's first visit with Dr. Gupta did not go how he anticipated, and it was unlike any other visit he had before. In the past weekend, he had seven on the list for reaping, leaving little time for him to tend to his mortal needs of food and sleep. He tried to catch up on sleep during his commute to the city and was awoken with a startle when he saw people shuffling their way through the crowd to exit the train. He quickly got up and made his way to the street. When he stepped outside, he realized he forgot one crucial item on the train, his umbrella. The rain was pouring so hard that it would splash back up a few inches off of the ground once it hit.

The line of people waiting for cabs reflected the rainy day. On a sunny day, there would be a line of cabs competing for him, but on rainy days it seemed there were fewer cabs and more people in need of a cab.

Lucas came to the realization that he would have to fight for a cab as he stepped towards the street with his briefcase over his head. The thought of taking a cab sent chills down his spine.

Since the night of the car crash, Lucas had avoided riding cars whenever possible

With the rain quickly soaking through his jacket, he had to make a quick decision.

*Do I show up to Dr. Gupta's soaking wet or do I get in a car, just this once?*

Lucas took a deep breath and fought the crowd to flag down a cab. To his surprise, he was able to catch one rather easily. Others in the crowd gave a few choice words to Lucas as he entered, claiming the cab was theirs. Lucas ignored their remarks and continued to climb into the cab.

"Where to?" the cab driver asked.

Before responding, Lucas took one quick peek out the window and saw something which made his heartache. A mother and her young son, who couldn't have been more than three years old, were standing in the rain, hopelessly waiting for a cab. Like Lucas, they must have left their umbrella elsewhere.

*Should I give up my cab for them? Was this a sign I shouldn't be in the car?*

The cab driver was getting irritated. "Sir, where am I driving? I have a lot of people to get to. Speak up or get out!"

He looked at his watch. He would never make it in time if he walked to the hospital. There was only one option. He rolled down his window and called out to the woman. "Ma'am!" he said, trying to catch her attention.

She looked at him and then looked over both of her shoulders, appearing unsure if Lucas was talking to her.

"You in the blue scarf with the boy. Do you want to share my cab? You're going to catch a cold sitting out there in the rain."

Lucas watched her as she hesitantly picked up her son and walked towards the cab. He pushed the door open, into a crowd which continued to elbow each other for curb space.

"Thank you," she said while entering the cab.

"My pleasure," Lucas replied as he scooted over so she and her son could take their seats. Though her hair was soaked from the rain and her makeup was smeared down her face, Lucas could tell she was quite beautiful. She looked to be of Indian descent and had the accent to support this assumption.

"Okay! Are we done saving the world? Can we get moving?" barked the cab driver.

"Ladies first," Lucas said as he looked at the woman with a smile.

The lady smiled back and replied to the cab driver, "Hospital please."

Lucas let out an audible laugh. The woman looked at him, slightly offended.

"I'm sorry. Did I say something funny?"

"No no," Lucas said, still laughing, "I wasn't laughing at you. It's just funny how things work out sometimes. You're going to the hospital. That is exactly where I'm heading."

The woman smiled, uncomfortably.

Lucas didn't talk much during the cab ride. He stared out the window, trying to give the woman and her son their privacy, while also trying to control his breathing. The rain pounded the windshield of the yellow taxi cab, similar to the way it pounded the windshield on the night of his accident.

"Are you a doctor?" the lady asked, eyeing Lucas's suit and briefcase.

"No. I'm not that smart. I'm only smart enough to talk to doctors. I'm a pharmaceutical sales representative."

The lady smiled and nodded her head. "Well, good luck today. You'll need it."

Lucas wondered what she meant by those comments. She spoke as if she had experience in the field.

*Was she also a rep? Or perhaps a doctor?*

Before he could ask, he was interrupted by the cab driver shouting back at them as he slammed the brakes at the entrance of the hospital. "$29.50."

To Lucas's surprise, they were already at the hospital. It had been so long since he had been in a car that he'd forgotten how quickly he could travel a couple of blocks in a vehicle.

"You go on in. I've got this," Lucas said to the woman.

She smiled at him and said, "No. Please, I can pay."

Lucas shook her off. "It's my treat. Go on and try to stay dry out there."

She smiled at him as she picked up her boy, who was about to fall asleep for a morning nap, and walked towards the hospital. Lucas then reached into his wallet and grabbed thirty dollars for the cab driver.

"I said it was $29.50," the driver said as he turned to look at Lucas while Lucas exited the cab.

"You're right, keep the change. You were a real treat," Lucas said, closing the door and heading towards the hospital entrance.

Lucas reviewed his key talking points during the elevator ride to Dr. Gupta's office on the sixth floor.

"Our drug is 25% more effective than the competition's. It works faster and last longer. While the price may be a little bit higher, patients are recorded as being more satisfied with this prescription than any other medication on the market."

He looked to his right and noticed an elderly couple was staring at him.

*Was I talking out loud?*

Slightly embarrassed, he smiled as the door opened and said, "Sorry. It's my first day here, and I'm a little nervous."

The two gave him an understanding smile before the elevator door closed between them as they exited.

When Lucas arrived at Dr. Gupta's office, he saw him typing away on his computer. Lucas took a deep breath and knocked on the door.

*Here goes nothing.*

But when he opened his mouth to introduce himself, Dr. Gupta cut him off.

"I'm not seeing reps today. Come back next week."

Dr. Gupta wasn't the least bit apologetic about it. He held himself in the utmost regard professionally and felt his professional time was more valuable than other's, giving him the right to be outright rude to others if need be.

Lucas, caught off guard, regrettably said, "Your office hours are today, right? Or did I confuse them with another day?"

"My office hours are when I damn well please them to be! They could be tomorrow, they could be next week. But I can tell you one thing. They won't be any day with spineless sales representatives such as yourself! Now please excuse yourself from my doorway!"

Defeated, Lucas slumped his shoulders and began to walk away. He couldn't think of anything to say. He was usually very smooth and quick worded, but in this instance, he was left speechless, as if he'd never learned to talk. Retreating, he turned to walk away. But as he did, he accidentally bumped into someone behind him.

"Oh, I'm sorry," Lucas said, turning around. He was surprised to see it was the lady and the boy from the cab.

"Same floor too? It must have been destiny," the woman said. "I hope my husband wasn't too mean to you."

*Husband? That guy?*

It didn't make sense to Lucas that someone so painful to talk to could be married to someone as lovely as this lady. But he knew the world needed balance. The good must balance out the bad. Lucas looked at the woman in the eyes, but instead of letting her know how he felt, he said, "Oh, who? Dr. Gupta? Never. You've married a good man."

When Lucas left Dr. Gupta's office, he planned never to return. As a pharmaceutical sales representative, he had become accustomed to kissing ass and playing up to physician's egos, but he didn't want to waste another minute trying to kiss the ass of the lost cause in Dr. Gupta.

*No one else has been successful with Dr. Gupta. Why would I be any different?*

Later that week Lucas's cell phone rang while he was walking between offices. He looked and saw it was Steve.

*Probably calling to talk about a game plan for Dr. Gupta.*

Lucas reluctantly hit the answer key to take the call. He hadn't yet told Steve that he would never go to Dr. Gupta's office again, and he was prepared for Steve not to accept that decision.

"Cancel all your appointments this afternoon and meet me at Johnny's On The Corner. We're celebrating today, buddy!"

"Celebrating?" Lucas asked Steve, "What are we celebrating?"

"You did it. In just one week you convinced the largest prescriber of allergy medication in the Chicago area to begin prescribing our drug! I don't know how you did it, but all you have to do is keep him happy, and you'll be the top performer of the year. Not to mention, you saved my ass. So, in return, I'm going to get your ass drunk!" Steve exclaimed.

Lucas couldn't believe it. Dr. Gupta didn't even look up at him. He didn't even get the chance to mention the name of the medication.

*Did his wife convince him to begin prescribing? Perhaps she told Dr. Gupta of my random act of kindness and persuaded him to help me out?*

"Oh. Was that supposed to be challenging?" Lucas replied in an attempt to play it off as a small feat. "I'll see you there in an hour."

Ever since, Lucas had kept a careful eye around Dr. Gupta's office, hoping to bump into Mrs. Gupta. He wanted to properly thank her for saving his job, and with Dr. Gupta prescribing everything that Lucas pitched to him, Lucas could afford to arrange a driver to take her wherever she pleased. Never again would she have to wait in the rain for a cab. But he has not seen her since that rainy day, and based on his first impression of her, he concluded that she would likely decline the offer, claiming it to be unnecessary.

"Yes Lucas, please come in," Dr. Gupta said from his office, a greeting Lucas had grown accustomed to hearing from Dr. Gupta ever since that first encounter.

# Chapter 3

A magazine worthy view could be seen from the backyard of Lucas's one and a half story bungalow home. His grass was cut, his landscaping was in top shape, and the river, which he could view from his deck, reflected the orange and red color tones of a breathtaking sunset. On beautiful nights like these, Lucas enjoyed sitting out on his deck and having a beer while listening to a classical jazz sampler through his phone speakers. This Monday night, however, was not one of those nights. The week before, Lucas was at a sales training event in Orlando, which put him behind on his reaping list and forced him to catch up over the weekend. He executed four reaps in two days, concluding with Tom Dempsy on Sunday night. This was his first night home in over a week.

He wanted to try to catch up on laundry, but as Lucas dismantled the piles of clothes, he quickly realized he underestimated the amount that needed cleaned, pressed and stored away. He rubbed his hand on the back of his aching neck and looked longingly towards the steaks he set out for dinner. He was tired, hungry, and in need of a night of relaxing on his back deck.

*It looks like I won't have time to grill those steaks tonight.*

Lucas picked up a couple of strip steaks from the local meat shop located just a few blocks from his home. He always cooked for two. It was less depressing than cooking for one and leftovers were always a welcomed convenience for his busy schedule.

He brought his attention back to his mountain of laundry. For a single person, he could pile up the laundry rather quickly. Each day, Lucas was liable to go through four wardrobe changes. He'd begin with running clothes, then switch to his uniform for work, which consisted of a gray suit and a button-down shirt. After work, Lucas would get out of his suit as fast as he could and change into his favorite attire, corduroy pants and a t-shirt. Lastly, Lucas would change into a pair of pajama pants for bed.

As he was sorting his clothes into darks and lights, he heard a familiar voice calling from his back deck.

"Are you going to make me watch this beautiful sunset by myself?" It startled Lucas. He wasn't expecting company, but his friend Sam never came announced.

He stepped out from the laundry room to see his old friend sitting in one of his patio chairs. Sam was dressed in his standard attire, consisting of an untucked light blue button up shirt, a pair of dark denim jeans, and blue suede shoes. His blonde hair was combed over to the side.

"What brings you by this time? Kicked out of the house by the most recent fling?" Lucas teased as he walked outside to greet Sam. He smiled and opened up his arms to give him a welcoming hug.

Sam rose from the chair to return the hug. He was about the same height as Lucas, hovering around 6 feet tall, but he wasn't as slender. Lucas often asked Sam to join him for a run or a bicycle ride to help shed the extra baby weight, as he called it. However, Sam would always decline the invitation, claiming that he was far too busy to be concerned about a little bit of weight around his beltline.

"I just thought I'd stop by to check on you. You know, given what day it is and all," Sam said.

Lucas looked at his feet. He had stayed busy to keep his mind from thinking about what today represented.

"It's still just as tough for you now as it was twenty years ago," Sam said as he leaned against the railing of the deck, folding his arms over his chest.

Lucas paused for a moment before replying. "I feel like it should get easier over time, but it hasn't. I can't believe that today makes twenty years."

Sam returned to his seat on the patio chair. Lucas slowly walked over to sit in the chair next to him. It had been twenty years to the day since Lucas's parents passed away.

He remembered the rain. There was so much rain. He could still hear his mother's scream coming from the front passenger seat, "Frank watch out!"

Then there was the man. It was like he came out of nowhere. Everything happened so fast, Lucas didn't know what it was at the time. But as he reflected on the event, as he's done so many times, he could now see the man in the road, seemingly daring the car to hit him. When his father turned the wheel to avoid the man, he lost control, sending the car off-road.

What happened next was still a mystery to Lucas. He remembered the man, the rain, and the car losing control. But he didn't remember how he was the one who ended up on the edge of a creek bed while his parents were still in the car.

He recalled the feeling of waking up from a horrible nightmare. As he rose from the ground, he felt a sharp pain in his head and felt the blood in his hair when reached up to touch it. Panicked, he looked around for his mom and dad.

"Mom! Dad!" Lucas yelled.

But they never called back. He then turned his head towards the creek and saw the family sedan, upside down. Lucas rose to his feet. The adrenaline was pulsing through his body, and he no longer felt the pain in his head as he rushed through the waist deep water to get to the car.

"Mom! Dad! Can you hear me?" he yelled as he got closer.

Once he reached the car, he wished he hadn't. Inside the family sedan were his father and mother, still strapped to the front seats by their seatbelts with their heads submerged in water.

Sam was the only person who knew Lucas's viewpoint of the tragedy, and he was the only person Lucas knew who would understand. Sam was like Lucas, a reaper.

He was ten or so years older than Lucas, or at least Lucas estimated him to be. He graduated from the college with a computer science degree and was hired on at a startup as a developer. Sam stayed with them for five years before they were sold. Him and his other co-workers who were there at the beginning made out like bandits. Now, with no need for a steady income, Sam does freelance work. Companies call him, and if the job sounded interesting, he did it. This lifestyle allowed Sam the flexibility to carry on with his reaping quota as well as the additional responsibilities Sam carried. Not only did Sam reap, but he also managed. He oversaw other reapers in the area to keep things in check. Even death had an organizational chart.

"So. What do you say you transfer those steaks from your counter to your grill and we open some of those expired beers sitting in the icebox?" Sam said with a grin. "It's the perfect time of day to kick back and relax the best way we know how."

Lucas looked at the pile of clothes sitting on the laundry room floor. He didn't need a lot of convincing to put that chore off for another time.

*It can wait until tomorrow.*

Conversing with others was something he didn't get the pleasure of often doing. Sam was the one who showed him the ropes, acting as a mentor and becoming a friend.

A few years after Lucas's parents passed away in the car accident, Lucas received a letter in the mail. It was delivered in a manila envelope with no return address. It didn't even have a stamp. He concluded that someone hand-delivered it to his mailbox. Curious, Lucas took the envelope to his room and opened it up. Inside was a single sheet of cardstock with a red border around the edges. Written in cursive on the cardstock with red ink were the names of ten people, all of which he didn't recognize. Puzzled by the delivery, Lucas placed the letter in the top right drawer of his desk and locked it.

Shortly after the accident, Lucas was put in a temporary foster home. He wasn't yet entirely comfortable in his new place. Frank and Mary were Lucas's only family and when they passed there wasn't anyone left for him. The foster parents were an elderly couple who couldn't have children of their own. They were warm and welcoming to Lucas, but he could never fully let them in. To him, they felt more like roommates than family.

A few days later, Lucas was walking to the place he was staying. That was what he called it, the place he was staying. He could never call it home. To call it home would be like saying he had moved on. Lucas wasn't ready to move on. He couldn't move on. He still had too much grief and too many questions.

During that walk on that particular day, however, he was approached by Sam for the first time. "Do you understand what the contents of the envelope mean to you?" he said.

Lucas was taken aback by how direct this stranger was. He looked at him and said, "What do you know about an envelope? Were you the one who left it for me?"

"No. It was delivered by the service. I'm the one who has been assigned to you to tell you what it means and how to proceed with it."

*Proceed with it?* "What do you mean proceed? What is the service?"

Sam replied in a monotone voice, which was far less personable than the Sam who Lucas grew to know, "I realized this would be a lot for you to take in, and you've been through a lot already. Fifteen months earlier a similar list was delivered to a man. It had your name on it. Remember your car crash? How did you make it out of the car and onto the shore?"

None of this was making sense to Lucas. Why would his name be on a list?

Lucas asked, frantically, "What do you know about the car crash?"

"I know your time was up. But you didn't pass on. You were spared by the reaper assigned to the task. Normally you'd just be assigned to the next list, but sometimes the victims become the reapers." He said the words as if they were regular things for him to be saying. As if these types of things were taught in school and Lucas should be familiar with the concepts of reapers and lists of victims in relation to mortality.

"What the hell are you talking about?" Lucas exclaimed. "I think we are done here. I have to get going."

Lucas then took off, running the rest of the way to his foster parent's house.

*How could he know so much about the crash?*

As crazy as the guy sounded to Lucas, his reasoning was the sounder than anything he had come up with.

It wasn't until a few days later when Lucas again saw Sam, this time sitting on a bench at the park which Lucas walked through on his route to the place where he was staying. Against his better judgment, Lucas approached him.

"Look, I don't know who you think you are or what you think you know but…"

"I'm Sam," he replied back calmly. "I failed to properly introduce myself last time. My name is Sam, and I am here to help you through this difficult transition in your life. Since my transition began under similar conditions as yours, the council thought I'd be best for the job."

Lucas, taken aback by Sam's expression of empathy, took a seat next to him on the bench. Sam didn't say anything when Lucas sat down. He just looked ahead. Lucas stared out ahead too, allowing them to sit in each other's company in silence. The weather station said it was the hottest spring day in over twenty years. This park would generally be full of people and kids enjoying the outdoors, but that day few people were out.

"I don't understand how I ended up on the bank of the creek that night," Lucas said with a calm tone. "All I remember is it was pouring down rain. We were looking for a hotel and a man ran out in front of us. He came out of nowhere. The next thing I knew I was laying on the bank of the creek."

Lucas paused, waiting for Sam to interject and provide answers. But Sam continued to stare ahead as if he was just there to listen. His breathing remained steady, sitting perfectly still, so much to the point that Lucas pondered if he was meditating. Unable to handle the silence, Lucas continued with more questions, "Was the man who ran out in front of us the reaper? Did he pull me out of the creek?" His voice started to shake as the emotions he'd tried to keep tightly sealed inside began to slip through the cracks. "Are you the one responsible for my parents being dead?"

The last question broke Sam from his seeming state of meditation. "I am not the one responsible for your parents dying. What few people understand is that there are larger forces at play in this world. Most don't see them, and most don't know about them. People go to great lengths to understand how we got here, why we got here, and why we have to go. But few understand."

"Are you talking about religion and the after-life?" Lucas asked.

"There isn't an after-life. There is just life. It is nothing more than energy compiled together in a mold. When a person dies, the energy doesn't go away. Energy cannot be created or destroyed. It's all continuous."

Lucas was feeling more uncomfortable. His mind was telling him to get up and leave, but his body didn't listen, weighing him down as if he was glued permanently to the park bench. He had so many questions. The idea which Sam illustrated was familiar to Lucas. He was very bright and was able to take physics earlier in high school than most. The concept of not being able to create energy or destroy it was introduced in the first class, but he would have never dreamed people's lives were at play to keep things in check.

"Why should I believe you?" Lucas protested.

"Let me offer further explanation. Think about a bottle rocket. Have you ever lit a bottle rocket?"

Lucas thought back to the Independence Day celebrations he had with his parents. His dad would drive across the Illinois border to buy a box full of fireworks. Then, they would barbeque way too much food, and consequently, they would eat way too much food. After the food settled in their stomachs, they would get the box of fireworks and take turns lighting off bottle rockets, high-fiving after each explosion.

"Yes. I've lit bottle rockets before," Lucas replied.

"Think about what would happen if you didn't let it shoot up in the sky. What if instead, you held it in the palm of your hand and made a fist?" Sam asked, sounding sincerer the more he talked.

Lucas didn't know where Sam was going with this, but he replied, "It would blow your hand off."

"Precisely. If someone shot a bottle rocket and it hit you in the hand while it exploded, you would get a minor burn but nothing major. There was a place for the energy to go outside of your hand. However, inside of your hand, there would be nowhere for that energy to spread. Too much energy in one spot would create an explosion, and all you would be able to do is use your other hand to wave your hand that was holding the bottle rocket goodbye."

Growing impatient Lucas replied, "I don't understand what bottle rockets have to do with me, the list in my bedroom, or my parents."

Sam exhaled. "The world is like a hand, and it can only hold so many molds of energy at a time. There needs to be a proper balance of positive and negative energy. To keep the balance, some molds of negative and positive energy need to be redistributed. If they weren't, the earth would begin to close in on the population like a hand around a bottle rocket. I think we can agree that we don't want to be around for that."

Lucas let this sink in for a moment. He had no reason to believe anything Sam said, but he also didn't have a reason not to believe.

"Why are these forces at play allowing the population to snowball? Are they testing the limits? Are we close to the end?"

"The population growth is making it tougher for the reapers to keep up with quota, which is one reason why people are living longer these days."

The word reapers stuck out to Lucas. "Reapers?" he questioned. "How many reapers are there?"

"Not enough," Sam replied.

"Why would you agree to be a reaper? Why not just say no?" Lucas asked.

"I asked the same question when I was told that I would have to become a reaper. I was told if I said no I would be next on the list of a near-by reaper."

Lucas's eyes strained as he tried to contemplate his life, all in a matter of seconds.

"Wouldn't I be better off then?" Lucas's voice was quivering as he spoke. "Let them take me. There's no one here left for me. I could die as a decent person. Isn't that better than living as a murderer?"

"Is that what you'd be? A murderer? Is sacrificing the needs of the few for the good of the many the act of a murderer?"

Lucas stared back at Sam, dumbfounded.

"This is bigger than you Lucas. Bigger than me," Sam continued as he was now using his hands to help emphasize his words. "Reapers are not murderers. They are preservers, doing all of the dirty work it takes to make sure the world we live in can sustain."

Lucas opened his mouth to protest but before he could speak Sam interrupted, "It's like I said, life doesn't come and go. It's always here. The form it takes may differ from century to century, but it never goes away."

Lucas thought to the consultation his foster parents had offered him. "My foster parents tell me that about my parents. They say their teachings and characteristics live on through me."

"That's partially true," Sam replied. "When people pass on, they don't die completely. Yes, the body they lived in served its purpose and is buried, or cremated, or whatever it is that people want to do with their deceased. But the energy which fueled that body and mind lives on, and it can be transitioned to another form of energy."

*Great. What good does it do me if my mom and dad's energy was transferred to the grass growing from the ground? The grass can't hug me. The grass can't play catch with me. The grass doesn't love me.*

He looked at the ground, feeling as if had been put into a corner with no options for living a happy life. He wondered if it would be better just to ignore the list. If Sam were telling the truth, his time left here would be short. That didn't sound like the worst thing that could happen. But as Lucas was kicking his feet on the ground, Sam offered one more piece of information which lifted his spirit.

"I didn't finish telling you the whole story," Sam began, "The life of the reaper is hard, too hard for anyone to do for too long. And because of that, reapers are only obligated to perform the job temporarily. At some point, every reaper receives his final list, and when they do, they live on as better people than what they were before their assignments began."

"So, are you going to just stare at the grill or are you going to warm it up? We've gotta get that fire going. If you don't get the sear right, then everything will be off." Sam said, jarring Lucas back to reality.

Lucas didn't know how long he had been dazed off. He shook his head, blinked his eyes, and said, "Leave the steaks to me." He gave Sam a grin and walked towards the kitchen to grab a couple of cold beers.

"Here's a toast to better times ahead," Lucas said as he gave Sam a beer, their usual toast for when they got together. Lucas hoped his better times ahead would come sooner rather than later.

# Chapter 4

What do you mean by top forty under forty?" Lucas asked his manager, Steve Reynolds, over his cell phone as he walked the crowded streets of Chicago. The sun was out, and the temperature hovered around seventy degrees, making it a pleasant day for Lucas to walk between offices for his physician calls. It was about three in the afternoon when he saw his phone was ringing with the call from Steve.

"Forty Under Forty," Steve replied for a second time over the phone with Lucas, ignoring the displeasure in Lucas's voice. He had known Lucas for several years, and in that time, he learned Lucas had a displeasure for doing social events such as office happy hours or going to a Cubs game on the weekend. Talking to a reporter for a story was sure to be something on Lucas's not to do list.

"The paper posts an article every year of the top forty professionals under forty years of age. A reporter called and asked if we had someone in mind who would fit the criteria. You know, someone young and successful. There would be bonus points for someone with a strong and likable personality.

You have been the best rep in the company for years, so you were the first to come to mind."

"But I don't have a strong and likable personality," Lucas protested. "What about Jason? Everyone loves Jason."

Steve was shaking his head on the other side of the phone. Jason was like the guy in college who always seemed to sneak through each of his classes, barely passing them without learning a thing. He was the one who always had bigger and better plans and was always talking about his latest party or hookup. He was the kind of guy who people hoped would get what he had coming to him after college. But then, years later, he shows up at the class reunion in an 80,000-dollar car and a 3,000-dollar suit because he learned to read a script and smile for a sales company.

"Jason is average at best. If he didn't have his million-dollar smile to go with his two-hundred-dollar haircut, he wouldn't even be able to sell eggs to a diner," Steve replied.

Lucas's mind raced, trying to think of anyone who could do this besides him. Getting extra attention was something towards the bottom of his list of things he'd prefer to do today. Each year he would plead with the senior leadership of the company to not have an awards ceremony because each year he was forced against his will to go on stage and accept an award for being the best sales rep in the company. He'd much rather be just another face in the crowd instead of the face the crowd was looking at.

"Stacey," Lucas suggested. "Stacey has been hitting her target every quarter, and she is a proud mother of three."

Steve let out a deep sigh before saying, "Stacey is also over forty years old. I knew this conversation with you wouldn't be easy and I could have quickly gotten Jason or someone else to agree to the interview. But Lucas, you are the best. I think the world deserves to know that Lucas Braun was not only the best in the business but also the best the business had ever seen."

Steve paused, waiting to see if Lucas had a response. After a moment of silence, he delivered his final blow. "Look, Lucas. I can't make you do this, but you would be doing me a favor if you did."

He knew that Lucas had a soft spot for helping people. If he made it seem like he was doing it for him, he was sure Lucas would accept the assignment.

"I checked your schedule when I was on the phone with the reporter and saw you had time scheduled to enter your calls for tracking. I can fill the sheet out for you this week, based on looking at the calls on your planner. I agreed for you to meet the reporter at Clancy's at 4:00 and I gave her a description of you so she could pick you out of the crowd. Just go, have a drink, answer a few questions about where you went to college and what you've accomplished in your career, and then start your weekend."

"You've put me a tough spot here, Steve," Lucas replied, "The reporter is taking time away from his family to meet some stranger at a bar on a Friday night. It would be extremely rude of that someone to stand them up. I'll help you this time, but next time you do something like this to me, you'll have to do more than just fill out my call tracking report."

"Thanks, Lucas. I owe you. Have a nice weekend," Steve replied, hanging up the phone before Lucas could change his mind.

Lucas could picture the smile spreading across Steve's face. Steve was always pushing him to be more sociable, claiming it would be for his own good to get out of his comfort zone. He appreciated that Steve took an interest in his well-being, and he tipped his cap to him, knowing Steve won this battle.

# Chapter 5

Clancy's was one of the up and coming bars in Chicago. Opened within the last year, it was the place to be on a weekend night, often drawing a crowd so large that the building would exceed its capacity, forcing patrons to wait in line outside until others left. A Friday afternoon, however, was a downtime for the bar and Lucas was able to walk right in. He scanned the room and saw that nearly every table was empty. Unsure of what the reporter looked like, he decided to stand towards the front, hoping the reporter could pick him out. He eyed the specials, written on a chalkboard which hung near the bar. Craft beer, the cheapest drink on the menu, was priced at nine-dollars a pint. He didn't like to pay that much for a drink, but he did enjoy craft beer.

*Better that my money stays local with the craft beer as opposed to going to a global business and redistributed in the pockets of multi-millionaires.*

"Have a seat where ever you want," shouted the bartender. He was a mid-twenties man with his hair in a bun and a sleeve of tattoos running down his left arm.

Lucas gave the man a friendly smile and headed towards the table near the bar. As he was taking a seat, he heard a voice from the back corner.

"Actually, why don't you have a seat over here?"

Lucas's eyes went towards the voice. A woman was rising from her seat and approaching him. She was average height, slender, and both her long hair and bright eyes were brown. Her black yoga pants were skin tight, and her long baggy white shirt with a V-neck cut made it look as if she had either spent the day at home or was on her way to the gym.

"Are you from the paper?" Lucas asked, hesitantly. For some reason, he imagined the reporter was going to be a man, although Steve never mentioned a man or a woman.

"Yes. My name is Chloe Benedict. Thanks for meeting with me on such short notice," she said as she held out her hand, gesturing for a handshake.

"No trouble at all," Lucas replied politely, returning the handshake.

Lucas could feel his mood shift. He had come in dreading this interview, but after seeing Chloe, he was suddenly glad to be here, awestruck by her beauty.

There was a short pause as Lucas and Chloe stood in the middle of the bar, holding each other's hand during an extended handshake. Neither said anything while they slowly shook their hands up and down, gazing into each other's eyes.

Although Chloe was beautiful, she was often single. She never liked going out to the bars with the girls during college, and she never found a man who could keep her interest for longer than a couple of weeks.

Chloe shook her head, bringing herself back to reality, and said, "Well, should we have a seat?"

"After you," Lucas replied, gesturing towards the table Chloe came from.

After Lucas took his seat, Chloe jumped right into the interview and said, "So Lucas, tell me about why you are deserving of the honor of being in the *Forty Under Forty* article."

When Chloe decided to pursue a writing career, she dreamed of writing for a large magazine while working on a series of mystery novels. However, after she graduated from college, there were more writers for magazines than there were magazines. With rent and bills to pay, she took the first job she could get with the local paper. Six years later she was still writing columns, and her first mystery novel was left unfinished.

"Other than being under forty years old, I'm not sure what qualifications I have," Lucas replied. "My manager thinks I'm better than I am and signed me up for this interview."

"Your manager is Steve, right?"

"Yes. Steve Reynolds."

"He told me you'd be like this."

Lucas tilted his head and gave Chloe an inquisitive look. "What do you mean like this?"

"Modest. He mentioned you have been the top sales rep the company had ever seen and you single-handedly altered the market for allergy medication in Chicago. How could that not make you worthy of being in the article and not the first thing which comes to mind when I ask you why you are deserving of being in the article?"

Lucas sighed. "That's what the company says. But I didn't do it; I just got the credit for it."

He thought of Mrs. Gupta standing in the rain on a crowded sidewalk with her son. If he had never offered her his cab, he wouldn't be in this bar being interviewed for a newspaper.

Chloe shifted her position in her seat. "You took the credit for someone else's work?"

"Can I get you two something to drink?" The bartender asked as he stepped out from behind the bar and approached the table.

Chloe looked up and said, "Can I have a gin and tonic, please?"

"And I'll have a beer," Lucas said, grateful for the interruption.

"Ok. Sir, we have over sixty beers on tap. Do you know which you'd like or would you like to try a few samples?"

Lucas shook his head. "No samples. I'll take a pint of your favorite brew."

The bartender smiled at the idea and returned to the bar to prepare the drinks.

Chloe looked back at Lucas in anticipation of his answer to her question.

"I did take credit for someone else's work," Lucas said as he looked at his hands, which were folded together on the table. "I was assigned to make a sales pitch to the top allergy prescriber in the city. He prescribes more allergy medication than the next ten combined, and he never prescribed my company's medication. On my way to my first sales pitch to him, I helped a stranger by letting her and her young son share a cab with me on a rainy day. I picked up the bill for the both of us when we surprisingly realized we were traveling to the same destination. Later, I bumped into her on my way out the physician's office after the doctor belittled me and shut me out. As it turned out, the woman I helped was the physician's wife. Next thing I knew, the doctor was solely prescribing Cure-iosity allergy medication, and I have been the number one sales rep in the country since."

"Gin and tonic for the lady," the bartender said as he returned with the drinks. "And the local session IPA for the gentleman. I hope you enjoy it."

Lucas and Chloe both looked up and replied, "Thank you."

Chloe returned her gaze to Lucas, waiting to see if he had more to add. After a few uncomfortable moments of waiting, she replied, "Interesting," and she took out her pen and began writing in her notebook.

Lucas's foot was tapping softly on the floor between them. Her longing gaze made him nervous, almost as nervous as the fact he just told the local paper his secret to success.

"What are you writing?" Lucas asked with a slight panic in his voice.

*Should I have just told her everything I just said? Why am I so willing to open up with her?*

"Are you going to put that in the paper?"

Chloe smiled and said, "Your manager also mentioned you tend to give others credit for your success."

"What do you mean? I didn't do anything to sell that physician on my company's products, and he is now prescribing our drugs. Why would I deserve any credit?"

"Sometimes the things we do which we don't think matter, matter the most. You helped out a person in need, not looking for any kind of reward, but you were rewarded for it, seemingly against your will."

Lucas looked at Chloe with a confused expression on his face. Wasn't she supposed just to ask a few questions and take notes? So far this had felt more like a session with a therapist rather than an interview with the paper. He took a sip of his beer. It tasted slightly warm and overly bitter.

"Okay, so if you need something for your article, I'm the most successful rep in the Chicago area. Anything else you need for it?"

Chloe smiled. She had seen her fair share of people who didn't want to talk to the press over the years. These were mostly people who had things to hide. Lucas seemed different to her. He didn't seem like someone who didn't have anything to hide at all, but instead someone who just wanted to hide.

"Well, there is more to success than just professional success. How are things at home? Do you have a wife and kids?" Chloe asked.

"Unfortunately, the answer is no," Lucas said with a hint of regret. "Hopefully someday in the future, but my time hasn't come yet."

Lucas glanced at Chloe's hand and saw she wasn't wearing a ring. He liked Chloe. He didn't know why, but in the brief time he's been with her, he's felt better about himself. If things were different, he'd be tempted to summon the courage to ask her on a date.

"How about extracurricular activities? What do you do outside of work?"

Lucas paused for a moment, reflecting on his extracurricular activities.

*If she only knew what I did outside of work. She'd have the story of the century. The first documented interview with a reaper.*

"I try to give back as much as I can. My job pays me quite a bit of money. Much more than I need. I bought my home with cash and have no debt and enough in my retirement plan to where I just need to minimally contribute for the remainder of career. I'm not interested in traveling and live a modest lifestyle. A couple of years ago, I looked at the number in my bank account and decided I should do something with it. That was when I decided I would donate fifty percent of my income to different charities."

Chloe's jaw dropped unable to speak. She took a drink before saying, "I'm sorry. Did you say five percent or fifty percent?"

"Fifty percent," Lucas replied firmly. "As I said, I don't have a family, so I don't need as much money as I make."

"You mentioned that you just started donating this amount a couple of years earlier. Was this after you bought your yacht, sports car, and downtown apartment?" Chloe teased.

An assuring smile spread across Lucas's face while he nodded his head. "People jump to the conclusion that I am giving after I already purchased life's luxuries. I don't have a yacht or a sports car. I don't own a car. And I live in a modest, affordable home."

Chloe looked pleased with Lucas's response. "You are truly much different than the others I've interviewed for this story. Most talk about how much money they manage at the firm or talk about how they were the youngest to do this and that. The single men always manage to drop in how much money they make in an effort to impress me. I thought you might be one of those, but so far you seem to be more ashamed of the money you make than proud."

"Well, that's a relief. Hopefully, you have enough for your article?" Lucas said, hoping he could be excused from the questioning. He'd much rather enjoy his drink with Chloe without the fear of saying something that he didn't want to end up in the paper.

"Am I so intolerable that you have to rush away?" Chloe asked. "I talked to your boss. He assigned you to be here, and you don't have work to be getting to. You don't have a wife, and you don't have children. What's the rush?"

Chloe's forwardness brought a smile to Lucas's face, revealing his straight and perfectly white teeth.

"I'm sorry," Lucas apologized, "It's not you. You're actually quite lovely. I've never felt comfortable exposing more of myself than necessary to the public. That's one of the reasons why I haven't settled down with a wife. I'm reluctant to open up to colleagues and friends, let alone the press."

"I get it. This article is mostly bullshit. Your write up is the first genuine contribution to it. Honestly, I wish my editor didn't make me do it. Your manager already sent me your picture, so I have everything I need."

"Picture? Are you serious?" Lucas asked. It was just then that it dawned on him that Chloe was quick to flag him down when he walked into the bar.

"You have nothing to worry about. It's a charming picture," Chloe assured.

Lucas was getting the feeling that this interview was turning into a date. The reporter said she had everything she needed and yet she was asking Lucas to stick around longer. He had no immediate plans for the evening other than maybe catching up on laundry or sitting down and reading a good book. His plans for Chinese takeout could be postponed to another time. He had no reason to leave other than the one reason which always made him leave. If he stayed then him and Chloe might become friends. She might want to get to know him better. As much as Lucas wanted to stay, he was not in a position to be making any new friends.

"Well, if a picture is necessary, I guess whatever Steve picked will due," Lucas replied as he looked for the bartender.

"Let me just get your phone number in case I need to call back for clarification."

"Sure." Lucas pulled a business card from the pocket of his jacket and handed it over to Chloe. She looked at it and then put it into her navy leather purse.

"Do you ever get tired of wearing suits?" Chloe asked. "They just seem like so much work. You can't throw them in the washing machine. They look as if they rarely fit properly. And who wants to wear a jacket in a Chicago summer?"

Lucas smiled and took a sip of his beer.

*I should leave. She is too likable. If I stay, I may never want to go.*

"Suits are the worst. If it were up to me, sales professionals would wear corduroy pants and button up shirts. Corduroy pants are so easy to maintain. You never have to iron them. While a button up shirt is still somewhat of a chore, you have to keep it somewhat classy."

Chloe smiled. Her red lipstick complemented her fair skin tone beautifully.

Lucas nearly gasped as he took in her smile. At that moment he decided that Chloe was the most beautiful woman he'd laid eyes on. He couldn't imagine how anyone could look more attractive to him than how Chloe looks right now.

*What the hell? What's one night of cutting loose going to hurt? I should stay.*

"I take it you hate suits more than I do?" Lucas asked. "You appear to be dressed in the exact opposite of a suit."

"I like to be comfortable. Recent fashion trends have made it socially acceptable to wear skin-tight leggings as pants, a huge win for women since there is nothing more comfortable. Throw on a baggy t-shirt, and suddenly I'm what people our age refer to as fashionable.

"Do people our age say fashionable?" Lucas teased.

Chloe laughed. "I don't know."

Lucas smiled and looked at his beer. It was half empty. He didn't care to drink the rest of it as it was only getting warmer. He was also quite hungry. One of his calls ran late, and he had to rush to the next office before they stopped taking calls for the day, causing him to miss lunch.

"How's your gin and tonic?"

"It's decent. Not the best but not the worst. How's your beer?"

"Terrible. I'm trying my best to finish, but I don't know if I'm going to be able to. Have you been here before? How's the food?"

"The food is okay. I've gotten the fish tacos to go a few times."

"Are you hungry?" Lucas asked. "I haven't had much to eat today."

Chloe smiled, again. Each time Lucas saw it, he became more attracted to her. "Sure. Let's eat."

Lucas waved for the tattooed bartender to come back.

"Do you not like the beer?" he asked, sounded slightly offended that Lucas didn't share the same taste as him.

Lucas politely replied, "No the beer is fine, just not in the mood I suppose. Could you bring back a pitcher of margaritas and a couple of orders of your fish tacos?"

"Now we mean business," the bartender said. "I'll be right back with your order."

Once the bartender walked away, Lucas looked at Chloe and said, "I hope that order was okay. We can call him back if you want something different."

"It sounds perfect," Chloe assured.

Lucas leaned back in his seat in relief. The excitement of spending more time with Chloe was building in him. He wanted to learn more about what motivated Chloe Benedict.

"Great. So tell me, what made you decide to write about strangers under forty years old for a living?"

"Very funny," she replied.

It was a sensitive subject for her. When she was going to college and obtaining her degrees in journalism and creative writing, she never dreamed she'd be meeting strangers in bars to interview them about what makes them successful.

"I'll never again be in this scene once I finish my series of mystery novels," Chloe said as she looked at the floor.

"Mystery novels. My favorite. How are they coming?"

"They aren't. The further I get into a book, the more I hate it, and I throw it away. I've been doing that for the last six years."

"I can imagine that writing a novel would be pretty hard. I struggle just with writing emails."

Chloe gave Lucas an appreciative smile. "What about you? You don't seem like you were born to sell. You aren't overly assertive, and I can already tell that you have a tendency to second guess yourself."

Lucas wasn't surprised that Chloe was able to scan him. He had discovered that it is easy to learn a lot about people in just a short amount of time. If the situation were right, Lucas would sit down and have a conversation with the people he was about to reap. It was the only time he was allowed to be honest with other people. During those moments, he could quickly determine who the pricks were and who the good people were. He always hoped the person was a jerk. It made his job easier if he felt the person wouldn't be missed.

"Two orders of fish tacos and a pitcher of margaritas," said the bartender as he returned with their order.

"Looks great. Thanks," said Lucas as the bartender stepped away to return to his position behind the bar.

It was beginning to get busier in the bar with more people piling in after work. Visually, Lucas and Chloe fit in with the crowd as most appeared to be in their late twenties or early thirties. However, Lucas didn't share the same interests as his generation, and he was sensing that Chloe didn't either. Though Lucas was single, an increasingly common trait for his generation, he didn't want to be single. He yearned for companionship. He wanted someone to stroll hand in hand with throughout the rest of his days.

"I actually wanted to become a software engineer," Lucas said after taking a bite of the fish taco. "The idea of not being customer facing and behind the scenes was very appealing to me. I graduated with a degree in computer science when I was twenty-one and got a job as with a start up a month after graduating. The pay was great, and I could work from home on my own schedule. I thought I'd never quit."

"You quit?" Chloe questioned. "Why would you quit? It sounds like you got exactly what you were looking for."

"It was. But then I saw a news story which caught my attention. It was an interview with James Burke, Cure-iosity's founder. He spoke passionately about his company, and not in terms of dollars and cents, like most CEOs. He was fueled by the need to help people live better lives. He started the company and focused on developing medications to help people deal with the everyday struggles of chronic pain, mental illness, and my claim to fame, allergies."

"And you believed him? Lucas, I have interviewed a lot of professionals in my career, and they are almost always lying through their teeth when they talk to the press."

"I thought that too, but something about the way he talked made me want to believe him. That interview stuck with me, and I often reflected on him, wondering how sincere he was towards his cause. Then one night I went to a bar and grill to get dinner. Sitting at the bar with an open seat next to him was Burke himself. He was eating a cheeseburger and watching the

Bears game on the television which hung over the bar. Sitting at a dive bar in blue jeans and a plaid shirt, he didn't seem anything like the CEO of a multimillion-dollar company. I couldn't help but take the seat next to him."

"What did you say to him? What was he like?" Chloe asked as she bit into her second fish taco.

"I didn't want to bother him with too many questions. He seemed to be enjoying his dinner in peace. I only asked him one question. I said – Mr. Burke. I saw your interview on the news a few months ago and thought you were great. I'm new to the professional world. If you could give me one point of advice, what would it be? He set his cheeseburger on his plate, wiped his face with his napkin, looked at me in the eyes, and said, one thing I live by and what I look for in people is how they treat people who can in no way help them. You can tell a lot about some who helps others in need when he knows the people he's helping have no means to return the favor."

"He sounds pretty special, but I don't know if it would be enough for me to give up a good job and change my career," Chloe said.

Lucas hesitated. Sam said the same thing to him when he told him of his plans. He tried to get the idea out of Lucas's head.

"Lucas, you have a great job with a rising start-up. I was in the same position as you at your age. You've followed my footsteps, step for step. You're about to get your big payoff when that company sells. Don't throw that away. You can help others after you make your money," Sam said to him all of those years ago.

Lucas grabbed the margarita pitcher and refilled their glasses. "There's more," Lucas said with a soft tone. "Later that evening, James Burke was walking home, and he witnessed a lady being assaulted by a man on the street. The man was reportedly dragging the woman to a car while she was screaming. James ran over to help and was able to separate the two, allowing the woman to get away. Before James could get away, the man pulled out a gun and shot him in the chest. James passed away within minutes. Several months later, reports came out about his trust fund, or to better put it, lack of a trust fund. There was the perception that James had over a hundred million dollars put away in savings, given he founded a successful corporation, and he lived a modest lifestyle. However, when the trust numbers came out, people were shocked at the little amount that was to be divvied out. It turned out he had been donating 90% of his earnings to cancer research as an anonymous donor. When people donate the type of money he was contributing, they usually get a wing of the hospital named after them. Even smaller contributors get a plaque. But he didn't want any credit associated with his name."

"This man sounds familiar," Chloe said with a wink. "What about his family? What do they do now that the money was spent?"

"I heard that he took out a considerable life insurance plan on himself to protect his family in the event he would pass too soon."

Lucas took a sip of his margarita. He thought of James's last moments, the moments he must keep to himself. As James was bleeding on the street and trying to catch his breath, Lucas rushed over to him to give him an injection which would induce an excess amount of trauma, ultimately leading to his passing. He was on the list. Lucas didn't want him to be, but that was part of the deal. James didn't say anything as he struggled for his last breaths. His eyes said it all as they looked towards the direction of the woman to see she had gotten away.

"After I heard that news, I became convinced that James Burke should be someone who everyone should look up to as a role model. I try, but even I am not as good. You were impressed that I donate half my income to charity. If I were as good of a man as James, I would have never shared that information with you."

Chloe ran her hands through her long brown hair. "Well, I think you seem decent enough."

"I'm still working on it. I didn't know where to start on changing my life for the better, so I decided I'd start where

James left, and I applied for a position with his former company. While I work on what I ultimately want to do with my life, I figured I could do good by convincing physicians to prescribe safer and more effective medications to their patients."

"Well that was quick," the bartender said as he came to clear the dishes. "Another pitcher for the table?"

Lucas would have liked to stay longer, but he knew he better stop while things were good. He met a lovely new person and shared a nice dinner with her. That would be it. He couldn't take the chance of getting to know her any better, or rather, he couldn't take the chance of her getting to know him any better.

"I think I've probably hit my limit," Lucas replied as he handed the bartender cash for the meal. "Thanks"

Chloe interjected, "Here. Let me pay my half. You were here because I needed an interview. I should be paying the entire bill."

"It's okay," Lucas assured. "I don't mind."

The bartender had already walked away. Chloe slumped her shoulders conceding the battle. "Well, thank you."

"It was a pleasure meeting you today, Ms. Benedict. This evening surprisingly turned out to be quite enjoyable," Lucas said as he rose from the table and reached his hand out to shake Chloe's.

It was my pleasure," Chloe replied, giving Lucas a warm smile as she shook his hand.

After exiting through the crowd, Lucas gave Chloe one last wave goodbye. She returned the gesture with one last awkward wave of her own before turning to pave her way through a crowd of pedestrians.

Lucas's mind was telling him to walk towards the train station, but his legs weren't moving. He watched as Chloe walked swiftly between pedestrians, wanting to soak in as much of her as he could before he'd be forced to close the book on this chapter of his life. His hand rose to his chest, feeling the speed in the rhythm of his heartbeat increasing. Though he'd only had known Chloe for less than a few hours, he felt at that moment he was watching "the one" get away.

# Chapter 6

You have my story yet!" shouted Terry Horn from his spacious office. He was an editor for the major newspaper in the Chicago area, and his office was one of the better offices in the building, which didn't match up with his rank with the paper. But he had been with the paper longer than anyone and was respected by everyone. Terry's seen a lot of change throughout the years during his thirty-five-year tenure with the paper. Digitalization, new forms of competition, expanded diversity throughout the workforce, and one change he his reluctant to give up, no smoking or drinking inside the building. When Terry first joined, he smoked a cigar every single day. It was one of the reasons he liked coming to work. To this day, he still walks around with an unlit cigar hanging from his mouth.

"You said to have it done by five," Chloe said from her cubicle, located directly outside of Terry's office. Her location in the office was one of the reason's she hated coming to the office. It put her directly in the line of fire. She also heard everything that went on in his room, and most of the time she didn't want to be hearing what was going on.

To most in the office, Terry comes off as incredibly intimidating. No one ever got the last word with him, and most weren't sure if he was capable of talking at a reasonable volume. He was always yelling in a thick and raspy voice he earned from all of the years of smoking. Terry was overweight, short, wore the same short sleeve white button up t-shirt and black slacks with suspenders every day. On Tuesday's, from 8:50 am to 8:54 am, Terry clipped his fingernails at his desk. He kept an electric razor in his drawer to shave with on Monday's and Wednesday's. He smelled of cigar smoke, and his teeth were as yellow as the paint on the roads. His black hair, or what was left of it, was now speckled with patches of gray.

"I'm going to need it sooner. We've got the annual News Reporters Association Ball tonight. I have to be out of here by four to pick up my wife. And you better have it to me by three so you can go find yourself a date, Miss," Terry yelled back through his office door.

*Great*, Chloe thought. She was hoping he'd forget about the event. She had been dreading it since she heard about it. Chloe hated small talk without a purpose. If it was for a story, she was one of the best at it, but listening to people talk about their kids or the hobbies put her to sleep.

"Three it is," Chloe replied. She tried to keep her conversations with Terry short and to the point, which was no small feat as he was frequently making inappropriate comments to her. He often concluded their monthly touchpoint meetings with, "Get that tight ass out of here and into the field." Chloe didn't take offense to the comments. He was like that with everyone, and, to her knowledge, he never made any unwanted physical advances towards another person. Plus, Terry was a damn good editor. He's saved Chloe on many occasions and in spite of Terry's shortcomings as a human being, she felt fortunate to be paired with him.

The article she was working on was already finished and had been finished for three hours. She didn't want to turn it in early because if Terry had too much time with any piece of work, he would tear it to shreds. The article was about a dog who smelt a fire coming from a family's basement and began barking to wake up its owners. It was just in time as they gathered their children and ran out of the house right as the floor started to collapse. She had to fluff it up for a thousand-word piece in which she praised the dog and warned everyone to change those batteries in their smoke detectors every six months.

It was those types of articles which ate away at Chloe's soul. How could she ever use her work at the paper as a reference to prior work when submitting her novels for publication? No one would take her seriously. Of course, Chloe wished she had that problem, to begin with. The series of mystery novels she set out to write have remained unsolved. She would routinely have a weekend where she finally felt like a breakthrough was coming, but by Monday she would be deleting the file, unhappy with the results.

Chloe could be described as a loner. If forced to provide a list of friends, she could provide the names of a few former college classmates. But she hadn't spoken to them in years. Outside of work, the only person who heard regularly from Chloe was her grandmother, Gammy. The result of a one-night stand, Chloe never met her father, and she never saw much of her mother. When Chloe was eight, her Gammy told her that mother ran off with a man to California. It wasn't much later when her Gammy and Papi sat her down in their living room and informed her that her mother passed away. That part didn't bother Chloe. The part which hurt was the time when her mother was alive but away. She always wondered what it was she could be doing that was more important than spending time with her daughter.

Four years later, Chloe's life was hit again with tragedy. Her Papi had a heart attack and passed away, leaving Chloe and Gammy to take on the world together. The two became inseparable, always reading and baking together. In Chloe's eyes, Gammy was put on earth just for her, healing her scars left from the parents who abandoned her and the loss of her dear Papi.

It wasn't until Chloe was fourteen when she noticed that Gammy began to worry about her lack of interest in other people. She was pretty, prettier than any of her classmates. Yet, Chloe wasn't getting phone calls from boys or going to school dances. She wasn't even hanging out with other girls from her classes. When Gammy pushed the subject on to her, Chloe would reply that all the girls are skanks or all the boys are losers. Gammy couldn't disagree.

"BUUURRRPP!" Chloe heard coming from Terry's office. The smell of grilled onions filled the air. Terry ate the same lunch every day, a cheesesteak sandwich with extra peppers and extra onions. Every day after lunch the same series of smells and sounds would escape into the common cube area. Terry wasn't shy about letting his gas out in the office, regardless of which end it exited his body from.

Chloe held her breath. Everything about the man disgusted her. She always told her Gammy that if he weren't the best editor in town, she'd be gone

Today, the smells and sounds were more disturbing than usual to Chloe. She needed to escape. As she heard the sound of gas exiting his rear, she said, "Done! The story should be in your inbox. I'm off to find a dress for the party."

She hoped he wouldn't remind her of bringing a date. Chloe was lovely and could easily find a date if she wanted to for the party, but she hadn't changed much from her teenage years. When her Gammy pushed the subject, she still gave the same response, "All the boys here are losers."

"Don't be afraid to cross the line a bit with your choice," Terry mumbled with the unlit cigar hanging from his mouth. "Many of the titans of the industry will be there tonight."

*How disgusting.*

One sure way to make the evening worse was to try to hold fake conversations with perverted older men staring down her dress.

"I'll see what I can do," Chloe replied, purposely not acknowledging the sexism from the comment in hopes that Terry wouldn't elaborate further.

"While you were taking your sweet ass time on your article, I took the liberty of finding you a date for tonight."

Chloe stopped in her tracks as she was passing by his door. She was desperately trying to get away without further damage, but this was the nail in the coffin. A blind date from one of Terry's pals was sure to be a night of ass grabbing and inappropriate remarks.

"Thanks, but I think I have someone in mind," Chloe lied.

"I hope that guy is Lucas Braun."

*Lucas Braun?*

She hadn't stopped thinking about Lucas since the interview. His phone number still rest securely in her purse, but she never intended to call. She was secretly hoping Lucas would find her number from his boss and track her down. But she never told anyone this. The fact that Terry was bringing up his name made her question the man she'd been thinking about.

*What does Terry know about Lucas Braun?*

"Lucas Braun? Who is Lucas Braun?" Chloe asked, trying to play dumb.

"Don't shit around the toilet, Chloe," Terry said.

Chloe rolled her eyes as she waited for Terry to continue.

"He's from your Forty Under Forty article. I'd never seen you write about someone the way you wrote about him. I've been reading your work for over five years, and I don't recall a time when you wrote the word remarkable about anybody."

Chloe was speechless. She felt like she was just caught committing a crime. Her eyes were wide as she tried to stutter a rebuke.

Terry smiled and said, "I'll see you at eight. Don't forget to strut your stuff."

Chloe walked away from Terry's office without saying a word. The shocked expression, frozen on her face, drew confused glances from the co-workers she passed during her route to the elevator.

*What does Terry know? He doesn't know anything about me. Who was he to decide who I should date?*

Chloe quickly stepped into an empty elevator to escape the nightmare. She stared at her reflection in the doors and grimaced at her appearance. She looked as if she wasn't trying, which was partially true. The mascara around her brown eyes was the extent of her morning preparations outside of brushing her teeth or putting her hair in a pony-tail. She brought her hand to the end of her hair.

*Eghh. This will be fun to straighten tonight.*

Her eyes then traced down her usual gray V-neck T-shirt and stopped before they reached her black yoga pants. They fixated on her leather purse hanging from her shoulder. She imagined Lucas' phone number written on a folded piece of paper she placed in the pouch with her loose change. Chloe asked Lucas for it after the interview, claiming she might need to call him back for further questions, though she knew there would not be a need for further questions.

As the elevator doors opened, she began to feel warm. It was hot outside, but the office was always known for overdoing it with the air conditioning. It wasn't uncommon for her to find her arms covered in goosebumps.

Chloe took a seat on a bench in the main lobby to cool down. She had always been very confident in herself, but as she pulled Lucas's number out of her navy leather purse, her hand began to tremble. She couldn't remember the last time she asked a guy out on a date.

*Have I ever done this before?*

At this point she didn't know what was more frightening, showing up alone to be harassed by Terry and company, or to call Lucas. Chloe inhaled deeply as she took one last look at the piece of paper.

# Chapter 7

The afternoon sun was beating down on Lucas's back as he peddled his way through one of his favorite bike trails. It was a hot August day, and not many people were out. When Lucas heard the meteorologist warn people to stay indoors and keep cool, he immediately thought it would be a good time to ride one of the of the best bike trails in the area, having it all to himself. Even the animals, which were frequently spotted along the path, were nowhere to be seen. The trail runs through a wooded area, providing magnificent scenery, and today it was all for Lucas to behold.

The opportunity for a leisurely bicycle ride presented itself to Lucas when Steve, his manager, had given him the week off.

"I've checked the numbers," Steve began when he called Lucas early in the morning. Lucas jumped to the conclusion that he was referring to sales numbers, but what he said next surprised him.

"I can't find any instance where you took five consecutive days off from the job. It's time for that to change. I don't want to see or hear from you for the rest of the week. I've talked to the I.T. department and confirmed that your email will be temporarily disabled from your phone and computer. Now go and enjoy yourself."

Lucas's instinct was to protest, and he made a faint attempt to do so by saying, "But I have a full week of calls."

"Never mind your calls. I've been itching to get out in the field a bit. I'll cover them, except for the infamous Dr. Gupta, of course. See you next Monday."

Steve was the kind of manager who any employee would be lucky to have. He was a top performer, so he had the respect of his superiors, and he always had the backs the people he managed, gaining their respect as well. Lucas dreaded the reality that it probably won't be too much longer before Steve earned a promotion into a new position. At which point he'll have to work to build a new relationship with his next manager.

Steve was right. Lucas hadn't ever taken a week away from work. He'd always used his vacation days sparingly, holding them back for when he had a surprise list to take care of. The idea of taking time for himself seemed foreign to him. But he had to admit; it couldn't have come at a better time. His travel and reaping schedule had been hard on him, and he could use some time to rest, clean his place up a bit, barbeque, and ride his bicycle.

Riding a bicycle through the woods was something Lucas had been doing since he was a teenager. His foster parent's house was near trails which led through a wooded area. Lucas spent most of his free time in it either clearing trails to make pathways or riding his bike through his recently cleared trails. There wasn't anything overly exciting about it, but it was a way for Lucas to escape the real world, the world which asked him to be there for people's last moments.

Lucas began riding the trails one day when he saw his old bicycle hanging in the garage of his new place. He looked at his bike and thought of his father. It was a gift from him for getting good grades.

"Son, I can't tell you how proud I am of you. I want you to have some fun this summer. Go out and play with friends, get dirty, get into trouble, just not too much trouble."

His mother was wary of letting Lucas ride away from home alone, but his father took the initiative to reward Lucas for always being good and for doing well in school.

"He needs to be out with friends, not stuck inside all summer while we are away at work," his father would plead.

Lucas's first ride started out better than he imagined. He felt free. The possibilities were endless. He took it around the block a few times to get a feel for how it handled and then he was off. Lucas didn't have a place in mind he wanted to go to. He just wanted to feel the wind on his face and the burn in his legs as he peddled faster and faster. But after about thirty minutes of riding, Lucas's vision began to blur.

*I must be dehydrated.*

He pedaled to a convenience store and left his bike at the designated bike rack. Lucas stepped into the store, feeling the dehydration catching up with him with every step as he walked towards the back of the store to drink from the water fountain. After quickly gulping down nearly half a gallon of water, he felt like a revived person and was anxious to get back out to his bike. However, when he returned to the bike stand, he felt as if he was going to throw up. Not from the dehydration, but from the view of the empty bike stand. His shiny blue bicycle was no longer resting against the rack. He scanned the area and ran to the sidewalk to look down the street, finding that a boy was pedaling away with his brand-new bicycle.

"Hey!" Lucas shouted, frantically. "Hey, that's my bike! Stop!"

But the boy didn't stop. He kept riding away, faster and faster. Lucas could do nothing but watch. What started as experience with endless possibilities and hope quickly turned into the painful feelings of anger and guilt.

He walked home, planning to go straight to his room and never bring it up with his father. Hopefully, he won't notice, Lucas thought. However, when Lucas arrived home, he was surprised to see his father was already back for the day, dusting off his own bicycle. Of all days, he picked that day to come home early and ride a bicycle.

"Hey Lucas!" his father said with a smile. "I thought maybe we could go out for a spin. I could show you some of the trails I used to ride when I was younger."

"Hello, Dad," Lucas replied in a defeated tone.

His father quickly picked up that something was bothering Lucas. Lucas approached him looking at the ground with his back slouched.

"What's bothering ya, buddy?"

Lucas tried to think of a lie he could tell. But when he went to open his mouth, he looked at his father in the eyes. They were big and blue and looked concerned. His large frame towered over Lucas and the closer Lucas got, the smaller he felt. Looking into his father's big blue eyes, he could feel the tears forming in his eyes.

*I can't lie to him.*

"It's…it's gone," Lucas said as the tears started to come faster and faster. "I took the bike and went for a ride. I got thirsty and stopped by the gas station to get a drink. When I came back out it was gone. I'm so sorry."

The tears were pouring from Lucas's eyes, and his throat began to ache.

With a straight face, his father replied, "Go inside and get yourself a glass of water."

Lucas went inside and watched his father drive away in his old pickup truck, which was well past its prime, but his father kept it running like it was built just yesterday. Lucas wondered where his father could possibly be heading.

*What could he do? I did not describe the kid who took the bike.*

He thought about his summer ahead of him and how much better it would have been if he had that bicycle. Instead of riding around town and maybe making a friend or two, Lucas would be stuck at the house, alone, reading books from the library to pass the time.

About an hour later his father pulled into the driveway, and there was a new bike in the bed of the old truck. Lucas rushed outside to meet his father, full of hope.

"What happened? Where did this come from?" Lucas asked, anxiously.

His father stood at the side of the truck and smiled a large, soft, smile.

"Sometimes life will throw punches at you, and sometimes you have to punch back. But one thing I've learned over the years is that you don't have to throw all of the punches yourself. It's always good to have someone by your side to help you when you're down, and I won't always be here to help you.

I want you to take this bike and make yourself some friends who can help you through life's ups and downs.

Lucas stood speechless. He couldn't believe it. He wasn't in trouble, and his summer was saved.

"And here, take this with you."

His father handed Lucas a chain with a key combination to securely lock his bike at future resting spots.

Lucas remained speechless. There were so many emotions running through him, and he didn't know what to say. He felt anger towards the person who took the bike, guilt for taking his eye off of it and for costing his parents the price of two bicycles, but mostly he felt love for his father. He was always there for him. His father preached to go out and make new friends, but the truth was that Lucas's best friend was standing right in front of him. He was there to tell jokes, play catch, build forts, sneak pizza and comics to his room on dull summer nights, teach him to grill the perfect steak, and always offer encouragement to talk to the pretty girl in class, though Lucas was far too shy for that.

He went to his father and wrapped his arms around his waist. His father returned the hug, holding him tight and patting his back.

"Thank you," Lucas said with tears rolling down his cheeks.

"Thank you for being you," his father replied, rubbing his hand through Lucas's hair.

Lucas had arrived at the end of the trail. It was a loop which began and ended just a few blocks from his house. He considered going on another loop, but he could feel the summer heat weighing him down and decided to pedal home to get a head start on his barbeque. He rode his bike right up to his front door and left it on his porch before walking inside. The cold air coming from his air conditioner relieved his overheated body. After Lucas took off his shoes, he noticed that his phone was blinking, indicating he had a message.

*I wonder who would have called me? Steve supposedly blocked off my contact with the company.*

He picked up his phone to play the message, and to his surprise, he heard the voice of Chloe Benedict.

"Hey, Lucas. It's me, Chloe. From the paper. I have kind of an awkward question to ask, especially over a voicemail." There was a slight pause before she continued speaking. "Tonight is the Annual News Reporters Association Ball. It's kind of a big deal in the field. All of the reporters, columnist, and radio hosts will be there. I'm expected to bring a date, and I was wondering if you would be interested in going with me. I know it's last minute and I totally understand if you can't or don't want to…………but I thought I'd ask anyway. I enjoyed the other night at the bar with you, so maybe if you came with me tonight to this event, it wouldn't be quite as unbearable for me. Anyways. I'll talk you later. Bye."

Surprised, Lucas took a seat in his living room to gather his thoughts. He hadn't stopped thinking about Chloe since his interview with her. He could still imagine her brown eyes looking back into his. Even through his imagination, he would get lost in those eyes. He left his phone number with her and had been hoping and dreading she would call him. If she did, then perhaps it meant the feelings he felt that evening were mutual, that she too had an interest in a relationship. This was the same reason Lucas had been dreading the idea of Chloe calling him.

*How could I possibly begin dating someone?*

Getting involved in relationships, both friendly and intimate, was something Lucas had spent his adulthood avoiding. If he were lucky, the person would get suspicious of his frequent disappearances and eventually tire of his excuses. That was if he was lucky. If he were unlucky, that very person would somehow end up on his list. Reaping was already hard enough. He didn't need to make it any worse.

Lucas walked towards the bathroom to take a shower. He couldn't call her back right away. He had to think of something to say. Given that this was last minute, it wouldn't be unreasonable for him just to explain that he was busy.

After showering and getting dressed, Lucas went to grab his phone to return Chloe's call. It was 4:30 and she would need time to try to find another date at the last minute. He felt terrible that he couldn't go with her, but it just wouldn't work out.

*What if we hit it off? What if she started coming over to my place. What if she visited on a night when I had to do a rush reap?*

She would question where he was and what he was doing and probably assume he was having an affair and leave him.

*Or what if she discovered who I really am? How could she possibly be open to the idea of being Death's girlfriend? Even if she were, the higher-ups certainly wouldn't be open to the idea of a mere mortal knowing about the system.*

Sam's teachings came to Lucas's mind. "Don't get caught. Whatever you do, don't get caught. You'll surely be the next on a list, and it won't be pretty."

Lucas wished Sam were here right now. He could use his friend and mentor today. Unfortunately, Sam didn't carry a phone with him. He didn't like the idea of someone being able to call him at any moment.

Looking at his cell phone, Lucas wished he had taken Sam's advice and canceled his own phone plan. That would have prevented this unfortunate event from ever happening. Lucas took a deep breath and hit the call button.

One ring. Two rings. Three rings. Lucas began to feel hope.

*Maybe she won't answer, and I can leave a voicemail.*

Four rings.

*Almost there.*

"Hello."

*Dammit.*

"Um...Hey Chloe. It's Lucas." He was trying not to sound surprised and trying even harder not to let his voice shake.

"Oh. Hi Lucas," Chloe replied, waiting in anticipation of Lucas's next words.

Unsure of how to begin, Lucas opted to ease in with small talk. "So, it sounds like you have quite the event tonight?"

Chloe nervously replied, "Yeah you could say that I guess. Though, it seems more like a chore than an event."

As Lucas listened to her voice, he imagined her lips moving over her perfectly white and straight teeth. He wondered what she would wear tonight. She looked magnificent in yoga pants and a t-shirt. He couldn't imagine how beautiful she would look tonight at the ball. Thoughts of letting loose and trying to make this work out crept into his mind.

*Maybe we could just have tonight.*

He shook his head and reminded himself of Sam's teachings.

*This could never work out.*

"I'm really sorry. I would have loved to have gone with you but I just can't tonight." His stomach knotted up, similar to how it felt when he was reaping. Death had called, the love life of Lucas Braun must go.

Chloe quickly responded as if she wanted to escape the uncomfortableness as quickly as she could. "It's okay. Last minute. I understand. Maybe some other time."

"Yeah, some other time sounds great," Lucas said, regrettably. He didn't know when a better time would be.

*I shouldn't have led her on like that.*

"Well, I better go. I'll talk to you later, Lucas."

Lucas's shoulders sank. He could hear the disappointment in her voice. He wondered if she could hear it in his as he replied, "Yeah. Good luck and have fun tonight."

Lucas hung up his phone and tossed it on his kitchen counter. It echoed loudly throughout his empty house as it hit the stone countertop.

"I hope you break," Lucas said to the phone as he wandered around the house. He paced from room to room with no destination in sight. His heart rate was up, and his blood was pumping. His eyes then fixated on his refrigerator.

*A beer might help.*

But on his way to the stainless-steel doors of his refrigerator, he saw something out of the corner of his eye, resting next to his front door.

"What fresh hell is this?" Lucas said out loud.

It was a manila envelope. The all too familiar manila envelope which held the fate of others and acted as the barrier to Lucas's happiness.

*Of course, I get another list tonight. This is why I can't have anything real in life.*

He desperately wanted to be close to someone. To love someone and have them love him back. To start a family. To see the smiles on his children's faces when he surprised them with pizza and movie nights. Instead, he was only allowed to be closest to the people who are about to die.

Lucas picked up the envelope and could feel the weight of a piece of paper and a single vile.

*Likely another rush reap.*

He opened and saw the usual red border and read the single name on the paper. Written in perfect cursive handwriting was the name of one of the most popular sports writers in the area, Bernie Chapman. Lucas exhaled as he realized what this meant. He was going to have to go to the ball tonight, after all.

# Chapter 8

Bernie Chapman had been with the press for over twenty-five years, specializing in sports. Though he was never athletic enough to play sports competitively, he's had a passion for sports his entire life. He wasn't great at math or good with his hands, leaving only the option of using the two skills he had to provide a living for his family, which were talking and writing. Not only did Bernie have a daily sports column, but he also hosted a radio talk show in the mornings. He discussed sports, trending social topics, and issues which had little to no importance yet still captured his audience and left them wanting more. During one of his morning shows he was sidetracked on a topic and spent an hour of his two-hour segment discussing it. The subject was - how long was too long for a person to be naked in a locker room? The ratings spiked. His listeners were calling, emailing, and texting into the show to offer their opinions.

"It's a locker room. Get over it," one listener chimed in.

"You have the option to change in the covered area next to the shower. If you still choose to walk around the locker room naked, then you're just trying to make others uncomfortable," another listener offered.

He was a beloved member of the community, always willing to help for a good cause. Of all the writers and reporters coming to the event tonight, Bernie was by far the most successful. Fellow reporters will be keeping their eyes on Bernie, hoping for a chance to swoop in and have a conversation with the living legend.

"I'll have a vodka and soda please," Bernie said to the bartender. He was sitting at the bar set up in the center of the downtown hotel ballroom. The ceilings towered forty feet high, and the acoustics were tuned to accommodate some of the finest orchestras. Women wanting to have their weddings in the ballroom often had to book it in advance of even finding the person they will marry. The wait was four years for an off-season month and seven years for the month of June. The only reason the ball could be held here was because of Bernie. He hosted an event which raised over three-million dollars for the hotel owner's son, who was diagnosed with brain cancer. The money helped to cure the boy, and the owner had been forever grateful to Bernie for drawing in such a large crowd for the event.

"I'll have the same," said Lucas.

He arrived at the event early, which was actually fifteen minutes late. Lucas never understood the etiquette for the proper time to arrive at a house party or an event. When someone says six, they mean seven. Why not just say seven?

He was happy to see Bernie had also arrived early. *Perhaps I can get this reap over with before Chloe comes.*

He thought to call her back and say something like, "It turns out I can make it after all." But then he'd have to manage to sneak away during the ball for the reap. After that, he'd have to figure out how to handle the relationship with Chloe.

*Would she expect to see me again?*

Lucas examined Bernie from across the bar. He'd aged well, now in his late forties but could pass for someone in his mid-thirties. Known to always be in style, he was wearing a three-piece, modern fit suit.

"So, I take it you never got a taste for the brown stuff either?" Bernie said looking at Lucas's direction.

Lucas looked behind him, wondering if perhaps Bernie was speaking to someone else. When he turned, he saw there was no one else in the area.

*Brown stuff? What does he mean by that?*

Lucas could see Bernie was awaiting a response.

"I beg your pardon?"

Bernie laughed. "The brown stuff. Whiskey. Bourbon. Alcohol with color. They say that real men don't drink vodka, but I don't like the other liquors, so this is what I drink."

*Dammit*, Lucas thought. Not only was this man one of the most beloved celebrities in the city, but he was also genuinely good. It's not often that people reach out to comment on similarities with strangers, and it was even less often that a celebrity would show an interest.

Lucas raised his hands in the air, surrendering to the accusation. "You caught me. I've tried whiskey, but I hate the flavor. Why would I want to put myself through something that tastes bad and burns when I drink it?"

The bartender returned with their drinks.

"Two vodka sodas."

"Thank you," Bernie replied as he handed the bartender a ten-dollar bill.

"Oh, no." The bartender replied shaking off the offer to pay. "The drinks have been paid for as part of the package."

"Well, have you been adequately paid for? I know these people coming here tonight. There's nothing they like more than an open bar. On top of that, they are lousy tippers. You better take this so that you might make it out of here tonight with a little something in your pocket."

Bernie was very skilled at talking, both with people he knew and with complete strangers. It was the main reason he had been so successful as a radio personality. His voice was calm and engaging, and he could read a situation to always know which words to use to bring out the best of his guest on his radio show.

Lucas eyed Bernie's drink. Its contents bubbled at the rim of the glass. The ice transformed to water, and a saturated ring formed on the napkin from the perspiring glass.

*How can I get the serum into his drink?*

Bernie sat back in his seat with one hand wrapped around the glass. People were gathering into the ballroom faster and faster as the event began to shape up. Lucas wondered what he could say to Bernie to keep his focus on him and not drift off to converse with the hundreds of people hoping to get a few minutes with the beloved celebrity.

"Here's to a lovely night which we'll remember forever," Lucas said as he raised his glass towards Bernie. They were a few seats away from each other and couldn't reach to tap their glasses against one another.

"Cheers," Bernie said with a smile as he raised his glass.

"Oh, that was weak. We need to tap our glasses for a proper cheer," Lucas said promptly, seizing the opportunity to get closer to Bernie's drink.

Lucas rose from his seat and walked over to Bernie, taking the place next to his. If he could keep him close, he hoped he could discretely slip the serum in Bernie's drink. It was the fast-acting heart attack formula. If injected, his heart would stop immediately. If he drank it slowly, it would take about ten minutes to do the job. Given the public area, Lucas didn't think he would be able to get a needle into Bernie without someone seeing, especially given that people would be looking for Bernie to see if he was at the event.

"I have to say, Bernie, I don't know how you do it. You've never met me, and you probably see people just like me every day; people who listen in to your every word every single day, hoping for a chance to meet you in person. If I were you, I'd be looking at my phone or away, trying to avoid eye contact with strangers. Yet here you are, initiating a conversation with me about the vodka and offering an inviting look as I took the seat next to you. You truly are a gift."

Bernie smiled. He had a kind smile and showed it often.

"Twenty years ago, I was at an event like this," Bernie began. Lucas quickly picked up that Bernie was likely a man who had a story for every scenario.

"It wasn't quite as nice as this, but there were going to be a lot of people from the industry attending. I arrived at the event twenty minutes early. I was nervous and didn't know many people and no one had any idea who I was. I went to the bar to get a drink to calm my nerves. I couldn't believe it, but sitting alone at the bar was Mark Falcone. Do you remember him?"

Lucas nodded his head. Before Bernie Chapman, no one covered Chicago sports media like Mark Falcone. He was able to get exclusive interviews with the best athletes. Mark was trusted and respected by both athletes and the public. Not only did he tell the best stories but he also left some of the very best stories untold in respect of those he covered. Rumor has it that he was always the first to know when an athlete planned to retire, sometimes years before it would become known to the public.

Bernie took a sip from his drink before continuing his story. Lucas eyed it, longingly.

*How I wish I could slip something in that beverage of yours and get this over with.*

"Well, I took a seat next to him. Similar to how you and I came to meet each other tonight."

There was nothing similar between Bernie's encounter with Mark and tonight Lucas thought, but he couldn't tell Bernie that.

"He was the first to speak. He said well son, tell me about yourself. Let's have a drink and get to know each other. I was shocked. I sat there in my father's suit, which was three sizes too big, and Mark Falcone was talking to me. Not only talking to me but interested in hearing what I had to say."

Lucas didn't say anything. He watched Bernie as he told the story and could see how much joy was brought to him while he reminisced. The longer he sat with him, the more his stomach began to cramp at the idea of what he had to do to the man tonight.

"So, I told him. I just graduated from journalism school and was working a late-night  talk show. And when I say late night, I mean early morning. It aired from 1:00 am to 3:00 am. I couldn't take call-ins because the only people listening were drunk college kids. I tried it once, and it was a total disaster. Mark looked at me in a way I didn't expect. I just told him I was a nobody in the business and the only people listening to me were drunks. He smiled in admiration and asked for my business card. I wasn't high enough up to have business cards printed for me, but I printed some myself just in case I ever needed one. That twenty dollars paid off in priceless amounts. The next day he called me and asked that I take his daughter out to see the city. I was shocked. What could I have said that would cause him to trust his family to me? Of course, I agreed, and I met her at Union Station the next day. She was stunning. She had blonde hair, blue eyes, and was way out of my league. I took her out to see the pier and then to one of my favorite pizza places. We made small talk and joked around a bit throughout the day. By nighttime, I was in love. Two years later, I married her. The wedding invite list was full of some of the biggest names in the business. I was fortunate enough to make some contacts, and before I knew it, I was the next Mark Falcone of Chicago sports media. I now have two kids and am going on twenty years of marriage. I can die a happy man, and I owe it all to a guy who wasn't too big to have a conversation with the little guy. "

Lucas sat silently for a few moments to admire the story. It never ceased to amaze Lucas how the littlest of moments make the most significant impacts on people's lives. He often wondered if they are purely coincidental or if certain things in life were meant to happen.

*Could there be something which shapes the lives of people, similar to the force which shapes their deaths?*

"That's an incredible story," Lucas replied. "The littlest of moments sometimes make all of the difference."

Bernie smiled in acknowledgment. He was about to speak again, but an abnormally tall man interrupted him.

"Mr. Chapman!" said the tall man. He had a shaved head and was in peak physical shape. Lucas concluded that he must be a former athlete who took a job as a sports reporter when his playing days were over. He was accompanied by a woman who looked to be half his age and also looked as if she could have been on the cover of a swimsuit magazine. Her dress covered just about as much as a swimsuit would. Her back was completely bare, and the front V-neck went halfway down her waist. She had an even tan throughout her body. The diamond on her left ring finger was the size of a marble.

"Mr. Bradley. How are you doing this evening?" Bernie replied as he turned his back to Lucas to converse with the couple.

Lucas looked at the three as they talked. They were oblivious to Lucas. This was his chance. He could slip the serum in Bernie's drink and make a run for it before Chloe arrived. He scanned the room. People were pouring in, and the bar area was getting more congested by the minute. He pulled the serum out of his jacket pocket and opened the lid. He took one last glance at Bernie and the couple.

"Mr. Bradley, did you kidnap this lovely young lady. What's she doing here with the likes of you?" Bernie teased.

Now or never, Lucas thought as he eyed the drink. He began to reach for it. *It is so close. Be quick and get out.* But just as Lucas was a half an arm's length away from the glass, he heard a familiar voice, a voice he was hoping not to hear tonight.

"Lucas? What are you doing here? I thought you said you were busy."

Lucas turned to his right and saw Chloe looking at him in disbelief. She was wearing a black dress which went down to her knees. It had a strap over her right shoulder and fit her slender frame like a glove. Her brown hair was straightened and worn down, reaching midway down her back. Lucas swore he saw a sparkle in her eye. Her red lipstick highlighted her perfectly straight pearly whites. Awestruck, Lucas nearly forgot about the vile of serum in his hand. But he came back to reality and gripped it tightly so Chloe wouldn't see it. He missed his opportunity to quickly take care of Bernie.

"I thought about how you'd be left to attack the evening on your own. And I thought about how much I enjoyed our dinner together a couple of nights ago. I canceled my other arrangements and rushed to get here. I considered calling you on my way, but my cell phone battery died," Lucas lied.

Lucas felt the weight of his cell phone in his pocket. He'd need to turn it off so Chloe wouldn't catch it ringing and see that it was a lie. She stood next to Lucas speechless. Her mouth was held partially open. The moment of silence left Lucas's mind to wonder.

*Had she found another date at the last minute?*

"If you have a date with you, I understand. I can leave. No big deal."

But it was a big deal. He hadn't finished off Bernie yet.

"I don't. I came stag," Chloe said slowly as if she was still in disbelief to be seeing Lucas.

Lucas rose from his chair and in one motion put his hand in his pocket, closing the lid to the vile. He'd have to think of a way to get it into Bernie before the night was over. The task was now much more complicated, and the same could be said for his personal life. This night could add more fuel to the flame, further sparking Lucas's attraction to Chloe.

"Well then. We have a date," Lucas said with a smile.

Chloe wrapped her arms around Lucas and gave him a hug to show her gratitude. Lucas returned the hug, holding her close. His heart began to race, and for a moment he completely forgot about his purpose. He forgot about why he came here tonight. He forgot that he was a reaper, that his parents had passed away, and that he was utterly alone in the world. At that moment, the only thing he knew was that he was here with Chloe, and that was enough. Nothing else mattered.

"So how about a drink?" Chloe said as she motioned for the bartender.

"It's open bar tonight. Thank goodness. It would probably best if you had a drink or two before my boss sees us and makes his presence known. Just try not to take too much offense to how harassing he can be. Don't get me wrong, it will be disgusting, but deep down, he's decent, I think."

Lucas laughed, playfully, "Okay, I'll follow your lead."

He watched as her eyes locked with his for a few lingering seconds before she turned to order their drinks. The bartender brought over two light beers. Chloe handed one to Lucas.

"I hope beer is okay. I felt like hell the morning following those margaritas."

"Beer is perfect," Lucas replied.

As Lucas took a sip from his beer, he saw Bernie's friends were departing. Bernie turned back to his drink and downed the rest of it like a shot.

*Dammit. That would have been it.*

"So, what did you skip out on to be here tonight?" Chloe asked.

Lucas brought his attention back to Chloe and straightened his tie, a nervous twitch of his. He was wearing a modern cut gray suit with a white collared shirt and black tie.

"I have some presentations for work that I'm way behind on," Lucas lied.

It became apparent to Lucas that he had already lied twice in the first two minutes of this date.

*How can I keep this up?*

Lucas's attention went back to Bernie when he saw him rise from his seat and head towards the back corner of the ballroom. Lucas looked at the sign hanging over the doorway which read *Men's Restroom*. Perhaps this could be my chance, Lucas thought. If they were alone in the restroom, he could use the needle to inject the serum into Bernie. It was the less desirable method, but it might be his only option.

"Well, thank you for coming," Chloe said, bringing Lucas's focus back to her. "You want to walk the room? I know a few people who I can introduce you to."

Bernie was getting closer and closer to the restroom. Lucas desperately wanted to just get the reap over with and get out of here.

"Before we do, I really need to use the restroom. Do you mind? I'll be right back."

"Sure, go ahead," Chloe replied as she observed the distraction in Lucas's body language.

Lucas left his beer at the bar and gave Chloe a reassuring pat on her shoulder as he walked past her towards the restroom. Bernie was nearly there. He surprisingly hadn't been stopped by other guests at the event. People looked and pointed as he walked by, but no one dared to stop and say hello to him.

As Lucas turned the corner to walk into the restroom, he could feel the dampness of his underarms. The uncertainty and anticipation began to build as he approached the door. He pushed it open and crossed his fingers, hoping that no one else was in the restroom.

Bernie turned his head to look at the door. He was at the urinal, relieving himself. It was a large restroom, containing eight urinals and four-bathroom stalls. All of which were empty, except for the one occupied by Bernie.

"You again. Those vodka sodas go straight through me anymore. I'm going have to slow it down a bit if I want to avoid spending the rest of my evening in here."

Lucas approached Bernie the way a predator approaches its prey. Swift, fast, and decisive. Bernie's smile disappeared from his face. It was as if he could see in Lucas's eyes that something was now different about the man who he just met at the bar.

"I'm sorry it has to be like this. You possess a positive energy unlike most. That energy will live on, just not with your body."

Before Bernie could cry for help, Lucas pounced towards him and pushed the needle into his neck, injecting the full serum. Bernie fell to the floor. It was quick and painless.

Lucas put the needle back in his pocket and turned towards the door. He wanted to get out before anyone came in. He stepped out and was relieved to see that no one was coming towards the restroom. Lucas then straightened his jacket and headed back into the ballroom.

The reap went much smoother than Lucas thought it would. He had enough time to leave the scene and find Chloe before someone discovered Bernie's body lying in the restroom.

He spotted Chloe. She appeared uncomfortable as she stood next to a man who looked to be about thirty years older than her. He was laughing as he talked while Chloe looked down at her feet.

*He must be the pervert Chloe was talking about.*

As Lucas approached Chloe, he thought about what Bernie told him. How the smallest of moments can change everything. He couldn't help but wonder if the interview for the paper would be the moment that would change his life forever. Could he keep his secret and have a relationship with Chloe at the same time? He wanted that answer to be yes.

Chloe looked up and smiled at Lucas when he approached her. He put his arm around her shoulder. Lucas rarely offered physical contact with others, but putting his arm around Chloe felt as natural as breathing to him.

"This must be Mr. Braun," said the man acknowledging Lucas's presence.

Lucas looked at the man and then at Chloe for an introduction.

"Lucas, this is my editor, Terry Horn."

Lucas reached out his free hand for a handshake. Terry returned the gesture and grabbed Lucas's hand. Lucas had shaken a lot of hands in his profession, but no one had a firmer grip than Terry. His hands were about average length, but they were abnormally wide. Lucas tried not to wince as Terry squeezed harder and harder.

"That's a firm grip you've got there, Terry." Lucas finally said as a cue for Terry to let go.

Terry loosened his grip and let go. "I was just checking to see what kind of man Chloe was interested in. A pussy wouldn't have said anything. He would have just cried out in pain. You passed the first test."

Lucas tried not to roll his eyes, recalling that Chloe warned about Terry's tendency to harass people.

"How nice of you to look after Chloe," Lucas replied.

He took his arm off of Chloe's shoulder and placed it at his side. Chloe quickly reached out and held his free hand. She was holding her light beer in her other as she talked with Terry about who would be attending the ball this evening and who they need to try to network with. Terry was pointing out an editor for the major paper in New York when a series of screams were heard from the back corner of the ballroom.

"Call an ambulance! Hurry, please hurry! Bernie Chapman isn't breathing!"

People immediately rushed towards the back of the room. Chloe had an expression of horror on her face as she turned to observe the scene. Lucas held his head down, looking at his feet for several seconds, before bringing his head up to see

Terry's blue eyes staring at him. Lucas stared right back to see if Terry would shake his concentration. But he didn't. He stared deeper and deeper as if he was looking into Lucas's mind and seeing precisely who he was. It as if he knew that this was all Lucas's fault.

"We should get out of here. The event isn't happening tonight. It'd be best if there were fewer people in the way of the emergency crews," Chloe said, unaware of the awkward stare down between Lucas and Terry.

"You're probably right," Lucas said, holding his gaze on Terry.

Lucas didn't know what Terry could know about him or if Terry was just a man who enjoyed harassing people. Either way, Lucas knew that he would not forget the name, Terry Horn.

# Chapter 9

Arrghhh!" Lucas screamed, bursting to his feet from his bed. He was sweating and panting heavily as he came to the realization that he was in his bedroom.

"Another nightmare," he said out loud to his empty bedroom.

It was about his parent's death, a reoccurring nightmare for Lucas. But this time it was different. Instead of riding in the car, he was watching from the outside of the car. The car was moving fast, but Lucas was somehow able to keep up with it from the outside. He could see inside as his father and mother desperately tried to see through the pouring rain. All Lucas wanted to do was yell at them to stop. But he couldn't. He could only watch. The more he watched, the more he realized that something was different about this scene. His parents were trying to see through the rain, but they weren't in the front seats. They were sitting in the back.

This didn't make any sense to Lucas. Why were they in the back seats? Who was driving the car? Lucas tried to look in the front seat, but all he could see was a shape. He tried and tried to run forward to catch a glimpse, and he got closer and closer to the front window. He was just about to pear through the front window when it happened. Crash. The car lost control and smashed into the creek.

Lucas wondered what the dream could have meant.

*Why were they in the back seat? Why was I outside of the car? Who was driving the car?*

He rubbed his hands across his face and made his way towards the kitchen to start a pot of coffee. It was Sunday, the last day of his week away from work. Lucas concluded that his manager was right, he needed the time off. He was able to wipe down all of the surfaces of his house, scrub his hardwood floors, and declutter. His trash can was overflowing with things Lucas never used and never needed. Every sales conference had giveaways, and he was annually awarded a plaque for being the top salesman of the year. Lucas never knew what to do with the things, so he just put them in his closet. The number of items multiplied over the years as he went to more and more conferences. Seeing no end in sight for the junk, he decided to be proactive and discard of it all.

Once the coffee had finished brewing, Lucas poured himself a cup and then stepped outside on his deck to soak in the sunrise.

"Got a cup for me?"

Lucas jumped, startled from the surprise of someone being at his house. He looked over saw his old friend sitting in one of his patio chairs.

"Sam, I wish you'd get a phone," Lucas said as he exhaled in relief.

Sam, as usual, came unannounced. Lucas wished he could return the favor one of these days, but Sam never told him where he lived. When Lucas asked, Sam would reply, "Over to the west." At first, Lucas wondered if Sam was lying to him.

*Does he not value our friendship enough to give me his phone number and address?*

But as Lucas grew to know Sam over the years, he learned that he lived his life with rigorous order and precaution, starkly different from the casual impression he gave.

"Cell phones can track where you are at all times. Not exactly the best recipe for a reaper, don't you think?" Sam would say.

Lucas couldn't argue with the logic. But his day job required a cell phone, forcing him to take the chance. The phone had come in handy from time to time too, providing last-minute directions or fact checks as he hunted down his list.

Lucas went back inside and poured a second cup of coffee. He was happy to see Sam, but he had also been dreading bringing up Chloe with him. He knew Sam would never approve of Lucas having a girlfriend. Sam enjoyed the intimacy of being with a woman, but he limited his exposure to one-night stands. The idea of a one-night stand seemed too much like a reaping assignment to Lucas. Meet the person for a moment, sometimes learn a little about the person, do the job, then discard.

It had been a few days since the ball. Lucas hadn't called Chloe, and she hadn't called either. Lucas figured she was either busy with work or waiting for him to call. Thus far she had always been the one the call.

*Perhaps this was her test to see if I am really interested.*

"Here you go, pal," Lucas said to Sam, handing him a cup of coffee. The steam escaped from the maroon coffee mug, dispersing its concentration of heat back into the air around it.

As Sam reached for the cup of coffee, he looked through the patio door and into Lucas's house.

"I see you've finally cleaned up the place a bit. You've been getting any action?"

Lucas shrugged. "Had some time off work. Thought I'd take advantage and clean up a bit. They say the ticket to a clean mind is a clean space. We'll see if it works."

Sam took a drink of the coffee. He was wearing a plaid shirt, blue jeans, and sandals. He always looked as if he was ready to go anywhere but prepared to go nowhere at the same time. His casual attire could pass for going out to dinner or for staying at home and streaming movies on the couch.

"If your mind isn't cleaned up yet then it's never going to be, buddy. I'm sorry to say it."

Lucas was about to take a drink of his coffee but paused in response to Sam's comment. "That's a little harsh don't you think?"

Sam didn't respond. He looked out over the river as he talked. It was shaping up to be a beautiful day. The sun was shining on the river, and people were emerging from their homes on the side opposite of Lucas's house to make use of the scenic trails.

"Do you ever think about moving to the city?"

The question took Lucas by surprise.

*Move? To the city? Why would I want to move?*

Although life in the city would help with Lucas's aversion to riding in a car, his house, blocks from the train station, kept him close enough to the city. His home was paid off, and it had all of the finishings and fixtures he desired. He had good neighbors, though he doesn't know if they are good people. They kept to themselves, and he kept to himself, which was just the way he liked it.

"Why would I move?" Lucas asked.

"I just find it curious. Given your past and how your parents went. I wonder why you'd want to live so close to water."

"Oddly, water isn't the problem. It's cars that trouble me. I still get uncomfortable every time I have to get in one. That's why I live here, close to the train. No need for a car."

"I hope someday that changes for you," Sam replied. "Life isn't meant to be lived in fear."

Sam wasn't kidding around today, Lucas thought. He usually liked to joke around and live like there were not any problems in the world. Before Lucas could mutter a response, Sam jumped back into his interrogation.

"I still don't get it. Why are you afraid of cars? You know it wasn't really the car that took the lives of your parents. Their time was up. They were on a list. It would have happened to them whether they were in a car, on a boat, on a train, or even sitting on their front porch."

Lucas was well aware of these facts. He reminded himself of these facts every time he was about to get into a car. But no matter how hard he tried to think rationally about it, he couldn't stop the pain he felt each time he closed the door and fastened his seatbelt. His stomach would feel hollow but also full as it twisted in knots. His mind would replay the scene again and again. Every tap of the brakes drove a dagger deeper into his empty heart. Every push of the gas brought the walls of the car in closer and closer until it felt like his body was completely entangled with the vehicle.

"I had the dream again last night. Except for this time, it was different. I wasn't in the car. I was outside watching, and mom and dad weren't in the front seats. They were in the back of the car. Someone else was driving the car, but I couldn't see who it was. What do you think that was about?" Lucas said, ignoring Sam's question.

Sam shook his head. "I think you are overthinking it, my friend. I'm really sorry this happened to you, but I hate seeing you like this. I wish you could move on."

Sam's comments infuriated Lucas.

*What was Sam talking about? How could I move on?*

"Move on? How can I move on? That night I lost everything. I lost my family. I lost my freedom. I lost my identity. All I do is think about that night, and the more I think about it, the more it doesn't make sense. How did I end up on that creek bed?"

"You were saved. Your life as you knew it was supposed to end in that car. But the reaper showed you mercy. Your dream was likely a metaphor for reality. Your parents had no control over their destiny. You know how it goes, their name showed up on a list. Their car was driven into the creek by fate."

"Why me? Why save me?"

"Somethings will always remain unsolved," Sam replied.

They both sat in silence for a moment and let the warm sun soak into their skin. It offered a therapeutic calm to ease the tension between them.

"So, you took care of Bernie on short notice. That was good work. The celebrities can be tough," Sam said.

"He was a good guy. The good ones always hurt," Lucas said.

Lucas looked at Sam to see he was nodding in agreement. He wondered how Sam could keep up with it all. Sam was always well prepared to discuss Lucas's reapings during his visits. These encounters with Sam typically left Lucas feeling more upbeat. When he felt like the world gave him more than he could take, he could always rely on Sam to help pick him up. Today, however, Sam wasn't doing anything to help lift the weight of the world from his shoulders. Instead, he was adding more weight.

"Well I didn't come here just for coffee today," Sam said, rising from his chair. He reached into his back pocket and retrieved a familiar manila envelope, folded in half.

Lucas let out an audible sigh. "They are coming faster and faster these days."

He thought about Chloe.

*How could I ever expect to call Chloe when I live a life as unpredictable as this? If we were together, we might have made plans for this beautiful day. What would she think if I suddenly couldn't partake in those plans with no explanation?*

"Yes, they are. And you have been one of the best at it," Sam said in a reassuring tone. "I think back to when I first met you. You were young and broken. I honestly didn't think you'd make it this far. I thought you would have messed up along the way, ending up on another reaper's list. But you've been careful, quick, and clean."

Lucas wondered if he'd been as careful as Sam was suggesting. He thought back to the look Terry Horn gave him when he heard about Bernie's death. It was as if Terry expected Bernie to die that night and he suspected Lucas was the reason why.

"I try my best to get them over with as quickly as possible. No mess, no frills. Just get in and out and try to move on with my life."

"And I want you to move on with your life, Lucas. It brings me great joy to be here this morning with this list. You see, this list is unlike the others. For one, I'm hand delivering it. I can't recall a time that I've done this. Secondly, it is the last list you will receive. Once you complete this list, you will no longer be a reaper."

Lucas paused, wondering if he was dreaming.

*Did Sam really just say what I think he said? The words I've been waiting to hear for the past twenty years. The words that would set me free from the nightmare which has been tied to me like a ball and chain. Could this be real? Please let this be real.*

"Are you saying what I think you're saying?" Lucas asked, hesitantly.

Sam didn't reply. He merely smiled as he stood in front of Lucas.

Lost for words, Lucas shot up from his seat and hugged Sam. He could finally begin to live the life he dreamed of living for so long. No longer would he have to look death in the face every time he looked in the mirror. No longer would he have a lack of control over his life. He would be free as soon as he finished this list.

"I'm happy for you, Lucas," Sam said, handing Lucas the list.

Lucas took the list and began to peel open the envelope. He wondered how many would be on the final list. *Ten? Twenty?* As he pulled the list from the envelope, he immediately noticed something different about the letter. Instead of the standard blood red border, he saw a gold border. At the top, it read *Final.*

"This is really happening," Lucas proclaimed, still unable to believe that it could be true.

His eyes scanned the list, and to his surprise, he didn't see a page full of names. In fact, he saw only two names. Scott Banks and Bethany Mandel.

"You're probably wondering how to do it," Sam stated.

Lucas held the list with his left hand and ran his right hand through his hair on the back of his head.

"Umm. Yeah. Usually, I have some sort of clue, but I don't see anything on this list."

"You'll have to do the scouting for these two. You will need to find them, identify their habits and pick the right moments," Sam replied.

"How much time do I have for these two? "

"You have two months. The sooner you finish, the sooner your duty is up, but you have to be careful not to get caught. You've come so far. It'd be a shame to let something slip through the cracks this late in the game."

Lucas looked at the list. The time had come. He thought about Chloe. A future with her was now a real possibility. They could go on picnics, see movies, go to parties and everything in between. For the first time in a long time, Lucas could finally be happy.

It then dawned on Lucas that this might be the last time he sees Sam. He had only known Sam while serving as a reaper. Would this list be the knife which severs their relationship?

"Will I see you again, Sam?" Lucas asked.

Sam smiled and placed his hand on Lucas's shoulder. "I'm so proud of you Lucas. I'm going to miss you. I hope for nothing but the best for you. But until my final list comes, I don't think we will see each other again."

*Every rose has a thorn.*

The happiness Lucas felt moments earlier was now accompanied by the sadness of losing a mentor and friend. Sam was Lucas's light in the darkest hours. He always knew what to say at the right time. Lucas doesn't think he would have made it without Sam.

"Why me?" Lucas asked. "You've been reaping longer than I have. You have sacrificed more than I have. Why haven't you received your final list?"

Without hesitating, Sam replied, "There comes a time for all reapers. There isn't a rhyme or reason to it that is apparent to me. My time will come, and when it does, you'll be the first to know."

The humidity began to weigh down heavier as the sun continued to rise. Lucas could feel he was starting to perspire under his arms. He looked to his coffee and was no longer appealed by its deep flavor and warmth.

"Well, I need some water. You need one, or a refill on your coffee?"

"Nah. I'm okay."

"I'll be right back." Lucas walked through his French doors and into his kitchen. He felt a sense of relief to be walking into a clean place. He had been so far behind in keeping up with the place the past few months. The week off helped him get back ahead.

"You want to go grab a bite to eat? There's a place down the street that serves a good breakfast," Lucas said, turning around to walk back out on the deck.

When he stepped outside, he was surprised to see that no one was there. Sam had left.

*Typical Sam*

It was just Lucas now. No more Sam, no more guidance. The weight of the world rests again on his shoulders. But now it was different. It didn't feel as heavy. It was as if the upcoming freedom acted as a crane, lifting the weight of the world ever so slightly.

He looked across the river and saw an elderly couple walking hand in hand on the walkway. It was a pleasant realization of the life he could now live. Perhaps he could enjoy the company of other people and even grow old with a companion. For the first time in Lucas's life, his hopes were now a reality. He grabbed his list and reread it.

*Final.*

He still couldn't believe that he finally got it. His ticket to a new life. Lucas sat on his deck for another ten minutes, imagining what his life would be like once his reaping days were behind him, completely oblivious to the man who just took a seat on the bench across the river, watching his every move.

# Chapter 10

Sammy's Tavern was mostly empty, a common occurrence for the place. A few regulars come in to drink draft beer or whiskey and not much else. The lights were dim and the place smelled of body odor and smoke. Most of the patrons were male and at least sixty years old. They all looked even older than they already were. The years of smoking and drinking didn't help them age gracefully.

Sitting at a table in the back corner was Terry Horn. He was wearing black slacks, a short-sleeve button-up shirt, and black suspenders; all of which helped to blend him in with the crowd. If there was something that would make him stand out, it was the mobile phone next to his ear.

"What do you have for me this time, Terry?" said the man on the other side of Terry's phone call, Bryce Cooper.

Bryce was a retired detective, but he was still young, yet to turn fifty. His retirement took the force by surprise. Bryce was the city's best-kept secret, and he had a knack for solving murder cases which appeared to be unsolvable. He became friends with Terry Horn early in his career, who like Bryce, had a flair for solving cases. Until he met Terry, Bryce hated the press. He viewed the press as a roadblock, trying to get a bit to send out to the public without concern of compromising the case. But Bryce learned very quickly that Terry was different. He wasn't there for a story. He was there with hunches, which he called information. For the most part, Terry's hunches were right. Bryce called it Terry's sixth sense.

Terry took a drink from his pint of beer. Like most beers served in this tavern, it was warm. He took a deep breath and said, "I think I've found a serial killer."

Bryce ran his hand through his hair. He had trouble hearing Terry through the phone. He sensed that Terry was in a bar. Terry often called Bryce from the bar. Drunk men shouting in the background was his cue that Terry was about to drop a new case on his lap.

"Terry, I'm having trouble hearing you, but I can tell you are at the bar, so I'm assuming you said you found a murderer. Didn't you get the memo? I'm retired now."

Terry didn't take Bryce's retirement seriously. He thought he was much too young to retire and had too much passion left inside of him.

"You're too young to be retired. Hell, I've been working almost as long as you've been living. What did you retire for anyways? It's not like you've been off traveling the world."

Bryce walked to his liquor cabinet and grabbed a bottle of whiskey. He poured himself a glass and drank it in one gulp.

Terry had a point. Bryce did retire, but from an outsider's view, he retired to nothing. He never married, and he hadn't done anything to kickstart his ambitions of golfing every morning, traveling across the country, or starting a vineyard.

"If you go by years, then yes I retired too soon. But if you go by cases solved, I probably should have retired ten years earlier."

Terry shook his head in disagreement on the other side of the phone conversation. "Cut the bullshit, Bryce. You miss it. When you picked up your phone a few minutes ago and saw it was my name you felt excited for the first time since you retired."

Bryce poured another glass of whiskey. He only took a sip this time. It was far too expensive of a bottle to drink in shots.

"How'd you come about this one?"

Terry took the cigar from his front pocket and lit it up. *I've got him.*

"Do I hear you lighting up a cigar? I thought you were at a bar?"

"Nobody here cares. Everyone in this bar is in a perpetual state of drunkenness. They didn't even notice that I came in. The bartender has smoked two cigarettes since I arrived. You know, you should join me here sometime."

"Sounds lovely," Bryce said, sarcastically.

Terry took another drink of his warm beer before continuing.

"A few weeks ago, I was eating dinner alone in my dining room. Just as I was finishing up, I looked out the window. You remember my house? The dinner table sits at the front of the house and looks out the bay window to the subdivision."

Bryce smiled and replied, "Yeah, I remember your house. You live in a neighborhood much too nice for the likes of you. I bet your neighbors are thrilled to see you walk out each morning in your underwear to grab the newspaper, belching along the way and farting as you bend over."

"My neighbors are just like me. They just hide it behind closed doors. I'm as genuine as they come. It's unfortunate there aren't more out there like me. "

Bryce let out an audible laugh. "You were eating dinner. Where does the serial killer come into play?" he pressed.

"It had been a rough day, and I wasn't in the mood for watching the bullshit they put on the television. I stayed at the table to enjoy my scotch instead of drinking it in the living room. I was watching out the window when I saw a man I hadn't seen before across the street. I didn't see a car and was concerned he was a door-to-door salesman. I hate it when those people come. You don't see me interrupting their evenings. My neighbor, Tom Dempsy, opened the door and looked as if he was trying to figure out who the person was. They had an exchange for about a minute while Tom guarded his front door. But then I was surprised to see that Tom let him inside. I figured Tom was either a sucker or he did indeed know this guy. Fifteen minutes later I saw the man leave the house.

After a couple of hours, I heard sirens across the street. They were at Tom's house. The next day his wife informed me that Tom had a stroke and passed away."

Bryce paused, waiting for Terry to continue. After a few more seconds, Bryce ended the silence and said, "Thus far, your story doesn't lend itself to a serial killer case, or even murderer. Do you think that man was somehow involved? Did you get a good look at him?"

"The timing seemed suspicious to me. I reached out to Bob from the station and asked for surveillance footage from that night."

Terry brought his smartphone down so he could see the screen and sent Bryce an email containing several pictures.

"You should have just received an email from me. Open it up."

Bryce walked to his couch and grabbed his tablet. He opened his email and saw a message with no subject line from Terry just came through. He opened it and began looking at the pictures.

"Well, what do you think?" Terry asked, growing impatient.

Bryce replied, hesitantly, "This is the man?"

Terry nodded his head in agreement, though no one was there to see his nonverbal cues. "That's him. I'd bet my bottom dollar on it."

"Do you recognize him? Have any idea who he is or where he lives?"

A broad grin spread across Terry's face as he brought his phone down and forwarded Bryce a second email. It was the Top Forty Under Forty article with the picture of Lucas Braun circled.

"I just sent you another email. Don't you think there is a similarity between the two?"

Bryce studied the two for several minutes. He had twenty years of experience of looking at surveillance and trying to identify a match. Rarely did it work out that he could get a positive I.D. from a surveillance camera and this case was no different.

"I can see they are similar, but it's not a slam dunk. And what if they were the same? All you have is that this man was at Tom's around the same time that Tom died of a stroke. It doesn't prove that any foul play occurred."

Terry conceded, "You're right, it doesn't."

Bryce paused, waiting for Terry to continue. It was unlike Terry to give up so quickly.

"You have more, don't you? I've never known you to give up a hunch just like that."

Terry took a long puff from his cigar and exhaled towards the ceiling.

"Last week, Bernie Chapman died of a heart attack at the Ball. Did you hear about it?"

"Yeah, I heard. It was all over the news. Terrible loss."

"Guess who was at that party?"

"I'm going to assume your boy, Lucas, was there."

Terry grinned and forwarded Bryce a third email.

"Yes, he was. I reached out to some contacts for footage of the ballroom from the event. Take a look at these photos."

The photos were of Lucas sitting next to Bernie at the bar followed by photos of him entering the restroom shortly after Bernie and then leaving minutes later before joining Terry and Chloe.

"I gotta say this is suspicious, but you still don't have any proof," Bryce replied as he looked over the photos. "This would never hold up in court."

"If I had proof we would be having a very different conversation. I tracked down where he lives. He has a nice place in St. Charles. I watched him from a distance yesterday morning. You should see this schmuck. He was out on his deck enjoying a bottle of water on a beautiful Sunday morning. It looked like he'd been there a while and possibly even had company as I saw two coffee mugs sitting on the deck. He looked completely relaxed and free, oblivious to the fact that people have been dropping dead around him. This is where I need your help. I've been trying to trail him, but I haven't got the time with my day job. I need you to take over the investigation for me."

Bryce leaned back on his couch and took another drink of his whiskey.

"Terry, I've retired. I've moved on from the life of crime. Call the station. They'll be able to set you up with someone."

"Don't play with me. You know you miss it. What else are you going to do with your days? And what if this guy is the real deal and getting away with murder right before our eyes? How would you feel about him being loose and on the streets?"

Bryce looked at the floor, shaking his head.

"If I'm going to do this, you're going to have to send me a bottle of the scotch you seem to enjoy so much."

Terry had a large grin on his face, revealing his yellow stained teeth.

"Welcome back, buddy."

Terry hung up his phone and went to the bar for another large draught beer.

"Another cold one," Terry requested, sarcastically. The bartender took the mug and poured him another beer. Her style was sloppy as most of the mug filled with foam. She still had a cigarette hanging from her mouth. But for two dollars, Terry wasn't going to complain. Plus, he was able to get away with smoking his cigars in this place. He gave the bartender a five-dollar bill and walked towards his seat to see that his phone was ringing.

"You miss me already?" Terry said, smiling as he sat down.

"I was thinking the occasion calls for us to meet in person."

Terry smiled and took another long drink of his warm beer.

# Chapter 11

Lucas's heart fluttered as he thought about his next move. He felt as if he was seated on a roller coaster, waiting nervously for the ride to spring into motion. He knew his fear would be overcome once the ride began, but the anticipation continued to build as the time passed. Once he set this in motion, there would be no turning back.

It had been over a week since he saw Chloe at the Ball. He didn't know the rules of dating or how many days a guy was supposed to wait before calling a girl, but he had a feeling that he had waited too long. Up until a few days earlier Lucas was prepared to let Chloe go. He didn't want to go down the path of lies and deceit. However, all of that changed when Sam stopped by and delivered his final list. Just two names stood between him and freedom. He had scouting to do and two months to execute on the list, but when Lucas considered his options, he felt he'd rather take his chances with Chloe while completing his obligations rather than take the chance of completing his list before calling Chloe.

*If I wait too long, she may no longer be interested.*

It was late in the afternoon on a Friday. The breeze coming off the lake was refreshing. Lucas imagined it would be jacket weather once the sunset, a welcomed event after a long and hot Chicago summer. Lucas had brought a backpack with a change of clothes and had already swapped his suit for the pair of corduroy pants and a T-shirt.

Casual clothes and an afternoon coffee had become Lucas's new Friday tradition to help ease him into the weekend. Instead of catching the train to head back to his home, Lucas sat at a table outside a coffee shop in the city.

*Just do it. How is it I can track people down and reap their souls, but I can't call a girl?*

Lucas closed his eyes and hit dial. His heart began to race, and he immediately regretted dialing.

*Voicemail. Voicemail. Please don't pick up.*

"I don't want to talk to you," said a voice, interrupting what Lucas thought to be the last ring before the phone went to voicemail.

It was Chloe, and as Lucas thought, she was pissed off at him for not calling her sooner. He debated whether to try to come up with an excuse or to apologize.

"I'm sorry," Lucas stated. "I don't have a good excuse for why I haven't called. I could make up some excuse about work, which you would have no way of proving me wrong about, but

I figure I'd cut the bullshit and just start with saying I'm sorry and I hope you'll let me make it up to you by taking you to dinner."

Chloe smiled as she sighed into the phone. "It better be a damn good dinner."

Lucas was now smiling as he spoke into the phone. He had her. Not only had he found a girl who he couldn't stop thinking about since meeting her, but he was also going to take her on a date.

"Only the best will do," Lucas replied.

"Okay. I guess I'll see you at seven." Chloe said.

Lucas hesitated. "Seven?"

"Yeah. I'm free tonight, and I'm hungry."

He was hoping she would say she's free tomorrow or even the next weekend. He wasn't anticipating meeting for dinner tonight.

*Take what you're given. Don't risk proposing a different time.*

"Seven sounds great," Lucas replied.

"I live on the corner of Wacker in the apartment building next to the new coffee shop. Do you know where that is?"

Lucas looked at the street sign near to him. He was sitting at a new coffee shop on the on the corner of Wacker. Next to him was an apartment complex going up at least fifty stories high. Lucas didn't believe in coincidences, but if he did, this would top his list.

"Yeah, I can find it."

"Great. Just let me know when you arrive. I'll meet you downstairs."

"I'll see you soon," Lucas said as he hung up his phone.

He looked at his watch. It was four-thirty in the afternoon. There was no chance he'd make it home and then back to the city in time.

*Thank goodness I brought a change of clothes.*

The last thing he wanted to do was wear a suit during his first date with Chloe. She'd already expressed her distaste for them. He pondered where he should take her for dinner.

*Italian? Mexican? A grill and bar?*

He thought back to his father telling him the story of his first date with his mother, a story Lucas heard on several occasions. He could see his father's eyes light up every time told it.

"It was a chilly summer evening. I had been courting your mother for quite some time, but she was playing hard to get. She was every bit as beautiful then as she is now. She had men trailing her at every corner, and I was one of them. One day we crossed paths, and I was fortunate enough to hold eye contact with her. She looked right at me and smiled. I couldn't pass on the opportunity to ask her to go to dinner with me. I stopped her and told her she was absolutely beautiful and that I'd be honored if she'd join me for dinner. I didn't think there was any way she would say yes but to my surprise, she agreed.

I didn't have much money and couldn't afford to take her to a nice restaurant. It was then that I decided I needed to find a different way to be romantic. I stopped by the local burger joint on my way to pick up your mother and grabbed a couple of burgers and shakes. I put them in a picnic basket in the trunk of my car. Boy was she regretting her decision when she saw that I pulled up to the park and opened my trunk. She probably thought it would be the place where she'd die.

I then pulled out the picnic basket, a flower, and two shot glasses. I gave her the flower, a purple dahlia. She said she had never been given anything like it. Even the florist said it was a rare pick for a first date, but something about the deep purple color it exuberated struck me.

I then poured us two shots of the cheap bourbon, and I told her I heard a rumor that if you take a shot of bourbon, it makes eating cheeseburgers in this park seem like eating a steak in a five-star restaurant.

She smiled her breath-taking smile, the one that still lights up my world every day, and then we drank our shots. They were terrible and burned all of the way down. But she didn't care. She said the cold, soggy cheeseburger tasted just as good as a filet mignon from a five-star restaurant. Of course, it didn't. She was just being nice. But to this day, cold soggy cheeseburgers hold a place near and dear to our hearts."

Lucas loved thinking about his parents falling in love. Even at a young age, he could see they never lost their love for each other. He hoped to one day find that for himself.

*Maybe Chloe is my chance to have the happiness my parents had.*

He could think of nothing better than to pay tribute to his parents by recreating their first date. He stopped at a convenience store and purchased a blanket, the cheapest bottle of bourbon the store carried, and two shot glasses. He then stopped by a burger joint and grabbed a couple of double cheeseburgers but put a little twist on the order and opted for sodas instead of shakes for fear the shakes would be melted by the time they reached their destination.

He stopped at the florist on his way back towards Chloe's apartment. He searched through every flower they carried.

*Roses. Tulips. Daisies. Where are the dahlias?*

Then he saw it. In the back corner of the store was a single purple dahlia.

Everything was coming into place, perfectly.

Lucas looked at his watch and saw it now read fifteen till seven. He was a few blocks away from Chloe's and decided to head her direction. He would be right in time for their date. The streets were less congested now than what they were a couple of hours earlier. The rush hour traffic had passed, and it was just before people began to go out for the evening.

Lucas pulled out his cell phone to inform Chloe he was at her building as he approached her apartment complex.

She answered her phone after a single ring, almost sounding surprised to hear from Lucas. "Wow, you called. I like that. Most people just text these days. Okay, I'll be right down."

Lucas had an aversion to text messages. He felt he missed too much of the conversation by not hearing the cues coming from the person's tone. He was happy to hear Chloe was in favor of his aversion.

As he waited on the street, he looked at his reflection in the window and wondered if he had made a mistake. He was wearing corduroy pants and a t-shirt on the first date.

*What if Chloe wears a dress? Would it make her feel uncomfortable to be overdressed? Would she look down on me for being underdressed?*

The door to Chloe's apartment complex swung open, and Lucas's anxiety quickly disappeared. Chloe stood there wearing form-fitting jeans, a pink blouse, and a jacket. Her hair was worn down, reaching the middle of her back and her brown eyes were subtlety lined with eyeliner. She looked stunning.

"Hey, there. You ready?" Chloe said, approaching Lucas.

He nodded, awestruck by her beauty.

He wondered if he should give her a welcoming hug. She was standing just a foot away from him. Unsure, Lucas opened his arms and gave Chloe a wide-armed hug, and Chloe awkwardly returned the hug.

"Well, we can work on that later," Lucas joked, realizing the exchange wasn't as smooth as he hoped it would be. Without overthinking it, he grabbed Chloe's hand and led her in the direction of the pier, which was only a few blocks away from Chloe's apartment.

"Where are we heading?" Chloe asked.

While she joked that the dinner better be good, she hoped they wouldn't be going to a place with overpriced food and menus with words she couldn't pronounce. Her typical dining out experience consisted of her being greeted by the hostess while she picked up her to-go order. Chloe debated wearing a dress in case Lucas was able to secure a reservation to one of the nicer restaurants, but dresses weren't her style, and she didn't want to risk being overdressed and uncomfortable tonight.

"It's nice out today. I thought dinner at the pier would be perfect."

Chloe smiled. "Dinner outside sounds great."

"How long have you lived here?" Lucas asked. "It's a great location."

"I've lived here for two years. The location is great. A couple of blocks in the opposite direction is my office. It's nice not to have to spend time commuting to work. But it comes at a price."

Lucas shook his head in acknowledgment. Walking and talking with Chloe felt natural to him. There was no hesitation to his questions or his thoughts. Being with her gave him a sense of relaxation which he couldn't find elsewhere.

"Does your family live near-by?"

Chloe looked at the ground before answering the question, appearing as if her breath had been taken from her.

"My grandmother lives in St. Charles. She and my Papi raised me from birth. I never met my father, and from what I gathered, my mother had only met him once, during the night I was created. When I was just a couple of years old, my mother ran off to be with some other guy. Papi later passed away when I was in junior high. It's been just Gammy and me since. I'm so lucky to have her. She's been my rock and best friend my entire life."

Chloe looked at Lucas and gave him a reassuring smile while shrugging her shoulders. He could see she seemed upset at the topic of her parents. He wondered what was worse.

*To have love but lose it or to never be wanted to begin with?*

Though his parents had moved on, he could still remember them. He remembers their lessons, the smell of his mother's perfume and his father's cologne, and their laughter. Chloe likely didn't have any of these memories of her parents.

"I'm sorry to hear about your parents. When I was a young teenager, my parents passed away in a car accident. I miss them every day. I was raised by foster parents for the remainder of my teenage years. They were an elderly couple in the twilight years of their lives who couldn't have children of their own. I was lucky to have them, but they later passed away after I went off to college.

Chloe squeezed Lucas's hand tight as she looked into his big brown eyes.

"You don't have anyone left?" Chloe asked.

Lucas looked back into Chloe's eyes. In the few occasions he's seen her, he's found himself being trapped in her gaze. He could stare into her eyes for hours. Like his, they were brown. But hers had a sparkle to them like he hadn't seen in anyone else before.

Breaking his gaze, Lucas looked to change the subject.

"I wonder if I had ever run into your grandmother around town?"

Chloe looked at Lucas curiously and asked, "Why would you have run into her?"

"You mentioned she lives in St. Charles. That's where I live."

"You live in the suburbs? Don't you work in the city?"

Lucas nodded. "For the most part. The city is nice, but I prefer the peace and quiet of my backyard. Something I couldn't find in the city."

Smiling, Chloe replied, "You are full of surprises, Lucas Braun.

Lucas brought them to a stop as they arrived at the beach. It was modestly crowded. Lucas could see there were other couples on dates, children splashing in the waves as they came to the shore, and people sitting amongst themselves taking in a book or just enjoying a few moments of peace.

"Well, we are here."

Chloe had a surprised expression on her face. Her eyes looked to where the restaurants were located. They were still four blocks away.

"Did you bring fishing poles in that bag of yours?" Chloe asked.

Lucas couldn't help but take in her smile. Her red lipstick was calling him in. The fluttering wings of butterflies made their presence known inside his stomach as he resisted the temptation to lean and press his lips on to hers. Instead, he merely returned the smile and led her to the sandy area which would serve as their dinner table. Sliding his backpack off his shoulder and bent to the ground to take out its contents and saw the purple dahlia resting on top.

"Oh. This is for you." Lucas said, pulling the flower out of the backpack and handing it to Chloe.

Chloe's eyes beamed as she looked at it. It was in full bloom with seemingly hundreds of small petals layered on top of each other, forming a circle as it surrounded the stem of the flower. As she stared into the deep purple color of the flower the tiny hairs on the back of her neck began to rise.

"How did you know purple was my favorite color?"

Lucas shrugged, "Lucky guess I suppose."

"It's magnificent. Thank you."

Lucas looked at Chloe and gave her a big, closed mouth, smile before looking back to his bag to retrieve the blanket to lay on the sand. He spread it out and grabbed Chloe's hand to help her to her seat. Lucas then pulled out the bottle of cheap bourbon and poured the shots.

Chloe watched Lucas as he prepared the drinks. "Shots? I never pegged you for the type."

"I promised you the best dinner for our date tonight," Lucas said, noticing Chloe's uneasy gaze at the shots of bourbon. He imagined his mother giving his father the same look at this point on their first date. "The word best is a relative term, and our perceptions define it. We are not at a five-star restaurant tonight. We are not drinking fine wine, and we are not being served by a wait staff. But if we drink a shot of this cheap bourbon, our sense of tolerability can change, making these soggy, lukewarm double cheeseburgers in my backpack become just as enjoyable as the filet mignon served in the finest restaurants. If we perceive this to be reality, then who's to say that it isn't?"

Chloe laughed. Lucas looked into Chloe's eyes, trying to gauge her thoughts towards the gesture.

*Was she happy with this date? Should I have arranged for something more traditional?*

Afraid that he made a mistake, Lucas broke character and asked, "Do you like cheeseburgers? I'm perfectly fine with scratching this idea and going somewhere to grab a bite?"

Chloe smiled and grabbed the shot of bourbon from Lucas's hand.

"Bottoms up."

Lucas and Chloe both took their shots and began coughing as the liquor burned down their throats.

"Aghh that's terrible!" Lucas exclaimed.

Chloe chimed in with, "It burned all of the way down."

"I don't ever drink bourbon, and I can't imagine I'll begin anytime soon," Lucas replied, coughing as the alcohol continued to burn his throat.

"How about those cheeseburgers?" Chloe asked, as her empty stomach growled louder than ever with the bourbon now swimming inside. "I think you might be right about things tasting good after this bourbon. I'm seconds away from putting a handful of sand in my mouth to get the taste out."

Lucas reached for the cheeseburgers. He looked back at Chloe laughing as she joked about eating sand. The butterflies began to flutter in his stomach again. He looked towards the lake and saw the sun was beginning to set and could no longer resist the temptation as he eyed Chloe's lips, covered in red lipstick.

"How about we try this instead?" Lucas said.

He leaned in and pressed his lips to Chloe's, kissing her softly. He placed his hand on her side as she placed hers on the side of his face. They gradually began to kiss each other deeper and deeper. Lucas felt as if he had found what he had been looking for his whole life. Everything he's been through led him to this. He didn't want it to end, but as their tongues began to touch ever so slightly, Lucas pulled away from the kiss and swiftly gave Chloe a soft peck on her cheek before sitting back.

Lucas looked around. The publicness of the area became very apparent to him. He looked towards his right and saw a woman quickly look down to her book, trying to hide the fact that she was watching them. A slight embarrassment for him, but one which he'd endure every time if it meant he got to kiss those lips.

"Well, that didn't work. You're mouth reeked of cheap bourbon," Lucas joked, sharing a lingering look smile with Chloe.

He pulled out a cheeseburger and soda from his bag and passed them to her.

"This was my parent's first date," Lucas said while he opened his cheeseburger from the paper wrapper.

"My dad told me the story several times when I was young. He loved telling the story, and he loved my mother very much. He said he knew he was in love with her before they even finished their first date. My mother said the same."

Lucas and Chloe exchanged an extended glance, each appearing as if they could relate to the feeling. Chloe repositioned herself on the blanket so she could rest her back into Lucas's chest while they ate their dinner and took in the beach.

The demographic makeup of the beach was changing as it got later in the evening. There were fewer kids playing and more couples enjoying each other's company and the beautiful weather. Lucas felt relief from the cool breeze coming from the lake, but when he looked at Chloe, he could see she had wrapped her arms around her stomach. He pulled his suit jacket from his backpack and placed it over her to keep her warm while they continued sitting together in peace.

"What do you suppose their story is?" Chloe asked Lucas as she motioned towards a couple further down the beach. There was an overweight man sitting next to a very slim, supermodel-like woman, who also appeared to be much younger than the man.

"It's not all that common to see such an attractive woman with a man of that stature."

Lucas agreed with Chloe's thought. He looked closer at the couple, seeing something familiar in the woman before realizing that he knew exactly who the couple was. The woman was Dr. Kelley, one of the physicians on his call list. She was a lovely woman and often spoke of her husband and family. Lucas could see in her eyes that she was genuinely in love with the man she married when she spoke of him, and he recognized the man from the pictures he had seen in her office.

"Funny you bring it up. I actually know that couple's story. The woman is one of the physicians who I call on. Based on the conversations I've had with her, I'm led to believe he stays at home to take care of the kids. The children were a product of her first marriage. Her husband tragically passed away years earlier, and she remarried."

"You're kidding," Chloe challenged. She rose from leaning back on Lucas's chest to look at him in the eyes, searching for a tell that he was lying.

"I swear on it. This is one of the best examples of beauty being in the eye of the beholder. Not everyone will see things in the same light as the everyone else. Everyone else sees a man who is significantly overweight and seems to have lost his drive for taking care of his appearance. But when she looks at him, she sees something different than what everyone else sees. The world is like a painting in a museum. Many people conform to see the same thing in the painting, but not everyone. Some people will see something new and exciting. It makes you wonder who is right, the minority or the majority." Lucas paused. "Perhaps both could be right."

Lucas found himself thinking about Dr. Kelley quite often. He wondered if perhaps the overweight man was just a transfer of energy from her deceased husband. Sam told Lucas that the energy must move on and take on a different form. He wondered if it was possible that energy could take on the form of another human. Sam always brushed the subject off when Lucas brought it up.

"We don't know what happens to the energy once it leaves a human." Sam would say.

"I don't think I've ever met someone quite like you," Chloe said, "You have a perspective on life that is uncanny to anyone else's."

Lucas smiled and gave Chloe a soft kiss, something he now determined should be done as often as possible, and then rose from his seated position.

"Well, it's getting dark out. Perhaps we should head back."

Lucas held out his hand to help Chloe rise from the blanket.

"Where do you want to go?" Chloe asked.

"I thought we'd head back towards your place. The coffee shop near your apartment complex is pretty good. Maybe we could grab a cup of coffee?"

"A decaf coffee sounds great."

Chloe enjoyed a cup of coffee every morning, but she tended to avoid it in the evenings. On evenings when she had a cup after dinner, she would spend the remainder of the night staring at the ceiling in her apartment, trying to fall asleep.

Lucas wrapped his arm around Chloe's shoulder as they embarked on the short journey back. The top of Chloe's shoulder rested just beneath his shoulder. He couldn't help but notice how their bodies fit together perfectly. He was beginning to feel as if they fit together perfectly emotionally. It was still very early in their romance, and he didn't have an extensive history with women to compare his feelings too, but he thought it would be unrealistic for him to feel this way about other women this quickly.

The walk went by faster than Lucas had hoped. He took a mental note to pick a location further away next time so he'd have more time to hold Chloe close during the walk back. They turned the corner and were on the same block as Chloe's apartment and the coffee shop. Up ahead, Lucas recognized a man walking towards their direction. He seemed to be in a hurry and was approaching quickly.

"Hey. Isn't that your editor?"

Chloe looked ahead and saw Terry Horn walking in their direction. He was wearing his usual black slacks and suspenders. The cigar hanging from his mouth was lit. A man in a pinstripe navy suit was walking next to him.

"It is. He must have met a friend after work," Chloe speculated.

Lucas recalled the uncomfortable way Terry stared at him the last time they were together. He wondered if he would be greeted similarly on this occasion.

"Hey, Terry. How's it going?" Chloe asked, with a hint of nervousness in her voice. She rarely ran into Terry outside of work or a work event. During those occasions, Terry was known to make inappropriate sexual comments. Sometimes they were about her, and other times she wasn't sure what they were about.

Chloe had a look of surprise on her face when Terry and the man walking next to him stopped in their tracks. They both looked like deer in headlights.

"Ughh. Hello, Chloe." Terry said, giving a polite head nod.

Lucas noticed the awkwardness of the situation. He could see that both of the men were staring right at him with a look of shock on their faces. He studied the man in the pinstripe suit. He had light blue eyes, and his sideburns ran down to the bottom of his ears. He was the same height as Lucas and was relatively slim for his age. A scar, about two inches long, ran down his face beginning at the corner of his right eye.

*Why are these men staring at me like this? They look like someone who's spotted a celebrity.*

Before Lucas could say anything, they broke their stare and moved on past them.

"Well, that was unexpected," Chloe said to break the silence after they passed. "I was expecting Terry to make some comment about my ass or my legs. Instead, he looked like he'd seen a ghost."

Lucas nodded, agreeing that Terry was acting peculiar. He thought back to the way Terry stared at him while the crowd went into a panicked frenzy after they found Bernie laying on the bathroom floor.

"Time for a coffee?" Chloe said, breaking Lucas from his train of thought.

"Sure, this way," Lucas said, motioning towards the door. After ordering two decaf coffees, Chloe and Lucas took seats outside. The cool air, which was a welcomed change from the summer heat for Lucas when the evening began, was now getting too cold and he could see goose bumps forming on his arms. He ignored them and listened attentively to Chloe as she talked about her dreams of being a novelist.

"My grandmother and I had a book club when I was growing up. It was just her and me. Each month we would pick a book, and once we finished, we would make tea, eat banana nut muffins, and discuss the book. We cried and laughed together discussing hundreds of books."

Lucas watched Chloe's face as she talked of her grandmother. Though she never said it out loud, Lucas could see that she loved her dearly.

"I knew when I was very young I wanted to be the one behind the words. I dreamed of being the one to keep people up late into the night reading a suspenseful twist. I wanted to be the one who made people laugh and cry together, and the one who brought people together for tea and muffins. If I could do that for people the way hundreds of authors did for me, then I could die happy."

Lucas smiled, letting her words sink in before responding. "I hear that a lot, die happy. I often wonder what it is that people are afraid of. Are they afraid of death? Or are they afraid of not living a full life? Death is something that is certain. It will happen to all of us. But living a happy and full life isn't as certain."

Chloe shrugged, looking as if she was searching for an answer. "I guess if I spend more time around you I'm going to have to get used to the fact that you'll be bringing deep meaning to seemingly common phrases."

Lucas smiled.

*Perhaps I'm letting on too much for a first date.*

"Please forgive me. I don't often date." He raised his coffee cup as if giving a toast and said, "Here's to living life fully."

Chloe smiled and raised her cup to Lucas's. "To living fully."

There was a moment of silence as the realization sunk in that the date was coming to an end. Lucas leaned back in his seat and glanced at his watch.

"I guess I better get moving to catch my train back home."

Chloe sighed and said, "Yes, I suppose it is getting late."

Lucas looked into Chloe's eyes and sensed that she too didn't want the date to end. "I had a wonderful time tonight," Lucas said, lost for words on how to depart.

"Me too. You picked a great place to eat. From my perspective, it was the best five-star restaurant I've ever dined at."

Lucas laughed, "I'm glad you enjoyed it."

He walked Chloe across the street to the door of her apartment building, and Chloe turned to look at him before entering the building. They both stood speechless for a moment, waiting for the other to make a move.

"Well." Chloe said, pausing as she searched for the words she wanted to say, "Have a …."

Before Chloe could finish her sentence, she was interrupted by Lucas lips being pressed firmly against hers. As Lucas felt her soft lips kissing his, he was tempted to cut ties with his reservations and ask to continue the date up in her apartment. But deep down he knew he couldn't, and he abruptly pulled away and brought Chloe's head to his chest, holding her close for a hug.

"Have a great night, Ms. Benedict."

Before she could reply, he smiled and turned towards the train. As he walked, he concluded that he was right, there was something special about Chloe Benedict. For the first time in his life, he was in love.

# Chapter 12

There was an irritating hum coming from the fluorescent lights hanging from the ceiling. It was the type of hum people hear every day, one which they eventually learn to tolerate. Lucas had been sitting in the room for over two hours, and he still could hear the hum. He had asked the staff about it, but they didn't offer any help.

"I don't notice it," they offered, seeming to play dumb.

Fourteen-year-old Lucas sat in a chair in the front of a room. To his right were two caskets holding his parents. Lucas was left with the burden of planning and coordinating the funeral procession. He was the only remaining member of the Braun family.

His throat ached from crying. He had been drinking glass after glass of water in an attempt to sooth it. Within a few hours, the water filled up his bladder, and he left the empty room to use the restroom.

After he was finished, he zipped up his pants, hung up his jacket on the coat hanger, and rolled up his sleeves to wash his hands. Lucas closed his eyes as the warm water ran over his cold hands. Initially, the warmth was soothing, but it soon turned too hot and began to burn his skin. He didn't care. He wanted the burn. He stood at the sink and forcefully held his hands under the water until it was too much to take. He then took his hands and splashed the hot water on his face. With his eyes closed, he reached and grabbed a towel to dry off. His hands and face still burned, even after patting himself dry.

Lucas had a theory that a person could only be allotted a certain amount of pain, and that the person could potentially redistribute his emotional turmoil into physical pain. He was dead wrong. Not only was he a wreck on the inside, but now he felt like his skin was on fire. Lucas opened his eyes to assess the damage and gasped in horror.

*The towel is blood red. Did I burn the skin off of my hands?*

He looked at his hands and arms. They too were covered in blood.

*My face? What about my face?*

When he looked in the mirror, he couldn't see anything but steam. Lucas frantically began to wipe it with his burnt hand. It felt as if his skin was peeling away with each stroke.

*My face. What does my face look like?*

He confirmed that his fear was a reality as he cleared the mirror. Blood dripped from his cheeks, falling into the white sink he stood before.

*How am I going to explain this to anyone who might come to the funeral?*

Lucas tried using cold water to rinse away the blood, but it acted as a tour guide, directing more blood to flow from his skin. He then reached for more towels and began to pat gently at his tender skin to soak up as much of the blood as he could. He first needed it just to stop bleeding. After that, he could figure out how to handle any people who come to pay their respects to his parents.

As Lucas dabbed at his face with the towel, he looked carefully at his skin, trying to identify any signs of improvement. But the closer he looked, the more panicked he became.

*I don't even look like myself.*

He took a step back from the mirror to get a better view of what he was seeing. Looking back at him was not Lucas at all. It was a familiar face, smiling right at him and covered in blood.

*Sam?*

Buzzzz Buzzzz Buzzzz Buzzzz. The alarm clock in Lucas's room was sounding off. He quickly rose from his bed to stop the ear-wrenching sound. Though it was Saturday, a day when most people don't set alarms, Lucas was glad he set it. His dreams about his parents were coming more frequently and getting even more confusing.

*Why was Sam looking at me through the mirror? Why was he covered in blood?*

In the back of Lucas's head, he had always speculated if Sam was the reaper sent for his family. He wondered if Sam was supposed to reap him but then changed his mind. Sam always seemed uneasy when Lucas talked about his parents, notably when it was about their deaths. But he couldn't verbally accuse him of being the reaper. Sam was the closest thing Lucas had to a friend. He didn't want to risk damaging their relationship. He sighed in sorrow as he thought about Sam and how he'd likely never see him again now that he had his final list.

Lucas rose from his bed and grabbed the full glass of water resting on his nightstand. He drank the entire glass in one drink. It was lukewarm and went down quickly. Though he only had one shot of the lousy bourbon last night, he could still feel the lasting effect of dehydration this morning. He walked towards the bathroom and refilled his glass from the sink before settling down at his desk to retrieve his final list from the manila folder. Scott Banks and Bethany Mandel. He had been researching Scott Banks on the internet over the past few days. Scott owns a diner just a few miles away, and it supposedly it serves an excellent breakfast. Lucas set the alarm so that he'd be up in time to eat breakfast and look for a way to execute on his list.

*Just two more names stand between me and freedom.*

He drank his second glass of water before putting on a light green pair of corduroy pants and a dark blue t-shirt. He then laced his brown suede shoes and grabbed his backpack, which was filled with a couple of books, a bottle of water, and two serums for his final reapings. It was still early enough in the morning to not be too warm for the bicycle ride to the diner, and Lucas rolled his bicycle down the steps and began to pedal.

As he made his way towards the diner, he couldn't help but think of Chloe. The way she lingered at their departure. It was as if she wanted him to come up to her apartment with her but didn't want to ask.

*Want to go up and watch a movie?*

That was the type of question he could ask if he didn't have people to reap. If he didn't have to take care of his final list, he could be waking up in bed next to her this morning after holding her in his arms all night while they slept to the sounds of the city. They could then get out of bed to walk to the pier to watch the sunrise before going back to her place for breakfast.

*Soon. Soon those dreams will be a reality.*

The diner was conveniently located just a few miles from Lucas's house, and he arrived there in little time. Despite being early, the diner was full of patrons. The small gravel parking lot was filled with old pick-up trucks. Most of the people who ate here worked in the local steel mill or were farmers. There wasn't a place for parking bicycles, so Lucas chained his to the pole with the handicapped parking sign on it and walked inside.

"Please have a seat wherever you'd like," said the waitress with a friendly smile from across the restaurant.

He eyed the place, looking for an empty table. The first one he saw looked to still have dirty dishes on it. Then he spotted an empty two-seater in the back and headed for it. As he walked, he got a growing concern that he wasn't going to be eating for a while. The waitress who greeted him appeared to be the only person serving tables.

It was a small diner, likely only able to seat thirty people at a time. Lucas counted them up. He was patron number twenty-nine. But to Lucas's surprise, the waitress arrived at his table just after he took his seat.

"Would you like some coffee?" asked the waitress.

Lucas didn't know why, but the sound of her voice made him feel at ease. She was wearing a yellow dress underneath a baby blue apron and had white tennis shoes laced around her feet. Her brown hair was worn in a ponytail and her bright blue eyes shined through her glasses.

"Yes please," Lucas replied.

"You having the special, sweetie?"

Lucas's eyes went to his table and searched for a menu. He didn't see one. But he had no idea what he'd want even if he did have one. Fearful of how long he'd have to wait if he didn't order at this moment, Lucas looked at the waitress and nodded in agreement.

She walked to the back and informed the cook of the new order before moving on to take care of other patrons. He watched as she made her way to the coffee brewing area. The stream of fresh coffee pouring into the carafe made him painfully aware of his full bladder.

*Two glasses of water and no bathroom break. Go figure.*

His eyes fixated on the restroom across the diner and he walked towards it. Despite the diner being small, Lucas had a clear pathway to the restroom. He made his way in quickly, with the burning sensation growing in his bladder with each step. He was greeted by the color of white when he opened the door. Not only did white tile cover the floors in the small restroom, but it also ran up the wall to the ceiling. Lucas looked at the two urinals and saw there wasn't a privacy wall between them and opted for the stall. To his surprise, it was relatively clean for a public restroom. The smell of bleach made it evident it was recently cleaned.

After Lucas emptied what felt like a gallon of urine into the toilet, he lifted his foot to press the lever to flush the toilet. Even though everything looked to be clean, Lucas still didn't want to physically contact a toilet in a public restroom. He then walked to the lone pedestal sink, which was also white, and turned on the hot water to wash his hands. The steam rose from the hot water, reminding Lucas of his dream. He placed his hand in it for a few seconds, until he felt a burning sensation, and then pulled it back. His skin was red from the hot water, but unlike his dream, there was no blood.

A layer of condensation began to form on the bottom of the mirror. Also unlike his dream, it wasn't Sam looking back at Lucas. It was just him. The only thing which bothered him about what he saw in the mirror was how much of a mess he looked today. He didn't bother to take a shower or fix his hair because he anticipated he would be a sweaty mess when he rode his bike home in the mid-morning sun. He turned on the cold water and splashed some on his hair in an attempt to weight down the pieces of hair that were sticking up. It was a failed attempt as it only seemed to make the hair appear greasier.

*Oh well, it will do. I'm here for research, not a modeling gig.*

Lucas left the restroom to return to his small table in the back of the restaurant and saw he had a fresh cup of coffee, a plate of French toast, bacon, sausage, hash browns, and eggs waiting on the table for him.

*Wow. That was quick.*

He didn't expect to get so much food. There was no way he'd be able to eat all of this and keep it down while riding his bike back home. He started with a sip of his coffee. It was awful. It was burnt and tasted artificial.

*Hopefully, the food is different from the coffee.*

He cut a piece of French toast and took a bite. It melted like butter in his mouth and tasted warm and sweet. Like a hungry teenage boy home from school, Lucas began to quickly devour the French Toast, unable to slow down. It had been a long time since he had tasted French Toast which tasted this good. It was his mother's secret Saturday morning recipe. He had a habit of waking up early to watch cartoons in the living room. While he tried to be quiet, he was never successful. His mother would always be up within five minutes of the television being turned on.

"Good morning, sweetie," she would say as she greeted him with a kiss on the top of the head. "How about some breakfast?"

Lucas, not looking up from the cartoons, would give a nod of the head to indicate he would like some. His mother would then go to the kitchen and come out 15 minutes later with a plate of French Toast and a glass of milk. It was at about that time when Lucas's father would crawl out of bed.

"Do I smell your famous French Toast?"

His father and mother would exchange a kiss and a hug and join Lucas on the couch for cartoons and French Toast. It was the tradition Lucas missed the most. At that moment every Saturday morning, everything was perfect. He had the whole weekend ahead of him, a delicious meal on his plate, cartoons on the television, and his loving parents sitting on each side of him.

"Well, that was quick. You must have been hungry," the waitress said as she came to check on Lucas.

He was impressed with her ability to ensure that this entire diner was well attended to. Whatever she was getting paid, it wasn't enough, Lucas thought.

"It was delicious," Lucas said, looking up from his plate which no longer had French Toast on it.

Feeling nostalgic, Lucas asked, "Can I trouble you for a glass of milk?"

"Sure thing, sweetie."

*Sweetie. Just like what my mother would call me.*

There was something about the way she called him sweetie that triggered him lean forward for a kiss on the forehead. But the waitress didn't notice as she walked away.

*What am I doing? Good thing she didn't see that.*

Lucas began to feel warm. Similar to how he felt on those Saturday mornings, sitting on the couch between his mother and father. He watched as she smiled at other patrons, making her way back to the kitchen to retrieve the milk. She walked with the same style and grace as his mother. It was like she was sent from her grave and into this restaurant to serve him his favorite meal. When she reached the kitchen, Lucas's nostalgia was interrupted. Scott Banks walked out with his full head of thick red hair. He was short, shorter than Lucas. But that was the only thing smaller about him. His chest looked as if it could rip through his yellow shirt at any moment. If his chest didn't do it, then his biceps would surely begin to tear apart the seams.

The research Lucas conducted on Scott showed that he was a bodybuilder. His public social media page had pictures of him at the gym and of him oiled up and flexing with no shirt on. He also gathered that Scott was divorced and had a son who was going to college in Arizona. It suddenly dawned on Lucas as to why his breakfast included so much food. It was probably the size of breakfast which Scott ate before his workouts. Lucas put his hand in his pocket and could feel the reaping serum he put there as he entered the restaurant. He brought it just in case, not expecting to have an opportunity to use it today.

Lucas considered it. Getting this one out of the way so he could focus on his final reap, Bethany Mandel, would make life simpler for him. Lucas hadn't even begun his research on her. That was a mistake. She could have been laying right before his eyes, and he wouldn't even recognize her. His mind had been preoccupied with the thrill of seeing the finish line, dating Chloe, and trying to make sense of his puzzling dreams.

"My compliments to the chef," said a man in a baseball cap and a stained white t-shirt. He was sitting at the bar when Scott walked passed him.

"Thank you. It was my pleasure," Scott replied as he set the apron he was holding in his hand on the breakfast bar and walked towards the restroom.

*This could be it. This could be my chance.*

The waitress had yet to return from the kitchen. He began to feel guilty for asking for a glass of milk which he now would not likely be around for to enjoy. Not knowing how much his breakfast would cost, Lucas took out a thirty-dollars and left it on the table. He wanted to be able to leave immediately after he finished.

As he walked to the restroom, he reflected on how he frequently found himself in public restrooms for reasons other than using the restroom. It was rare that he could find someone in a private setting. A public restroom was often the most privacy he could find.

Just before Lucas entered through the restroom door, he caught eyes with a man. He was sitting alone. He stared at Lucas intensely as he passed. The strangely familiar blue eyes sent a chill down Lucas's spine.

*Why is he staring at me?*

Lucas shook it off and continued to the restroom. He saw they were alone when he entered the room. Scott was in the bathroom stall. Lucas wondered why Scott hadn't installed privacy walls between the urinals if he even didn't feel comfortable using them.

He looked to the sink and read the sign above it. All employees must wash hands. It amazed him that there are employees out there who wouldn't wash their hands if it weren't for a sign telling them to do so.

*A person's conscious needs continuous reminders of morality.*

He went to wash his hands to make it appear as if he had a reason for being in the restroom. He didn't want Scott to come out and see someone standing and staring at him. It was easier when the person felt comfortable around Lucas. They were less likely ready for what was coming, making them less likely to put up a fight, something Lucas wanted to avoid with someone the size of Scott.

But as Lucas waited for Scott, he got the feeling that something was off. Nothing about this scene seemed right. He felt as if he shouldn't be there, like this was a trap for someone to catch him. He heard the toilet flush. Scott was coming. Lucas turned off the water and began to slowly dry his hands while he gathered his thoughts.

*Who was that man staring at me? Why did he look so familiar?*

"How's it going, chief?" Scott said as he walked past Lucas to the sink.

"What's up?" Lucas tried to say casually.

*What's up? Do people still say that?*

He watched as Scott scrubbed his hands vigorously under the hot water. He was standing there, unaware of who Lucas was, ready to be taken. Lucas reached for his syringe. Just a lunge away from being one name away from a free life. Lucas's arms began to shake. His feet felt like they were encased in five-gallon buckets of cement.

*This isn't right. That man out there. I recognize him.*

He recalled the scar running down the side of his eye. It was the man he bumped into who was with Terry Horn. The two of them stared at him as if they could see right through his flesh and bones. To Lucas, it seemed like they were looking right into his soul, seeing precisely who he was.

Feeling like today was a lost cause, Lucas tossed his paper towel in the trash and returned to the diner. Sam always warned him never to get caught. Being so close to the end, Lucas now had more to lose. He looked right at the man as he exited, but the man didn't look at him. He stared down at his coffee, almost as if he was purposely trying to avoid eye contact.

*Was this in my head? If he thought I was a murderer, why wouldn't he have looked at me as I left? Did I miss a perfect opportunity?*

While he walked out the door towards his bicycle, Lucas looked back and saw an ecstatic look on his waitress's face. She quickly put the tip money in her apron and moved on to tend to her other tables with a smile on her face. Lucas smiled as he imagined the waitress stopping by the toy store to buy something new for her son with the unexpected increase in income for the day, just as his mother would have done for him.

*At least today's visit wasn't a complete waste.*

# Chapter 13

Monday came at Lucas like an unforgiving storm. The place where he picks up bagels for his morning calls had problems with its oven and was forced to close until it could be repaired. One of his physicians was out sick and a second couldn't take calls because she had too many unexpected patients due to an outbreak of a stomach virus.

After a couple of misses, Lucas took his usual coffee break early.

"Medium coffee one cream," said the smiling man behind the counter.

Lucas came to this place a few times a week and always ordered the same medium coffee with one cream. The barista had caught on, and Lucas barely even had to speak to get a coffee in his hand.

With today's stresses wearing him out, Lucas let out a sigh and said, "Better make it a large today, please."

The barista could see the exhaustion in Lucas's eyes and quickly poured the coffee and handed it to him.

"Here you go, pal. On the house today. You look like you need it."

Lucas smiled. "Thank you."

He left a five-dollar bill in the tip jar and took a seat near the window. He usually drank his coffee while on the run to his next appointment, but today he needed a break to regroup. Lucas opened his laptop and considered doing administrative work for the remainder of the day. He had a presentation due in a few weeks, and it seemed the universe was telling him to put his efforts into it instead of to trying to sell physicians on allergy medication. The presentation was part of a teaching series. Each rep in the district was assigned a topic, and every month the district would gather for a presentation. Lucas's was covering the best practices for handling physicians whose patients don't have health insurance which covers the cost of the company's drugs.

He opened a presentation template and stared hopelessly at it. The cursor pulsed like a heartbeat on the screen. Even though Lucas knew exactly what to present to the team, the idea of putting it into a formal presentation exhausted him. He tried to reason with his manager, Steve, by suggesting he merely uses the handout outs and sells to the team in the same manner that he sells to physicians.

"Lucas, I know that you could sell the team in less than a minute. But my goal of this presentation isn't for the team to be better on this topic. It's for you to go through the exercise of presenting to co-workers and management, something you'll do a lot of when you are promoted up."

Lucas admired Steve for taking an interest in developing his team, and he didn't want to let Steve down, but there was no way in hell he would ever accept a position which required him to be in an office. Prior to having his final list, Lucas could never dream of being reliable enough to appear at a desk from eight to five each day. Once the list was complete, he could theoretically take the position. But he didn't need the money, didn't want the fame, and thinking of playing corporate politics for the rest of his career sent his stomach into cramps.

After a few minutes of staring at the pulsating mouse cursor, Lucas allowed himself to be distracted by searching for Scott Banks on the internet. He needed to learn more about him.

By looking at Scott's public social media posts, Lucas gathered that Scott worked his mornings at the diner and then headed to the gym in the afternoon. On Tuesdays, he played darts, and on Wednesdays, he looked forward to watching a television series about zombies in space. He was planning to appear in a bodybuilding competition in Florida in a couple of weeks.

*Is the diner the best place to do this?*

As Lucas thought about his options, he wondered what his best opportunity would be. He wanted to complete the job before Scott left for the competition. There wouldn't be much time once he returned from his trip.

*If I do this at the diner, will the blue-eyed man be there?*

Lucas had always been so careful. He found it difficult to believe that anyone would be on to him.

The ring coming from Lucas's phone startled his train of thought. He quickly pulled it out of his pocket, expecting to be hearing from his manager, but to his delight, it was Chloe calling.

*What could this be about?*

Anxious to hear why she was calling, he clicked the answer button and lifted his phone to his ear.

"Hello."

"Hey, Lucas. It's Chloe. How's it going?"

Small talk, Lucas thought to himself. He had become quite good at it over the years, talking to nurses and office personnel while he waited to be seen by the physicians.

"Oh, you know. It's a Monday."

Chloe laughed, "Yeah I hear you."

Chloe paused for a moment, and Lucas waited for her to speak, curious what it could be that would cause her to hesitate.

"I have yet another request of you, Lucas."

"I would be surprised if you didn't," Lucas said, playfully.

Chloe let out a laugh and replied, "I'm going to visit my Gammy this evening. She is always asking me about when I'm going to meet a boy and settle down, and I keep telling her that I'm waiting for Mr. Right."

Conflicting emotions encompassed Lucas. He could see where this was going, and he was thrilled that Chloe thought so much of him, but he was also concerned it was too soon for him to be meeting her grandmother.

Aware of Lucas's hesitation to respond, Chloe broke the silence. "Don't take this the wrong way. I'm not saying you are Mr. Right. I'm not even planning to tell her that we have gone on a date. It's just that," Chloe paused, "I don't know how much more time she has, and I think it would mean a lot to her if she saw I was at least trying."

Lucas sympathized with Chloe. He knew what it was like to lose loved ones.

"I'll do anything I can do to help."

"Thank you. She lives in St. Charles at the new assisted living center. I was planning to be there at five, but you don't have to be there right away if you can't make it back from work that quickly."

"I'll see you there at five."

"You're the best. See you there."

Lucas hung up his phone and looked back at his laptop. He hadn't met with any physicians, and he hadn't made a shred of progress on his presentation today, but he felt as if he'd been working for twelve hours. He was happy Chloe had called. He could use a friendly face today. He took one last look at Scott Bank's social media page before shutting down his computer.

*Scott Banks. How can I earn your trust and lure you in?*

He packed up and hopped on a train. Before leaving to meet Chloe, Lucas stopped at his home and changed into his usual pair of corduroy pants and a t-shirt. He then grabbed his bicycle and pedaled towards the assisted living center. The air outside felt like a sauna. He could feel his armpits dampen in under a minute.

*What happened to the cool weather from the other night? I'm going to be drenched by the time I arrive.*

Pedaling slowly to avoid breaking into too much of a sweat, Lucas arrived in fifteen minutes. He pulled out his phone and saw he had a text from Chloe which read - Let me when you get here. I'll come out and meet you.

Unwilling to text back, Lucas dialed Chloe's number.

"Hello."

"Hey Chloe, I'm here."

"Okay, I'll be right out."

Lucas waited for her in the lobby. He had never been in an assisted living center that was this warm and welcoming. He imagined it to be the same gloomy feel as a hospital, but it couldn't be anything further from that. In place of stick on tiles lining the floors were dark oak floors. Instead of white and beige, he was greeted with blues, greens, and purples. To his right, Lucas could see the natural light beaming in through the windows which made up the walls in the common room.

"Hey there," Chloe said as she wrapped her arms around Lucas.

Lucas hugged Chloe back and kissed her on her cheek. He liked the way she felt in his arms and he liked the way being in her arms made him feel. He didn't have anything to compare it too. Nothing he had experienced had made him feel the way that he feels when he was with Chloe.

"Thanks for coming. I ended up getting here earlier than I anticipated and we are just finishing our book club meeting. Gammy is down the hall."

As Chloe led Lucas to Gammy's room, she gave him a warning by saying, "Just an FYI, Gammy is in pretty bad shape. She's had a few medical issues and broke her hip a couple of months back. She's in good spirits but hasn't responded well to treatment."

Lucas nodded in acknowledgment. "Well, I'm glad you're bringing me to meet her. If she's half the woman you paint her out to be, I'll be in for an enjoyable evening."

Chloe smiled. "She's great."

They entered her room, and Lucas was greeted by a smile from an elderly woman sitting in a wheelchair next to a small table. She had surprisingly thick gray hair cut shoulder length. Lucas could see what Chloe was warning him about with her condition. Her body looked frail and weak.

"Well, who might this charming young man be?" Gammy asked, looking at Chloe.

"This is my friend, Lucas. Lucas this is Gammy."

Gammy held out her hand for Lucas to kiss the top of it.

"Hello, Mrs….?" Lucas asked as he held her hand and kissed the top of it, avoiding the diamond ring which rested loosely on her ring finger.

"Gammy. Everyone calls me Gammy, and you may as well too."

"Well, it's a pleasure to meet you, Gammy. Chloe has said a lot of great things about you."

Gammy smiled at Chloe, "He's a cute one."

Chloe's cheeks turned red. "Oh, Gammy."

Chloe motioned for Lucas to have a seat. There were muffins, tea, and two copies of Romeo and Juliet laying on the table.

"This must be the book club," Lucas said.

"The best there ever was," Gammy replied.

She had a lot of spirit in her. While on the outside she appeared to be frail and withering away, on the inside she was bright and strong.

"Have a muffin and some tea. We were just finishing our session," Chloe said.

Lucas took a seat and a bite of a banana nut muffin. It was warm and tasted freshly baked. Chloe must have come earlier to make the muffins, Lucas thought. He observed as Chloe and Gammy conversed. He could see that both had a sparkle in their eyes as they looked at each other. This was something that both looked forward to each month.

Though, he wondered how it came to be that they haven't already read Romeo and Juliet. It was one of the most popular stories ever written.

"Well, what do you think about the end?" Chloe asked Gammy with anticipation, "She killed herself because her love had died. Seems a little extreme to me, don't you think?"

Gammy's smile went away, and her tone became serious.

"I don't know if it was that extreme. She had lost the only person in her life who meant anything to her. He meant the world to her. He was the one that she was born to be with, and he was taken away. What else did she have left?"

"She was so young," Chloe countered. "How does she know that he was it. What if there was someone or something else?"

"One of these days, you'll know. Your Papi was my everything. It has been so hard without him. The only thing that keeps me going is the beam of light you bring to me," Gammy replied.

There was a look of surprise in Chloe's eyes after hearing Gammy speak. Chloe had described Gammy to Lucas as being so strong. He imagined it was hard for Chloe to hear that she has suffered.

Lucas observed as Chloe and Gammy looked at their feet. He could see that Papi meant a lot to them and it was difficult for them to talk about his passing. When he first entered the room, there seemed to be a vibrant energy with the way Chloe and Gammy smiled, but it now it seemed as if as if someone took a giant vacuum to the room and sucked out all of the joy. He felt the urge to try to bring some of it back.

"I read this book a few years back," Lucas began. Chloe and Gammy both looked at him with their teary eyes. They both had brown eyes. He imagined the faded color in Gammy's was previously as bright as Chloe's during her younger years.

"Romeo was everything that Juliet wasn't. He was the salty to her sweet, the ice to her fire, and the solid to her liquid. Together they were whole. Their sum didn't come to a negative or a positive number; it came to nothing. They were a perfect balance, not too negative and not too positive. When Romeo died, it left Juliet unbalanced, and after feeling what it felt like to be balanced, it became apparent to her on just how unbalanced she was."

Chloe and Gammy looked at Lucas inquisitively as he continued with his perspective.

"It all comes down to physics. All must add up to nothing. When Romeo died, he left Juliet to live the rest of her life trying to gain her balance. If she were lucky, she would find pieces here or there to help offset, but it would be unlikely she would find her full balance again."

Lucas examined the expressions on Gammy's and Chloe's faces. He couldn't tell if he had helped to ease the tension, or if he only provided a temporary distraction as they evaluated his sanity. After a few excruciating moments of silence, Chloe finally broke it by saying, "Well Gammy, you have been asking me to bring a guy to visit you for quite some time now. As you can see, I might not be the best at picking a romantic."

She gave Lucas a playful wink, easing Lucas's concerns.

"Oh, I think he's just charming. Lucas, would you like some more tea?" Gammy asked as she began to rise from her wheelchair.

"Yes please, but I can pour it," Lucas said quickly to prevent Gammy from struggling to get out of her chair.

Chloe opened her mouth to speak but was interrupted by a knock on the door.

"Knock knock," the lady dressed in scrubs said as she walked into the room.

"Time for your evening pills, Gammy."

Lucas smiled. Everyone really did call her Gammy. He studied the nurse as she walked into the room. She had long red hair and green eyes. She looked like someone he'd seen before, and by the way she was looking at him, Lucas concluded she was thinking the same thing about him. She must have been a nurse at one of the offices he called on.

"Lucas?" The nurse said as she entered. "It's me, Jessica. From Dr. Roy's office."

Lucas smiled, thankful she volunteered her name. "Yes, Jessica. How are you doing?"

"Good," she said with a playful smile. "Your Gammy here is my favorite."

Before Lucas could intervene and explain that she's Chloe's Gammy, Chloe rose from her seat, and, while giving Jessica a cold look, said, "I can help Gammy with her pills tonight. Thanks, Jessica."

Jessica looked at Chloe and then looked at Lucas, appearing as if she was figuring out that Chloe and Lucas may be an item. It didn't dawn upon Lucas that she may have been flirting with him. He was never good at picking up on queues, partly because he never tried.

"Okay. I'll see you tomorrow, Gammy," Jessica said, smiling at Lucas as she left the room.

Gammy had a smile from ear to ear. "And you said that Lucas was just a friend?"

"Okay, Gammy. Here are your pills and your water. I'll see you next week, and we can talk about which book we want to read next," Chloe replied, ignoring Gammy's remark.

She gave Gammy a long hug and kissed her on the cheek. "I love you, Gammy."

"I love you too, my dear."

Lucas stood and walked towards Chloe." It was a pleasure to meet you, Gammy. "

"Same too you. I hope to see you again, darling."

Chloe grabbed Lucas's hand to hold as soon as they were out of Gammy's site.

"She's great," Lucas said to Chloe as they walked down the hall.

"Yes, she is. And so are you. Thank you so much for coming and for saving us from the impending tear bath."

"I'm glad you invited me, and you're welcome."

The hot, humid air hit them like a wave as they exited the building. The initial relief of warmth quickly went away as Lucas could already feel his skin was preparing to perspire.

"Well, I'm sorry, but I'm going to have to take off to finish my story for the paper. I left work early today so that I could come before Gammy took her pills. They make her drowsy, and it's best to come before she takes them."

"It's okay. We'll catch up soon. I'll watch for your story in the paper."

Chloe rolled her bright brown eyes. "Don't waste your time. It's about rising gas prices. Most of it is just interviews with people saying they are trying to drive less and keep fewer things in their car to get better gas mileage."

The concept was foreign to Lucas. He never drove and thus never monitored the price of gasoline.

"Well, they can always try riding one of these instead," Lucas said as he unchained his bike from the bike rack.

"You rode your bike today? It's over ninety degrees outside."

"Beats the alternative. I hate cars."

She gave Lucas an understanding smile. Lucas had mentioned that his parents passed away in a car accident. It made sense that he would develop an aversion to cars.

Chloe leaned in to kiss Lucas. Lucas didn't want it to end, but as the seconds passed he sensed that the kiss goodbye was lasting longer than most. He wasn't about to stop it, but then Chloe pulled away slowly and said, "Maybe we can get together this weekend. I think it is my turn to pick the date."

"That sounds great," Lucas replied.

———

Chloe turned around and made her way towards the train station. While she walked, she thought of Lucas. He was sincere, kind, charming, and breathtakingly handsome. The feelings now encompassing her are feelings which she had rejected throughout her life. She didn't want to allow herself to feel them. Her mother and father left her. Her Papi died while she was young. Only one of the four people who were supposed to love her was still around. She didn't want to risk loving someone else for the chance that they too may go away. But she could no longer hold back her feelings for Lucas. At this moment, as she walked through the blistering heat to the train station, Chloe realized that she was unconditionally in love with Lucas Braun.

# Chapter 14

The diner was just as crowded today as it was on Saturday. With most of the patrons being over retirement age and the place having the best breakfast money could buy, the diner was seldom left with an abundance of empty tables. Lucas was again seated at the small table in the back of the restaurant.

"Well hello to you again, sweetie," said the waitress as she greeted Lucas.

He was surprised she remembered him. They barely spoke last time. But he indeed remembered her. The way she carried herself and her ability to keep the entire diner attended to and satisfied on her own sent him back to his childhood. His mother walked around the house with the same grace, taking his dirty dishes from him when he was finished eating, picking up the house, then resting next to him on the couch for some snuggle time.

"Coffee and a special today?"

Lucas looked at the waitress and smiled. "The special sounds great, but instead of coffee may I have glasses of milk and water?"

Lucas recalled his last visit. The food was spectacular, but the coffee tasted like burnt acid.

"Sure thing, sweetie."

The waitress went back to the kitchen to put in his order. Lucas looked out the window and saw Scott's truck in the parking lot. It was a monster of a truck, featuring a lift kit and a giant pipe coming out of the truck bed. Scott frequently posted pictures of it on social media with the caption, "Just gave the kid a bath."

The bell hanging over the door jingled as a customer walked in. Lucas saw that it was again the blue-eyed man with the scar on his face coming into the restaurant. He didn't make eye contact with Lucas as he took his seat next to the restroom.

*Is he following me?*

He didn't recall any of the other patrons from last weekend, but the crowd felt the same. Most of the men had on hats and most had voices which sounded as if they had smoked cigarettes their entire lives. It's possible they could be the same people as last time.

"Water. Milk. Special. Anything else I can get for you, sweetie?"

Lucas looked at the mountain of food in front of him. "No thank you, ma'am."

He took a bite of the French Toast. It was every bit as good as the last time. The bread melted in his mouth. He wouldn't even need teeth to enjoy this breakfast, just like the French Toast his mother would make for him and his father on Saturday mornings. Lucas's heart sank as he thought of them. Many years have passed, and he still hasn't been able to move on. He missed the way he felt safe in his mother's arms and his father's loving smile.

On Friday nights, his father would always make a stop on his way home from work to pick up a movie from the video rental store. His mother would also make a stop, picking up an extra-large extra cheese pizza. It was a tradition which Lucas looked forward to every week. By Wednesday's his mouth would be salivating at the thought of the mounds of melted cheese. He tried to recreate this night on his own, stopping to get a movie and a cheese pizza. But without his parents, the movie seemed dull, and the pizza tasted like cardboard.

Lucas's mind went to Chloe. He hoped she could be the one to fill the holes in his life. Maybe they could one day have children, and he could play the role of stopping to pick up a movie while Chloe picked up a pizza. They could sit on the couch with their children in their laps, laughing at goofy comedies and eating way too much cheese.

"Here's you another water, sweetie. Is there anything else I can get for you?"

Lucas looked at his table as he was awakened from his daydream. He hadn't even touched his other water.

*Perhaps I did leave too large of a tip the last time I visited and now she is giving me extra attention.*

There was one thing the waitress could bring him. His hand instinctively went to his pocket and felt that he had the two vials.

"Yes, actually. Could you I speak to the cook? This French Toast is phenomenal, and I'd like to personally give him my compliments."

The waitress smiled and said, "Sure thing. And I'm going to leave this here. There's no rush." She placed the bill on the table and went back to the kitchen.

Lucas looked at the array of beverages on his table, and his heart began to beat faster and faster. Everything was coming into place as he had hoped. If these next few minutes went as planned, Scott Banks would be crossed off his list, and he'd only have one more to go before he could free himself from his curse.

Lucas saw the waitress was pointing him out to Scott. He was wearing a skin-tight black polo shirt and a black hat, covering his red hair. He looked stiff as he walked over towards

Lucas, with his biceps and chest appearing as if they could burst out of his shirt at any moment.

"I hear you enjoyed the breakfast," Scott said as he approached Lucas.

His voice was thick, but it sounded forced. Lucas wondered if his natural voice didn't match the body which he worked so hard to build, leaving him to now work on strengthening it to match his appearance. Lucas pulled a vial from his pocket and began to pour it in one of the glasses of water. He checked his other palm and verified the cap was black.

"Sorry, just one second. I have a workout in an hour, and I need to get this started," Lucas said as he took the glass and drank it all without taking a breath.

"Awww. That's better. Sorry about that. Judging by your build, you know how it is when you get into a workout routine."

Scott smirked. "What was that? I haven't seen it before."

Lucas smiled. What he poured into his water was water. He had filled a vial with water and placed a black cap on it to distinguish it from the actual serum, which contained a red cap. He had been thinking about how to get Scott ever since his last visit, and it dawned upon him as he was searching through Scott's social media pages; the man loved his body and loved working out. But he wasn't like your typical health enthusiast.

Scott took it to a whole other level by entering into bodybuilding competitions. He'd been entering for the past five years, and he had yet to win one. The latest series of pictures he posted featured him with a different beverage in each one.

"Trying a new mix. I can see the gold," read his latest caption.

"It's not out to the public yet," Lucas lied. "It is scheduled to be released next month. My company developed it, and I have been stocking physician offices with samples in anticipation of its launch. Don't tell anyone, but I saved a few back for myself. The stuff is intense. After just one dose I went from running a twenty-one-minute 5k to a seventeen-minute 5k."

Lucas embellished his running ability. He could, at best, complete a twenty-five-minute 5k, but he needed to broadcast numbers he thought would be respectable to Scott. He considered talking about weights, but Lucas figured his physic could never be mistaken for a weightlifter.

Scott looked intrigued. "So, you'll need a prescription for it?"

"Yes. Big business, you know? They gotta take their share."

"Yeah, I hear ya," Scott replied as he let out a deep exhale in disappointment. He was willing to try anything to get an edge.

"You don't happen to have any extra samples? I've got a competition this weekend."

Lucas sighed, looking away from Scott. "I shouldn't give these away just yet. I could get in big trouble."

He paused, watching Scott's eyes as the information sank in before saying, "But I've never had a breakfast as good as yours. When's your next workout?" Lucas asked.

Scott's smile spread across his face. "I'm going to clean up a few things here and then hit the gym within an hour."

"Okay. You've still got time. It's prescribed to take an hour before your workout. The formula is slow to kick in, but it has an extended release to keep you going."

Lucas pulled the second vial out of his pocket. He could feel that his nerves once again caused his hands to perspire, making gripping the lid and twisting it off more difficult than necessary.

"You better only start with a half dose," Lucas warned as he pulled the second glass of water towards him and emptied half of the contents of the vial into the glass. Everything was coming into place perfectly. The second glass of water was delivered to his table without Lucas even asking, and he had the victim salivating at the chance to drink his death.

Lucas instinctively checked his surroundings as he closed the lid on the vile. The blue-eyed man was staring at him with great interest. Lucas stared right back, unwilling to give in.

*What does he know about me?*

"Come on, man. I can handle the whole dose," Scott pleaded.

Lucas gave him a grin.

"I know you can handle it while it's active, but the side effects can be intense. Studies show that those who work out the hardest have the highest probability to wake up with a debilitating headache the next morning. Try the half dose, and we can see how you feel tomorrow morning. I'll be back here for another helping of this delicious French Toast."

Lucas would have loved to have given Scott the full dose and crossed him off his list on the spot, but a full dose would have dropped Scott to the floor before he could make it back to the kitchen. The half dose will kick in later in the evening, or perhaps over-night. There will be no way to trace this back to him. The autopsy will reveal that Scott suffered a stroke. The blue-eyed man can stare all he wants. There will be no way to prove a cause and effect with this one. It was perfect.

Scott held his hand out in a fist towards Lucas. Lucas made a fist and bumped it. He then watched as Scott's enlarged Adam's apple went up and down rapidly as he drank the glass of water without taking a breath.

"Dude, I already feel like I could kick some serious ass. Thanks, man."

Lucas nodded, "The least I can do for the best cook in the state."

Lucas could feel the muscles in his back loosen as he watched Scott head back to the kitchen. He already felt a little more-free, as if a metaphorical weight was lifted from his shoulders.

*One more to go.*

He picked up his bill. It read that he owed five dollars and sixty-four cents.

*I was right. I did leave too much money for his bill last time.*

It was no wonder the waitress remembered him. He looked at the waitress and felt a bit of sadness when he realized she would have to find a new job after today. He thought of how his mother would have felt if she had lost her job and was no longer able to provide for her family. He pulled two twenties out of his wallet and left them on the table.

*This will help her get by. And if she is truly like my mother, she'll be back on her feet in no time.*

As he walked out of the diner for the last time, he met the stare of the blue-eyed man and smiled. Lucas was one step away from freedom and whether this man was watching him or just a peculiar individual, there was nothing that was going to get in his way.

# Chapter 15

W hat have you got for me?" Terry said to the phone as he sat in his cluttered office. There were papers scattered throughout, empty cans of soda piled in the trash can and stray fingernail clippings along his floor.

"We need to keep an eye on Scott Banks," said Bryce on the other line.

He was calling from his car, which was parked outside of the diner. The heat of the day was already beginning to makes its presence known and Bryce had the car idling so he could run the air conditioner.

"Who is Scott Banks?"

"He runs a diner here in the suburbs. Lucas had eaten here twice in the past week. Today he had an interaction with Scott, and it looked as if he poured a small vial of something into a glass of water for Scott to drink.

"Interesting," Terry replied.

He stood up and closed his office door, which was a rare event. Terry had been known for saying some of the rudest and inappropriate things in an open setting. The office staff often wondered and feared what he might be prompted to say behind closed doors.

"Did Scott see Lucas put the contents into the drink?"

"That's the part I don't understand. He did. It almost seemed as if Scott asked for it."

Terry ran his hand through his thinning hair.

"I don't know what this proves. If Scott drops dead today, all we have is that he willing drank something which Lucas put in his drink. It would be Lucas's word against ours on what it was that he put in the drink."

Bryce sighed. "I know. We've got nothing. He also poured a vial into his own drink, making it seem even stranger and tougher to prove. Do you think we are grasping at straws with this one? Could he be a victim of unfortunate coincidences?"

"You've seen the pictures. It would be an awfully big coincidence. We'll see what turns up with Scott Banks tonight."

"He's been spending more time with your co-worker, Chloe. Do you think she can provide us information?" Bryce asked.

Terry sighed and said, "I want to wait until the time is right before I play that chip. She is rebellious, and if I suggest anything towards her new boyfriend, we'll lose her forever."

Bryce pulled out a napkin from his glove box and wiped the sweat off of his forehead.

"Well, if you are right about Lucas, we better not waste too much more time."

"Thanks for the heads up on Scott. We'll watch for him in the news. If he winds up dead in the next day or so, I'll see what I can fish out of Chloe."

Terry hung up the phone and rest his feet on a pile of papers on his desk. He had been on the job for over forty years, and his hunches were rarely wrong. He often wondered if he should retire while he was still ahead. But he was only gone for a few months when he tried to ease out of the job with an extended leave. It didn't take long before his wife begged the paper to take him back, or so that's what he says. If Terry were honest with himself, he'd admit that he needed the paper more than it needed him.

He looked through his office window at Chloe. She had seemed happier over the past couple of weeks. Terry would never tell this to Chloe but seeing her happy made him happy, like a father for his daughter. He hoped for her sake that he was wrong about Lucas Braun.

# Chapter 16

Clouds filled the evening sky, and a fresh breeze was blowing through Lucas's backyard. He watched from his deck as a storm threatened to emerge at any moment. Chloe was on her way to his place. It was her turn to pick the date. She wouldn't give Lucas any details as to what they would be doing tonight. She said she wanted to surprise Lucas the way he surprised her. He didn't mind. He didn't care what they did. He was just happy to see her.

While he waited on his deck, Lucas's thoughts went to the waitress from the diner. Last night, the local news ran a story reporting that the owner of a local diner had a stroke and passed away in his sleep. The lovely waitress was now in need of a job. It was always overwhelming for Lucas to think about all of the lives his jobs impacted outside of the lives he took. But soon that will all be over. Soon the only lives he will affect are his and those close to him. He hoped one of those close to him would be Chloe.

He pondered the possibilities of where his relationship with Chloe might go tonight. Would she want to stay the night at his place? It was a Thursday, and he had to work the next day. Lucas assumed Chloe did too, which made him question why she would pick a night in the workweek for the date. Lucas flattered himself with the thought that perhaps she picked tonight to help her resist the temptation to stay over.

He still needed to restrain from progressing too quickly with her as he had one name left on his final list and he had yet to do any research on the victim, Bethany Mandel. But he had time, nearly a month and a half, and he didn't want that distraction to get in the way of tonight.

Though Lucas was expecting Chloe, the sound of the doorbell ringing startled him. He looked at his watch and saw it read six-fifteen. Chloe was early by fifteen minutes. He walked from his back deck through his kitchen and living room to the front door.

"Hey there!" Chloe said from his front porch.

She leaned in and gave Lucas a welcoming hug and long kiss on the lips. Her tennis shoes, khaki shorts, and t-shirt gave Lucas the impression that they were in for a casual evening. Lucas was beginning to realize that it didn't matter what Chloe wore. He's seen her in shorts, yoga pants, and a formal dress. On every occasion, she took his breath away. Lucas's attire was on the border of casual and professional. He wore his usual red corduroy pants, but instead of a t-shirt, he wore a blue-button up t-shirt.

"You look amazing," Lucas said to Chloe as he motioned for her to come inside.

Chloe looked at her clothes and replied, "You're too kind."

She placed her backpack on the bench in Lucas's entryway.

*Is there a change of clothes in that backpack?*

"You place is gorgeous," Chloe exclaimed while she took in the scenery.

The main floor of Lucas's home consisted of a small living room, a small dining area, a small kitchen and a powder room. The word small was a reoccurring theme, but it was perfect for Lucas since he didn't need to much space, and it made it easier for him to keep the place tidied up.

"Thank you. Would you like a tour?"

"I'd love one," Chloe said, grabbing his hand for him to lead her throughout the house.

Lucas started with the living room. It consisted of a couch, loveseat, and a television, which was hung over a wood burning fireplace. The dark oak floors in the living room also ran throughout the remainder of the main floor. He then took her to see the kitchen. It had an L-shape granite counter top and stainless-steel appliances.

"I love all of the detail. Did you pick everything out yourself?"

Lucas sighed and looked at his bare feet. In theory, he was the one who ordered all of the materials and colors. But he wasn't the one who chose the design.

"My mother did."

Chloe gave Lucas a confused look as she asked, "Was this your parent's house?

"It wasn't their house. But my mother dreamed of this house. She subscribed to an interior design magazine and left post-it notes on the pages she was interested in. Growing up we could never afford the renovations, so they never happened. But her taste for design was decades ahead of its time, as it is now in style. When I bought this place, it looked nothing like it does now, but it had the bones to be what my mother would have wanted."

"Did you do all of the work yourself?"

"I wish I could take the credit for that. But one thing you'll learn about me is that I'll never be confused as handy. Years ago, I helped a man. His wife was ill, and I offered to cover the medical bills. He was persistent on repaying me, so I finally gave in and allowed him to put in the labor towards my renovation. He did a phenomenal job."

Chloe smiled and gave Lucas a quick kiss.

"You continue to amaze me, Lucas Braun."

Lucas grinned and said, "You haven't even seen one of the best parts."

He led Chloe through the French doors in his kitchen to the deck outside. There wasn't a building between him and the river which ran through the town.

"Every night that I get the chance, I watch the sunset over there," Lucas said as he pointed to his right.

Pointing to his left Lucas continued with, "And each morning I get to see the sunrise over from over there."

"It's perfect," Chloe replied. "I wondered why you didn't live in the city, and I'm quickly learning why."

Lucas looked at the sky and observed the gray clouds covering Chloe and him.

"Unfortunately, I don't think we will get to see a sunset tonight."

"You're right!" she exclaimed as if she came to a sudden realization. "We better get going with our date. We can finish the tour when we get back."

"There won't be much to finish when we get back. Just two bedrooms upstairs. One is used for an office. Where are we going?"

"I still want to see those," Chloe said with a grin. "And there is a Chinese restaurant just a few miles away that serves the best kung pao chicken. I brought my bike so that we can pedal to it."

Lucas appreciated the sentiment. She remembered his distaste for riding in cars.

"I know the place. You're right. The kung pao chicken is the best. Nice choice."

The ride to the restaurant took more time than it usually would for Lucas when he was riding alone. He rode his bicycle frequently and was fast enough to race competitively if he desired. Chloe didn't ride often, and Lucas didn't want to make the ride strenuous on her, so he kept his pace slow. He didn't mind. When he was with Chloe, he didn't have any concerns. He felt butterflies in his stomach, through his veins, and in his head when she was around. When she touches him, he feels as if he is in a dream that he never wishes to end.

"Do you eat here often?" Chloe asked as they parked their bicycles at the restaurant.

"Every week," Lucas said as pulled out his bicycle chain and tied the two of bicycles to a *No Parking* sign.

"Do you think someone would take our bikes?" Chloe asked.

Lucas thought back to when he was a young teenager when his bicycle was stolen. A chance he never wanted to take again.

"I don't know," Lucas admitted. "Just a habit I guess."

Lucas put his hand on Chloe's back and led her to the restaurant. The smell of ginger and garlic tingled his nostrils as he walked through the door. It featured one large, dimly lit room with an isle in the center, tables on each side, and a bar in the back of the room.

"Mr. Braun?" the hostess said with an inquisitive look on her face.

Lucas noticed the confused look on her face. He had been coming here for years and never with anyone else. Occasionally he would have a drink at the bar while they prepared his food, but in most instances, he picked up his food to-go.

"Mrs. Chang. How's business?" Lucas said in an attempt to make small talk.

"Two tonight? Are you dining in?"

Like usual, Mrs. Chang didn't make an effort to return the gesture of small talk. She had a habit of being blunt and to the point. But she always welcomed Lucas with a smile and would occasionally sneak in a couple of crab rangoon into his order.

Lucas, not fully aware of Chloe's plans for the evening, looked at her to answer.

"We'll be dining in. Thank you."

Mrs. Chang grabbed a couple of menus and led them to a table for two in the back corner of the restaurant. Lucas pulled a chair out for Chloe and helped scoot her seat to the table. As he walked around the table to take his seat, a waiter arrived to take their orders.

"Are we ready to order, Mr. Braun?"

Lucas looked to Chloe for reassurance. Despite not having a chance to look over the menu, he sensed he knew what she wanted to eat tonight.

"I believe we are. Can we get two orders of your kung pao chicken, an order of crab rangoon, and a pot of the herbal tea?"

Chloe gave a reassuring nod and handed her menu to the waiter.

"They don't waste any time here," Chloe said. She took the napkin from the table and set it on her lap.

"No, they don't. The first time I came in, I was new to the area, and I thought I'd try their place out. Despite the temperature hovering around twenty degrees outside, I rode my bike to their restaurant. It was at their previous location, and the place needed some work. Panels were missing from the drop ceiling, the wallpaper was peeling off, and most importantly, the furnace wasn't running."

"Wow, I probably would have turned right around."

"I was about to. But I before I could turn around, Mrs. Chang called me from behind the counter."

"I'll take your order." Lucas did his best to imitate her accent. He sounded less like Mrs. Chang and more like an Italian mobster from the movies. Chloe laughed at his attempt.

"I obviously didn't have a chance to look over the menu, so I decided to order something with a little heat to try to warm up. I asked for the kung pao chicken and took a seat. As I waited, I began to worry about the quality of the food I just ordered while I took in the deteriorating look of the place. For the second time, I nearly left. Then Mrs. Chang came out of the kitchen with a pot of fresh herbal tea. She told me I looked cold and to drink up. I took a sip, and it was as if all of my senses stimulated. Never had I tasted anything so pure. I could feel warm blood flowing from my heart and through my veins to the tips of my toes. Moments later she came out with my food, and once I tasted it, it was game over. I knew then that this would be the place where I'd be ordering my takeout for the rest of my life."

The waiter came back with the pot of tea and two cups. Lucas thanked him and poured a cup for Chloe and a cup for himself.

"I can't wait to try this tea now. You better not have oversold me, Mr. Braun."

She had a playful smile as she teased Lucas. He watched as he took a sip of the tea. Her brown eyes became enlarged as if she was surprised. She then closed them and took another sip while leaning back in her chair. Chloe looked as if she had traveled away from this world, to a place where she felt she was in peace. She then opened her eyes and said, "You really aren't a good salesman."

Lucas leaned forward in anticipation of what she was going to say next.

"This tea is like drinking straight from a stream of mountain water mixed with freshly picked herbs and tea leaves. I've never had anything like it. Your upsell was actually an undersell in this case."

Lucas let out a soft laugh. "I told you when we first met. I'm not good at my job, and I wasn't worthy of being in your Top Forty Under Forty article."

Before Chloe could respond, Mrs. Chang came to the table with two glasses of white wine. She set them on the table and turned away before Lucas could thank her. Chloe looked at the wine and then at Lucas.

"You must be their favorite customer. Don't tell me; you helped them out in the same way you helped the man who did the work on your house?"

Lucas looked at his hands on the table, embarrassed to respond. His eyes then went to Chloe. She was shaking her head at him with a closed lip smile.

"I don't understand. How is it that you are single? You're successful, genuine, kind beyond belief, and breathtakingly gorgeous. It doesn't add up."

*If she only knew who I really was.*

"If there is a mystery to be solved tonight, Ms. Benedict, it is the mystery of how you have managed to remain single," Lucas responded in an attempt to change the subject.

Chloe took another sip of her tea and closed her eyes, appearing as if she was soaking in the experience.

"Well, we all have our demons," she said.

Lucas smiled.

*She has no idea.*

"Two orders kung pao chicken. One order crab rangoon," The waiter said as he set the dishes down on the table.

Steam was pouring from the food. It looked as if it was only seconds removed from a five-hundred-degree wok. This was one of the reasons Lucas enjoyed take-out over dining in. The ride home gave the food time to cool to a temperature that would only slightly scald his mouth.

"Well, we may have to wait a few minutes on this so that our tongues don't catch fire."

Chloe nodded and took her fork and spread the food on her plate in an attempt to expedite the cooling process.

"I have a question for you," Chloe said with a sincere look on her face.

"I introduced you to my only remaining family. I was wondering, do you have any family?"

Lucas sensed she had been thinking about this. He wished he had a family to introduce Chloe to. Or anyone in that regard. The only real human contact he's had over the last decade had been with Sam, and he was now absent from Lucas's life too. If it weren't for Chloe, Lucas would have no one.

"I wish I did have a family to introduce you to. My mom and dad would have loved you. I'm sure my father would have pulled out embarrassing pictures of me and my mother, desperate for another woman in the house, would have smothered you with kindness."

Lucas paused before continuing. He could feel tears coming to his eyes as he thought about the idea of introducing Chloe to his parents. A joy he'll never get to experience. Chloe reached out and took hold of Lucas's hand.

"My foster parents, Bill and Denise, also would have been thrilled I had met you. They wanted nothing but the best for me. They went above and beyond their end of the bargain in fostering me. One of my biggest regrets is that I didn't hold up my end of the bargain. I never really let them in. They could see I was a troubled teenager who lived through a horrible accident which took the lives of the only family I had, and I was holding it all in."

Lucas tried to fight it off but lost the battle and let a single tear ran down the side of his face. Chloe squeezed his hand tighter, fighting tears back from her sympathetic eyes.

Lucas took a drink of water , looked at Chloe, and said, "This may scare you off, but as of this moment you are all I've got for personal social interaction."

Chloe let out a sigh.

"Lucas, I'm afraid that I can tell you the same thing. Outside of Gammy, you're the only person I look forward to seeing."

Lucas and Chloe smiled as they looked at each other. She was the missing piece in his life, and Lucas was beginning the believe that he may be the missing person in her life.

"Why you no eat?" Mrs. Chang asked abruptly, ending the moment of silence.

"Oh, just letting it cool down a bit," Lucas replied, "It looks great. Thank you."

Though still very hot, Lucas and Chloe began eating their dishes. He wasn't accustomed to enjoying this meal with company and forgot how much the spicy food made his nose run. He could see Chloe was also sniffling.

"How did you discover this place? You live within walking distance to some of the best restaurants in the Midwest. What inclined you to pick up Chinese food from the suburbs?"

"Gammy. Her place has a nice cafeteria, but once a month they allow the residents to vote on take-out from a list of options. They picked this place one month, and it was all she could talk about for weeks. One day, I surprised her by picking up take out before coming over. We now eat it once a month. I think I'm going to have to come by and grab some of this tea for the next book club meeting. Gammy will love it."

"You save room for dessert?" The waiter asked, abruptly.

Chloe leaned back and put her hand on her stomach, shaking her head no.

"I think we've eaten as much as we can. As always, it was delicious," Lucas said to the waiter. He pulled out some cash for dinner and handed it to the waiter.

"No, I've got this tonight," Chloe protested, "It was my turn to pick and my turn to pay."

The waiter had already left with the money and their plates.

"It's okay. The convenience store paid me to take the cheap bourbon for our last date. You made the long journey here and respected my distaste for vehicles when you showed up with a bicycle. It's the least I can do."

Chloe folded her arms over her chest, looking defeated.

"I'm sorry," Lucas said. He could see Chloe was disturbed by his gesture. "I should have asked. Next date is on you. I promise."

He stood up and reached out his hand to help Chloe from her chair. She still had her arms folded, looking out the window. She then looked up with her bright brown eyes and smiled. Lucas sighed in relief, seeing he was forgiven.

A sudden thunder rumbled loudly, causing the whole restaurant to jump in surprise. Lucas and Chloe looked at each other and then out the window at their bicycles.

"We better hurry," Chloe said, pulling Lucas towards the door.

On the way out, Lucas spotted Mrs. Chang.

"Thanks again for the wine. I'll have to get it again. It was delicious."

As usual, Mrs. Chang didn't respond verbally or physically to Lucas's comment. She stood both motionless and expressionless. Chloe pushed the door open as another loud thunder cracked through the town.

"I don't think we are going to make it. It's okay. Sometimes I take a cab in emergencies. I can call one here."

"We'll never make it with you just standing there. Hurry, unlock the bikes. It's not far."

Lucas smiled and quickly unlocked the bikes. They jumped on and began pedaling. Goosebumps formed on Chloe's legs as the wind gusts were getting colder and stronger. BAAMMM! Another loud thunder shook the earth, this time accompanied by a bolt of lightning. They were still over a mile away from Lucas's home.

"This is a little dangerous, don't you think?" Lucas asked as he pedaled up to ride by Chloe's side.

"We'll be fine. The rubber tires will protect us from any lightning strikes."

Lucas didn't know if that was true, but he pedaled along anyways. It was then that the rain came. It wasn't a typical storm which started with a sprinkle before gradually getting heavier. This storm started heavy and stayed heavy. Lucas and Chloe were utterly soaked within seconds.

Lucas looked ahead as he pedaled. The scene reminded him of the night his parents were taken from him. Like tonight, it was a strong and unforgiving thunderstorm. The rain came suddenly and hard. His stomach felt tight as he recalled the event.

*Thank goodness Chloe insisted we remain on our bicycles. This would have been much worse in the cab.*

He looked over at Chloe. Water was pouring from her face. Her eyeliner was running down her cheeks. Yet to Lucas, she looked just as beautiful as ever. She then looked at Lucas and let out a laugh.

"What's so funny?" Lucas shouted.

"This is perfect," Chloe replied.

She took her hands off the handlebars and held her arms out towards the sky, holding her head back as she pedaled and letting the rain pour all over her body. Lucas was impressed that she was able to handle her balance so well on the bicycle.

She again looked over at Lucas, who was still looking rigid and uncomfortable.

"Come on! Embrace it!" Chloe challenged.

Lucas shook his head no and continued pedaling, but his non-participation didn't affect Chloe as she continued to look into the sky and let the rain pour onto her face. She waved her wet hair from side to side, looking as if she were dancing while riding the bicycle.

Lucas looked ahead, and to his surprise, they were only a few more blocks from his home. He watched as she continued to unapologetically dance on her bicycle through the rain. He couldn't help but smile. The knot in his stomach loosened. He pedaled up to be side by side with Chloe. She looked at him as he looked back at her with a serious look on his face. Then he let go of the handlebars and held his hands in the air as if he were playing a guitar.

"Rock on!" Chloe encouraged.

Lucas put his hands back on the handlebars and smiled at Chloe before saying, "Race you to the house."

They both pedaled as fast as they could. The rain came down so quickly that the road was already flooded, forming one large puddle for them to splash through as they raced towards the house. Finally, they reached their destination and rushed up his porch to take shelter on his porch.

"That was crazy! I don't think I've ever been in anything like that," Chloe said as she hurried inside.

"Neither have I," Lucas replied.

He walked to Chloe and gave her a soft kiss.

Chloe smiled and stared into Lucas's eyes. Water was dripping from the two of them onto the oak floors. Their clothes were drenched in water and clung to their bodies, revealing every curve.

"I'll grab us a couple of towels."

Lucas pulled away and hurried up the stairs to his linen closet. He grabbed four towels, but when he walked back down the stairs, he realized that they wouldn't be enough as he eyed the puddles of water he left during his journey up the stairs.

Lucas turned the corner and said, "You know I have extra clothes. These towels may not be en….."

He stopped mid-sentence because what he saw when he turned the corner left him speechless. Sitting on the floor were Chloe's socks, shoes, shorts, shirt, underwear, and bra. Chloe was standing before him, completely naked. Her hands rested on her hips. Her skin didn't have any imperfections, smooth and clear from head to toe.

Chloe broke the silence with, "I think I'm ready for the tour upstairs."

# Chapter 17

The sound of the alarm clock came much too soon for Chloe and Lucas. It was a night neither would forget and a night neither wanted to end. In an effort to prolong it, Lucas and Chloe didn't go to sleep until three in the morning. The events began when Lucas led Chloe upstairs for rest of the tour of his house. Lucas jokingly led her into his second bedroom, which he used as a study, and described the reasons for why he picked the décor for the room while Chloe continued to stand stark naked in his hallway upstairs. They then exchanged smiles and made love. The moment was nothing like Lucas anticipated it would be. He was concerned he would be awkward and unable to provide an enjoyable experience for Chloe. However, everything went smoothly, like a choreographed dance which they never practiced but were meant to dance their whole lives. In those moments, Lucas felt whole and at the same time felt like nothing. He was in perfect balance with Chloe, summing to zero.

Instead of lingering in the bed afterward, Lucas and Chloe put on sweatpants and t-shirts from Lucas's closet before returning downstairs to start a fire. The thunderstorm caused a cold front, and their damp bodies were covered in goosebumps from the cold air.

The next few hours were spent wrapped in each other's arms on the couch as they streamed movies and listened to the crackle of the fire. The movies weren't memorable, and Lucas and Chloe didn't say much during them while they soaked in the comforting feeling of each other's warmth.

It was roughly around midnight when their stomachs began to growl.

"How about some cheesesteaks?" Lucas offered.

Chloe nodded in agreement, and Lucas went to the kitchen to prepare the meal. It was one of his favorite meals. He had purchased the ingredients earlier in the week in preparation for his weekend lunches. He was more than happy to make different plans for those meals and instead enjoy this meal with Chloe.

Once they finished the cheesesteaks, they settled in for streaming some documentaries over the internet. Both eventually fell asleep on the couch. At around 3:00 am Lucas woke up and his slight movement awoke Chloe. They exchanged smiles and headed upstairs to sleep in the comfort of Lucas's bed.

"I wish we didn't have to go to work today," Lucas said while yawning as he reached to turn off the alarm.

"Last night was amazing. But I think I'm going to pay for it today," Chloe said as she stretched her arms. "Mind if I use the restroom first?"

"Be my guest," Lucas replied.

Chloe hurried downstairs and grabbed her backpack and then ran back up to the restroom. Lucas got her a towel and showed her the tricks of his faucet. While she showered, he went to the kitchen and made a pot of coffee and two bacon and egg sandwiches. He also got out his blender and made a couple of smoothies to give them a quick infusion of vitamins.

"All done," Chloe announced as she entered the kitchen. She was wearing form-fitting jeans a teal V-neck shirt.

Lucas walked over to Chloe and kissed her.

"I'm glad you had an extra set of clothes with you. I'm afraid your original clothes reek of smoke from the smoldering fire," Lucas said as he looked towards the mantle where their clothes were drying next to the ash from last night's fire.

"Always good to be prepared, I guess."

Lucas motioned towards the counter. "I made you a smoothie and a breakfast sandwich. Coffee is on the counter. Feel free to eat and drink as much as you'd like."

Lucas hurried upstairs and took a quick shower. The warm water provided a much-welcomed relief to his cold and muddy skin. He hadn't realized until now just how dirty he was from the bicycle ride in the rain. He scrubbed himself clean as fast as he could and went to his bedroom to put on his suit before returning to the main floor.

In the kitchen, Lucas saw Chloe's dishes were cleaned and drying on a towel. Chloe was sitting outside on the deck, enjoying a cup of coffee. He walked to her and kissed the top of her head.

"I hope you enjoyed breakfast."

"I could get used to this. Delicious breakfast, great coffee and a beautiful view."

"The view is even more breath-taking from my vantage point," Lucas said, standing behind Chloe.

"Do you have to go to the city today?" Chloe asked.

Lucas sensed she had playing hooky on her mind. The idea thrilled Lucas, but he had to drop off samples at some of his key accounts before an influx of patients filled the offices.

"Unfortunately, I do," Lucas said, reluctantly.

Chloe stared ahead at the river. The sun was out, but it had made little progress in drying the soil and grass from last night's thunderstorm. The river was flowing rapidly with the excess water coming in from the runoffs.

"You can say no to this idea, but I was wondering if I could work from your place today? It's my Gammy's anniversary date with my Papi, and I want to check on her in the morning. Then I thought I could write my pieces from here. When you get home from work, we could have dinner before spending the weekend together."

The idea caught Lucas by surprise. Though he hadn't known Chloe for long, he wasn't the least bit concerned about her staying at his place to work while he was gone. However, he was planning to research his final victim from his list over the weekend. But given that he still had over a month to complete it, he supposed he could make an exception. Last night he got a taste of how it felt to truly be happy. He didn't want that feeling to end.

"That sounds great."

Chloe, noticing the pause in Lucas's response asked, "Are you sure? I don't want to be too forward."

"You don't want to be too forward?" Lucas said with the hint of a laugh in his voice. "You asked me to the Ball after interviewing me. When I called you for a date, you said yes on the condition that the date took place within hours. When I went to get you a towel to dry off last night I came down to see that you were completely naked."

Chloe blushed. "Someone's gotta push the pedal on this relationship. If I left it up to you, we'd never get anywhere."

"Well, I guess it's my turn to be forward."

Lucas paused before continuing. Chloe leaned forward and watched as Lucas rubbed his hand through his brown hair.

"Before we move forward with this relationship, there is something you should know."

Chloe's eyes appeared to be filled with anticipation while she watched Lucas search for the words. Before he could find them, she said, "Don't."

*Don't?* Lucas thought.

Lucas watched as Chloe rose from her chair and closed the distance between her and him. He wondered what she was doing, and that perhaps his words gave her the wrong idea about what he was going to say.

"Lucas, I love you," Chloe said, looking into Lucas's eyes.

He let out a sigh and rolled his eyes before saying, "Even when I try to be forward, you beat me to the punch."

Chloe's serious face turned to delight, appearing to have figured out what Lucas was trying to say.

"I love you too, Chloe."

They embraced each other with a kiss and a long hug. They had lived their whole lives with a piece missing. She was a one, and he was a negative one. Together they summed to zero, a perfect balance.

# Chapter 18

Terry Horn was drinking a cup of coffee in his breakfast nook while reading the morning's paper when his cell phone rang. His general rule of thumb was to not answer his phone in the mornings. His doctor told him he needed to reduce the stress in his life, for his heart's sake. Between tight deadlines and dwindling budgets, it was impossible for Terry to avoid the stress while at work, so he compromised by taking time to drink coffee and read the paper in the mornings. He would mimic this behavior in the evenings, but instead of coffee, he would drink scotch. Terry's doctor argued that neither beverage was necessarily good for his heart, but none the less was satisfied that Terry was at least making an effort.

It was only a few seconds after he let the call go to voicemail when his phone began to ring again. It rested on the table a few feet from where he was sitting. Its vibration ran across the wood and through Terry's arms. He reached over to turn off the ringer but hesitated when he saw the name on the incoming call was Bryce Cooper.

*What the hell is he going to have to say at this hour of the day?*

Terry clicked answer and put the phone to his ear. "Hello."

He spoke in a soft voice, trying not to wake his sleeping wife. Though they lived together and have been married for over 30 years, they rarely saw each other. Terry was always gone before she woke in the mornings and his wife's schedule was always full of activities in the evenings. Even on weekends, she had a calendar full of plans. Terry would offer to go with her to wherever she was going on the weekends, but she would seldom welcome him along.

"It's a wine tasting; you wouldn't like it."

After a few lines similar to that from his wife, Terry eventually stopped asking. During his brief retirement, he discovered she had been seeing another man. He mistakenly picked up her phone one morning instead of his to listen to a voicemail and heard the man's voice. The kind and loving voice infuriated him. But before he could confront his wife, Terry took a look in the mirror. He hadn't been the best to live with for all of the years, and he hadn't exactly always been faithful. He was lucky she didn't leave him. Ultimately, he decided to let it slide, and a few weeks later he came out of retirement and rejoined the paper.

"She is at his place," Bryce said into his cell phone.

He was seated across the river, observing Lucas and Chloe share an intimate moment on the patio deck extending from his house, both oblivious to anything other than each other.

"Who is at his place?" Terry asked.

"Your coworker, Chloe. She stayed the night. Lucas just left, but Chloe stayed behind."

"Interesting. She's usually in the office in about an hour from now."

Terry didn't care when his employees came into the office. He didn't even care if they talked to him or if he even saw them as long as their work was timely and of good quality. But he's never seen Chloe not be at her desk by 9:00 am.

"It's time to deploy her. You saw the news. Scott Banks is dead. It's too much of a coincidence to deny any longer. Lucas is a killer, and we need proof. Maybe there is something she can find in his home."

Terry hesitated. He hated that this had happened to Chloe. He already felt bad enough for encouraging her to pursue a date with Lucas.

"She won't do it. I can't tell her I think her boyfriend is a serial killer. She'll never believe me. She'll probably cuss me out and threaten to quit. We'll lose our connection altogether."

Bryce protested, "What's the point of having a connection if you don't use her? How many people need to die while you worry about the feelings of your colleague? How do you know she isn't next?"

Those last few words resonated with Terry. It was something he had feared ever since Chloe became involved with Lucas. Though Terry came off as uncaring and unpleasant, he had a soft spot for Chloe. He could see she was damaged, but he also saw a brilliant individual who was a damn good writer. He was rooting for her to succeed like a father would for his daughter.

The vibration of his cell phone broke his silence.

*Another call this early in the morning. Give me a break.*

"Hold on a second. I've got another call."

Terry brought his phone from his ear and saw it read, "Incoming call from Chloe Benedict."

"It's Chloe," Terry said to Bryce, hanging up before Bryce before he could say anything.

"Hello," Terry answered.

Chloe paused. Terry rarely answered a phone call by saying hello. He usually replied in a tone as if the caller was rudely interrupting him and greeted the caller with a "What?" or a "Speak".

"Um. Hello, Terry. It's Chloe."

"What do you need?"

"I am going to work offsite today. I'll be visiting my grandmother in the morning, and then I'll send in my stories in the afternoon."

Terry considered asking Chloe where she was. The thought of probing her about her boyfriend crossed his mind, but he didn't think he'd garner the reaction he hoped for.

"What am I your father? Why are you calling me so early in the day to tell me this? I can't keep track of all of the stories for the paper as well as the whereabouts of the people writing the stories. Just get your work in by the end of the day."

He hung up the phone before Chloe could respond and took a sip of his cold, bitter coffee.

*This won't due for today. I'm going to need something stronger.*

From his liquor cabinet, Terry took out his bottle of scotch. The morning's events had already gotten on the wrong foot. He hoped the scotch could correct the course. This wasn't the first time and likely wouldn't be the last time Terry had a drink before going to work. After pouring himself a generous pour, Terry walked to his dining room table and looked through his bay window, noticing the garage door was open at Tom Dempsy's home. His blue sedan was still parked inside. Terry wasn't close with Tom, only close enough to the point that they borrowed tools from time to time and chatted about the weather. Yet, it angered Terry to think that Tom was murdered.

Lucas took that man from that family and to this point, he's gotten away with it. He didn't know what he could do to stop Lucas Braun, but he knew he had to do something.

# Chapter 19

Lucas was surprisingly full of energy as he walked the halls of the hospital towards the physician offices. He couldn't have slept for more than two hours last night, but he felt as if he had just woken from one of his best nights of sleep in years. He had just dropped off samples for a client and was off to Dr. Gupta's to drop off another large shipment. With an hour to kill between now and when Gupta's office began accepting sales reps for the day, Lucas took the time to touch base with his manager for his weekly review.

"How's the country's number one sales rep?" Steve answered.

It fascinated Lucas that Steve was always so genuinely kind. "You know what? I'm actually doing pretty well."

Lucas adjusted his wireless earpiece. He didn't like the way he looked when he talked using the earpiece, but he also preferred to keep his hands free while he was walking. The awkward glances from people he passed while speaking in the headset were the price he paid for convenience.

"Oh, sorry. I thought I was talking to someone else. Did you find this cell phone left behind on a train? Are you calling to find its rightful owner?"

While Steve was grateful for Lucas's job performance, he often wished-for Lucas to be more energetic and sociable. It was the reason why he submitted for Lucas to be interviewed for the Forty Under Forty article, and it was the reason for why he often urged Lucas to do lead team presentations and happy hours.

Lucas smiled. Steve had always pushed him to be more outgoing. It seemed to Lucas that Steve sensed he was lonely and that he wanted him to be happy.

"Hilarious, Steve."

"All kidding aside, I'm glad you seem to be doing well. I don't have much for you this week regarding performance. As usual, your numbers are great. However, I do have some news concerning the presentation you're working on which reviews strategies for selling to areas where we don't have strong insurance coverage."

Lucas's breathing stopped. He had been putting off working on the presentation ever since it had been assigned to him, six months earlier. Every time he opened his computer to plug away, he found himself being distracted and uninterested.

"We are going to push it back a couple of weeks."

Lucas sighed in relief.

*More time. Perfect.*

"Senior Leadership is interested in the topic and interested in you. They asked to sit in on it."

Lucas's heart began to race. Talking to Senior Leadership was something he tried to avoid. They were smart people, and they liked to let people know they were smart. Most were always full of irrelevant questions and comments, speaking only because they enjoyed hearing themselves speak.

"Why are they interested in me?" Lucas asked, unsure how to respond.

"Come on, Lucas. You've been the best for a long time. While they like the money you bring them in the field, they are interested in seeing if you can share your secrets with the rest of the field. This is a big opportunity for you, and it can pay off big in your bank account too."

Lucas politely replied, "Well, thanks for the opportunity, Steve. I'll give it my best shot."

"I know you'll crush it. Have a great weekend and stay happy, buddy."

Lucas didn't say a word before Steve hung up the call from his end of the line. He stood motionless in the hallway of the hospital until the sound of the robotic voice from his headset brought him back to life. "Call has ended."

He took a seat on the empty bench in the hallway. The call took Lucas by surprise. Not only was he going to have to prepare a presentation, but he was going to have to prepare it for a group of people he didn't care to talk to, and while presenting it, those people would be judging him on if he would be a good fit for a position which he had no interest in taking.

One of the things he liked most about his job was the independence it gave him. Most of the interaction was done through email. Outside of his weekly phone call with Steve, he rarely had a voice interaction with the company, and it was even rarer that he had in-person interactions. If he were to get promoted, he'd likely have to spend more time in airports traveling from territory to territory to mentor the other sales reps. Once he was finished with his final list, travel would no longer be a hindrance to his reaping obligations, but he had Chloe to consider now. Spending his weeks in other parts of the country didn't appeal to him. Spending time with Chloe did.

"You look like you've just seen a ghost."

Lucas was slouched over on the bench looking at his feet on the floor. The familiar voice sent a jolt through his body as he looked up to see his old friend.

"Sam!"

Sam smiled. He was wearing his usual button up shirt, denim jeans, and blue suede shoes. He patted Lucas on the leg as he took a seat next to him on the bench.

Lucas was still in shock. He thought he'd seen the last of Sam when he received his final list.

"What are you doing here? Are you okay?"

Sam shrugged his shoulders. "I'm fine, just taking care of business."

Lucas knew what that meant. He was often assigned to hospital assignments. The key was to give the patient a small dose so that they pass away long after you would have been seen at the hospital. That, combined with the fact that the patient was likely here because of a physical ailment where their survival chances were in question, helped to keep anyone from suspecting outside involvement in their passing.

"I can't tell you how great it is to see you. I thought I'd never see you again."

A couple of nurses walked by, giving an extended look at Sam and Lucas. Lucas smiled as they walked by. He tended to forget the effect Sam had on women. They attracted to him like bugs to a light.

"Listen, Lucas, it is good I ran into you. I have an update concerning your final list."

Lucas could feel his heart sink into his stomach. The light at the end of the tunnel. He only had one more name, and then he'd be finished, free to live a life with Chloe. He reflected on how quickly his motivations had changed since meeting Chloe, and also how quickly everything could be taken away from him if he wasn't relieved of his reaping responsibilities. He didn't think he could do it.

Lucas's voice shook as he asked, "What is it?"

"I saw you took care of the first one. Nice work."

Lucas believed that this quality in Sam was one of the reasons why he was cursed with being a reaper manager. He was always quick to compliment.

"Your last reap, I'm sorry to say, but things have changed," Sam paused for a moment. "She needs to go today."

*Today?*

Lucas was unprepared for the idea of reaping today. All he'd been thinking about was getting back home to Chloe.

*How could I pull it off today? I haven't yet begun researching the last victim. And what about Chloe? She's waiting for me at my house.*

"You mean Bethany Mandel?"

"Yes. The time has come, quicker than I anticipated," Sam replied.

"Do you have any information for me about her? I haven't had a chance to look her up yet."

"I'm sorry, Lucas. I don't have any further information. I have faith in you. Stay focused and finish the list. I know you'll do fine. This is the last day that you'll be under obligation with death. Tomorrow when you wake up, you'll be free."

*A free man. That would mean that this was sure to be it, my last interaction with Sam.*

Lucas had one thing on his mind, which he had to ask. *Sam knows what happened that night. I need to ask him one last time.*

"I guess this is it then?"

Sam smiled. "This is it, my brother."

"I got one last question for you."

Sam leaned his head back to rest on the wall behind him.

"I know you do, Lucas. And you know this is something I wish I could share with you. But I can't. I don't have that information. The time has come for you to put it in the past and move on."

Lucas protested, "But this person saved my life. I want to know what happened to him. In my years, I haven't saved anyone. What would have happened to me if I did the same thing?"

Sam shook his head. "I think you know the answer to that question."

Lucas looked at the floor. He suspected the reaper who saved him ended up on a list, then Lucas replaced him as reaper. Life and death are all about balance.

"Is this it then? Is this the last time I'll see you?" Lucas asked.

Sam nodded his head.

Lucas felt his energy escape him. He loved Sam, and it bothered him that their relationship wouldn't continue beyond this point. He'd wished that he could at least see that Sam made it, to see that he'd gotten his final list and was lifted from the curse.

He wondered if Sam felt the same about him.

*Would he like to know that I'm happy? That I've started a life?*

With a voice on the edge of quivering, Lucas said, "I've met someone."

Sam didn't say anything. But his eyes brightened ever so slightly and a small grin formed on his face.

"Her name is Chloe. She is a reporter for the local paper. She is the most remarkable woman I've ever met. I love her. Surprisingly, she loves me too. I don't know how I pulled it off. I didn't have any practice with dating. I was sure I'd mess it up. But I recreated my parent's first date for her. I bought the cheapest bottle of bourbon and a purple dahlia. It was a remarkable flower, and she agreed it was beautiful. And, as expected, the bourbon was awful."

Sam's grin grew as Lucas continued with the story.

"I told her that her perspective on everything else in the moment would change after drinking a shot of the cheap bourbon. The cold, soggy cheeseburgers in my backpack, would suddenly taste as good as a meal from a five-star restaurant. If we perceive this to be reality, then who is to say it isn't?"

Lucas looked at Sam, waiting for a response.

*Is he happy for me? Does he think I've been too reckless? Maybe he thinks I'm risking too much by beginning a relationship while still having loose ends to take care of.*

"You better get going. Remember to be safe and take precautions. This reap is rushed. Don't get lazy. I don't want to see your name on a list anytime soon," Sam urged.

Sam patted Lucas's leg as he rose from the bench, gave Lucas an extended smile, and walked away. It was in that smile that Lucas saw what Sam was feeling. He could see that Sam was happy for him.

Lucas reflected back on when he first met him. Sam encouraged that when Lucas was finished with his duties, he'd be left a better man.

*Perhaps Sam was right. All of this agony has led me to the light, to Chloe.*

Lucas checked his bag and saw he had a dose of serum with him. He was grateful he wouldn't have to go home to get one. Lying to Chloe was something he hoped to avoid.

Looking at his watch, Lucas saw it time for him to go to Dr. Gupta's to drop off the samples. He considered forgetting about the samples and getting to work on Bethany Mandel, but since he was close to the office, he decided he'd quickly drop them off. Not only would it help with his job, but it would also provide an alibi for his whereabouts for the day.

When Lucas walked into Dr. Gupta's reception office, he was greeted by the flirtatious receptionist, Rebecca.

"Woah watch out for Mr. Serious today."

Lucas always smiled when entering an office. He thought it was instinctive since he rarely thought about smiling but always did. Today's events have taken away his focus.

"Sorry about that. A lot of my mind."

Rebecca sat behind the counter. Her sandy blonde hair, generally put in a ponytail, was down today and she was wearing noticeably more makeup.

"Girl trouble?" Rebecca asked.

Typical Rebecca, Lucas thought. She was always trying to pry into his personal life.

"No. Just a busy mind," Lucas replied.

He paused for a second, wondering if he'd regret what he was about to say.

"You look nice today. What's the occasion?"

Her face lit up as if she were hoping he'd notice. "I have a big date tonight after work. My sister's husband works at a financial advisor's office, and they are setting me up with one of the guys from his work. He's taking me out for an expensive dinner and then we are going sailing under the stars on his boat."

"That sounds great! I hope he deserves you." Lucas replied.

He tried not to lead her on too much, but he gave her small lines from time to time to keep her in good spirits.

"Oh, he probably doesn't, but I'll give him a chance anyway."

"Well, good luck. You'll have to fill me in next week."

He smiled and went to the back to fill the sample closet with his allergy medication samples. It was a good thing he came today because the office was entirely out.

Rebecca was assisting a patient while he was walking out of the office. He smiled at her as he exited through the door. His duties as an ordinary citizen were over for the day. He now needed to shift his focus to learning about his final victim. There was a coffee shop just outside the hospital where he could eat a sandwich while conducting research.

His walking pace could nearly be mistaken for a jog as he raced the halls of the hospital. Lucas couldn't wait to get to the coffee shop to begin his research. It was starting to itch at him like a bug bite which he couldn't relieve. Just as he was near the exit and turning the last corner, he was stopped by someone calling his name.

"Lucas!"

It was Jessica. She was a nurse for Dr. Roy, one of the physicians on his calling list. And he just found out last week that she is also working part-time at the assisted living center in St. Charles, tending to Gammy.

"Hi Jessica," Lucas said as he continued walking.

He hoped that would be enough. He didn't have the time for small talk today. But Jessica continued talking and what she said next stopped Lucas in his tracks.

# Chapter 20

"What do I owe the pleasure?" Gammy said as she welcomed Chloe into her room.

It was mid-morning, and Gammy was reading her favorite book, The Princess Bride. She and her late husband read it together years ago. It quickly became their favorite book. They would often look for occasions where they could quote the book, bringing a smile to their faces every time. Gammy has read it each year since his passing.

"I had the morning off, and I wanted to come in and see the most beautiful lady in St. Charles."

Chloe walked over and gave her Gammy a hug and a kiss on the cheek, appearing to have more pep in her steps than usual.

"Well, aren't you in a lovely mood. What's changed? Did you meet a boy? What about Lucas? Tell me all about it."

Gammy loved girl talk. When Chloe was a teenager, she would often go to Chloe's room late at night to see if she wanted to talk about school or boys. Unfortunately for Gammy, Chloe never had a lot to say when it came to boys.

"School was fine. No, I don't have a boyfriend. I don't like any of the boys at school." Chloe would say to her prying grandmother.

Today was different though. Chloe had news, and she wanted nothing more than to share it with her grandmother. It was the day her Gammy had been waiting for ever since Chloe was a teenager.

"I have a boyfriend. And I'm in crazy in love with him. And yes, he's Lucas."

Chloe couldn't keep the smile off her face. Her eyes were beaming as she said his name. The word boyfriend and phrase in love were things Chloe hadn't mentioned in reference to herself in her lifetime, but both have come to feel natural to her.

"Oh, Chloe. I'm so happy for you. I want to hear all about it. Where did he take you for your first date? How did he kiss you for the first time?"

"Gammy," Chloe said, embarrassed to be talking about her intimate life.

"Oh, come on Chloe. I never get to have girl talk."

She shook her head reluctantly.

"Well, okay. He took me to the pier for our first date. We watched the sunset and ate cold, greasy cheeseburgers. "

Gammy smiled. "He seems different than most boys."

"He is. That's why I love him. He's unlike anyone I ever met. He's extremely successful, and, instead of splurging on himself, he gives all of his money away to help other people."

"Have you met his family? I bet they adore you."

"Well, that's another thing about him. He was an only child, and his parents died when he was a teenager. He was taken in by an elderly couple, but they too passed away. He doesn't have anyone to call family. I think that's why he tries to help so much with charities. It gives him a feeling of belonging."

"How about his closets. Have you checked them for any skeletons?"

"Oh, Gammy."

"Well you have to admit, he's just so handsome. And if he is as successful and good-hearted as you say, you have to wonder why he is still single."

Chloe protested. "What? Are you saying that I'm not good-hearted, successful, or beautiful?"

Gammy rose her hands in the air to surrender. "Okay, you got me. Maybe he just never found anyone interesting enough until he met you."

Chloe reached out and grabbed her grandmother's hand. "I think I've found my Papi."

Gammy smiled at the mention of her husband. She missed him every day. Everything they did together was in perfect harmony. On the nights she surprised him with his favorite dish, spicy hot wings, he surprised her with ice cream to cool the heat. He sang low, and she sang high. They still found ways to make each other happy during the most terrible years, when their only daughter ran off and eventually passed away. They didn't understand what they did wrong to make her want to run away. But life works in mysterious ways, and they were blessed with their perfect granddaughter, Chloe.

"I couldn't be happier for you. That is all I ever wanted for you. To find love as I did."

Gammy rose from her wheelchair and embraced Chloe with a long hug. Chloe hated bringing up painful reminders to Gammy about her Papi and his passing, but she knew Gammy would be thrilled to see that her granddaughter was in love.

Their extended hug was interrupted by the ring of Chloe's cell phone. She walked to her purse to retrieve it and saw it was Terry.

"Sorry, Gammy. It's work."

"Hello," she answered while she walked over to Gammy to help her back into her wheelchair.

"Clark is out today. Put your stories on the backburner and fill in for his work."

Typical Terry, Chloe thought to herself. He never asked for anything yet he always got exactly what he wanted. She didn't know what Clark was working on and hoped it wouldn't be anything that was too in-depth. Getting up to speed on a story with a tight timeline was not the most straightforward task to take on.

"Sure. What was he working on?"

"The obituaries for the Saturday morning paper. Everything you need to know is saved in the C drive."

"Sounds lovely," Chloe replied, sarcastically.

"I'm reading over the freshly printed Forty Under Forty article. You still seeing that Braun fella?'

*Is Terry taking an interest in my personal life now?*

"Umm. You could say that. Are you feeling okay, boss? It isn't like you to take up a casual conversation?"

"I didn't like the way he looked at me at the Ball. I got the uneasy feeling that he was guarding something."

*First Gammy, now Terry. Is there something I'm missing?*

"Well, I'll let you know if I find anything out," Chloe replied.

"Need it the obituaries by four. Thanks"

He hung up without a goodbye. She was, however, flattered that he said thanks. She can't recall the last time Terry said thank you to anyone. She once purchased a box of expensive cigars and a bottle of scotch for his thirty-fifth work anniversary, and, instead of thanking her, he asked if her buying those gifts were the reason he didn't have her column on his desk yet.

"Well, Gammy. I've been summoned."

"Don't you let them work you too hard, dear."

"Oh, I won't. I'm going to see Lucas again this weekend. I'll call you afterward to give you the scoop."

"I'm looking forward to it, darling," Gammy replied.

# Chapter 21

What did you say?" Lucas asked Jessica. She had a look of surprise on her face as Lucas questioned her. She had always known him to be calm and even-tempered. The man looking at her was full of horror and confusion.

"I asked if you were going to visit Gammy this weekend? I'm scheduled to work there Saturday and Sunday," she said, hesitantly.

Lucas shook his head. *That wasn't what she said just a few seconds earlier. What she said couldn't be right.*

"You didn't say Gammy?"

"Oh, sorry. Yeah, I still have trouble calling her Gammy. She is the only patient there who I don't refer to by her actual name. It's such a classic name too, don't you think? Bethany Mandel."

Lucas felt light headed as he leaned against the wall.

*This couldn't be the same person, could it? Bethany Mandel.* He could picture the name written on the list stored in the folder in his office.

"Are you okay? You look pale. Your lips are turning white."

Lucas nodded his head to indicate he was okay. He needed to get out of the hospital and into some fresh air.

"Yes. I'm fine. Sorry, you just reminded me that it's her anniversary today, and I need to send her a card. I'll probably see you there this weekend."

He rushed out towards the door, leaving Jessica behind.

*Bethany Mandel. Don't be the same person. Please be a different one.*

In all of his years, he never had to guess who the victim might be. There were always extra clues. However, this one was different. He was left to do the research.

*Please, let the spelling be different. Let her be a different person.*

He took a seat at the nearby coffee shop and pulled his laptop out of his bag. He opened a search engine and typed in *Bethany Mandel IL.* The first link pulled up a wedding announcement. It was dated September 2nd, 1957. His heart sank. That was exactly sixty years ago today. But he continued to search. It still didn't add up. Why wouldn't Chloe have the same last name? She never met her father. It didn't make sense for her to have a different last name.

He searched for Bethany Mandel, Benedict. The next link he clicked sent a chill down his spine. It was an article dated June 27th, 1988. Brittney Mandel, daughter of Bethany and Ryan Mandel, gave birth to a daughter, Chloe Benedict.

It was true then. His final victim was the grandmother of the woman he just fell head over heels for. He would have to reap Gammy or else face the consequences.

*Is this really something I can do?*

He had reaped outstanding people in the past, but he had never had a connection with them. One of the reasons he avoided getting close to people was because he feared they would one day be on his list. When he got his final list, he knew Chloe's name wasn't on it. She would be safe from him. But he didn't think to research the names to see if they had any relation to her.

*How could I be so careless?*

He considered his options. If he didn't reap Gammy, then his obligations would be left unfulfilled. He would then be on another reaper's list. He wondered what would happen to Gammy. Lucas was saved because another reaper spared him. Would Gammy be safe if he didn't reap her? How long would she have left? She's not the best shape for living the life of a reaper. It's likely that she would still be on a list, given her age and condition.

The buzz of Lucas's cell phone interrupted his thoughts, a welcomed distraction from his nightmare. He pulled it out of his pocket and said hello, never looking at the caller id.

"Hey," said a cheerful voice.

It was Chloe. Lucas regretted not looking at the ID before answering. He wasn't prepared to speak to her, given what he just discovered.

"Hey, Chloe. What's up?"

"I just left Gammy's. Terry called and demanded that I cover for someone and get a story in by the deadline this afternoon."

"That's a tough position to be put in. How was Gammy?"

"She was good. I could tell she had been crying. She was reading the Princess Bride. It was her and Papi's favorite book to read together. But then I told her about us. She couldn't have been happier that I found a decent man. You must have really done a number on her because she adores you."

*If only she knew what I'm considering doing to her.*

"But I was calling to see if you could do me a favor. I'm out of clothes for tomorrow. Would it be too far out of your way to stop by my place and grab some for me? That is, if you think I'll need clothes," she said flirtatiously.

"We'll see about that," Lucas said, trying to hide the anxiety in his voice.

"I can stop by. I was just getting ready to call you. It turns out that it is the monthly team building happy hour tonight. Totally slipped my mind. I would skip it, but it's my month to plan and host. Is that okay?"

He needed more time to plan what he was going to do. The happy hour was a convenient fib.

"Totally fine. I might try to do some writing while I wait. I'm feeling inspired today."

"That's great. If you find yourself getting writer's block, help yourself to any of the beers in my fridge. I'll pick up dinner on my way home."

"Okay. You'll need a code to get into my apartment. It's apartment 9F, and the code is 9-2-5-7. Can you remember it?"

Lucas wouldn't have any trouble remembering the code, Gammy's anniversary date.

"Yep. Got it. I'll see you later."

"See you soon."

Lucas hung up the phone. He was sitting right across the street from her apartment building. He had lost his appetite and left his table without ordering. He tugged on the exterior door to the apartment complex, but it didn't budge.

*Locked.*

He then saw the keypad next to it and wondered if she used the same code for both doors. He pushed 9-2-5-7 and heard the door click. It unlocked, and he walked to the elevator and rode it to the ninth floor. Her apartment was at the end of the hall. He punched in the code and entered.

It was a studio apartment. There was a twin sized mattress that was held in the air like a bunk bed. Underneath, instead of another bed, was a desk.

*Efficient use of space.*

She had a small kitchen to the right and a bathroom next to it. It was surprisingly spotless. Lucas had no reason to think that Chloe would be messy, but her place was tidied up as if she was expecting company at any minute.

He walked to her dresser and quickly grabbed a handful of clothes and carefully placed them in his bag. Before leaving, Lucas took one last look at the apartment. On the kitchen island rested the purple dahlia he bought for her on their first date. It was wilting away, already over a week old.

*Is my life about to expire in the same way as the dahlia's?*

Lucas then looked over to the living area and saw that Chloe had a sofa positioned in front of a television which hung from the wall. At that moment, everything became clear. He could picture himself staying here during weekdays, cuddled up on the sofa and watching movies together. On the weekends they could stay at his place, eating kung pao chicken and watching the sunset from his back deck.

Lucas decided what he was going to do. He didn't want to give up the life he recently imagined for himself. Lucas wanted to grow old with Chloe. They would date for a while longer, then get married and hopefully have children of their own. The happiness he would feel with her would outweigh the sorrow he would feel for being the one who had to reap her grandmother. Chloe will be devastated when she is informed that her grandmother has passed. But if he didn't do it, he would be reaped, and Gammy would likely also be reaped soon by someone else. At least this way Chloe wouldn't be left alone.

Lucas left the apartment building and headed for the train station. The next few hours would be some of the most difficult in recent memory. But he knew it was always darkest before the dawn. The sun will rise, and he will be a free man.

# Chapter 22

Chloe was eager to finish her work for the week. The picture-perfect weather she experienced during her bicycle ride back to Lucas's had her itching to relax on his back deck. She considered working from outside, but she feared that it would be too distracting. Given that her deadline was within a couple of hours and that she had never put together the obituaries previously, she figured she should endure the work inside and reward herself afterward. She opted to work in Lucas's quiet, upstairs office.

Like the rest of Lucas's house, his office had dark oak floors. The room was surrounded with crown molding around the ceiling and wainscoting around the walls, all of which were white. All four corners of the room were occupied. The door she entered occupied one of the corners, to her right was a chase lounge, straight ahead was a desk and chair, and diagonally ahead was a closet. She thought back to her Gammy.

*Any skeletons in that closet?*

Chloe shook her head and smiled as she walked towards the small desk. It was made of solid wood and looked to have centuries worth of wear and tear. There were two drawers built in on the right side, and the legs on the side facing the door were made of small porch columns. The stain on this wood was much darker than the stain on his hardwood floors, and it changed color along the top, soaking deeper into different grains and knots in the wood.

*Absolutely beautiful.*

This room lived up to the standards that the rest of the house set. Though it was an hour from the city, Chloe could see herself being very happy in this house. Everything about it invited her in. The warmth of the hardwood floors, the beauty of the molding, the simplicity of the furniture, and the cleanliness throughout called for her to come in and relax.

She opened her laptop to get to work. Using her cell phone as a hotspot, she connected to the paper's VPN and navigated to the obituary database. In it she saw that each folder was labeled with a year, dating back to 2002. Every death which was published in the paper over the last fifteen years was in the database.

Chloe double clicked the folder which read 2017 and saw that it had a folder for each week of the year. She then clicked last week to see what Clark had done before. To her relief, the process was surprisingly simple. All of the entries were put into the entries folder, and the output folder contained the document for printing. All she would need to do was go into the latest week's entries and organize the pictures and write-ups so it all would fit in section D6 of the paper.

In the entries folder, Chloe read each obituary and quickly realized she didn't want to cover for Clark too often. His job was quite depressing. Most were elderly, but there were a few middle-aged people who were leaving family behind. She thought of Lucas. He was once one of the family members left behind. After a terrible car accident, killing two, his parents left behind one incredible individual.

To Chloe's surprise, she was able to put together the obituary section in just under thirty minutes. Most were elderly people who had moved on, leaving behind children, grandchildren, and great-grandchildren. There was one man, a local diner owner, who stuck out to her. He passed away from a stroke.

*So young.* Chloe thought to herself.

She looked at her watch. It was one-fifteen. One thing she learned in her years working with Terry was to not turn in her work earlier than needed. He would either rip it apart, finding things which would want to tweak, or he would think she needed more work and give her another assignment.

To avoid both of those certainties, Chloe switched over to her desktop on her personal computer and began to type away at her novel. She found herself feeling more inspired since meeting Lucas. In her previous attempts, she hadn't yet eclipsed the one-hundred-page mark, always running out of ambition or interest. Over the last week, she's written fifty pages. Her latest premise involves a detective who is always able to solve the case because he has the unique ability to see ghosts. He finds the ghosts of the deceased people and trades them the favor of tying up their loose ends in exchange for information about the person who murdered them.

Though the temperature outside was in the low-seventies and there wasn't a cloud in the sky, Chloe didn't leave Lucas's desk for the next two hours. She wrote twenty pages on a case involving a woman who was murdered by her husband and in return for the information, the ghost asked that the handsome, mid-forties detective seduce her husband's mistress before turning him into the police.

The alarm on her phone went off, reminding her that her section was due to Terry in thirty minutes. Before turning back to the paper's VPN, Chloe decided to take Lucas up on his offer of drinking one of his bottles of beer, rewarding herself for a productive afternoon. She headed down the wooden staircase and into the kitchen. The contents of the refrigerator were similar to those in Chloe's refrigerator at her apartment. A pizza box with a few slices of pizza, some condiments, bread, deli meat, cheese, milk, and beer.

She grabbed one of the beers and began opening the cabinet drawers in pursuit of a bottle opener. In the first drawer were towels, the next was a junk drawer, and then the third was a utensil drawer. She dug around and found the bottle opener. She put the bottle on the countertop and pried off the cap. It was an early release of an Octoberfest beer. The cooler weather made it feel appropriate to be drinking a beer with this combination of malt and hops.

Before Chloe turned to walk back upstairs, an open manila folder caught her attention. Inside of it was a stack of papers, and each paper had a list of names.

*Is this Lucas's call list?*

She thought it was strange that a twenty-first company would still print out its call list on paper. Even for a company which made money off of paper, Chloe used surprisingly little of it. She flipped through a couple of pages and quickly concluded that Lucas's company wasn't concerned about wasting paper. Some pages were full of names while others only had a couple of names. The company was also into showmanship as names looked to be written in impeccable cursive handwriting.

After a few minutes of flipping through the lists of names, she began to feel embarrassed for looking too much into Lucas's personal documents. She closed the folder, but as she did it shifted on the counter slightly, revealing that another piece of paper was left underneath. Chloe picked it up to put it in the folder, but before she did, she read a name which didn't belong with a group of doctors.

*Bethany Mandel? Why is Gammy's name written on a piece of paper in Lucas's kitchen? Is there another Bethany Mandel in the area?*

The other name on the list sounded familiar to her too. *Scott Banks. How do I know the name, Scott Banks?*

It then hit her like a ton of bricks falling from the roof of a skyscraper. She dropped her beer and the glass bottle shattered on Lucas's oak floor as she gasped in horror.

# Chapter 23

The assisted living center was full of people who didn't look anything like a group of people who needed assistance in their lives. The energy at the outdoor patio was beaming from people laughing as they were playing cards while enjoying iced tea. The pathways were occupied by couples taking advantage of the perfect weather and enjoying afternoon walks. Lucas could even smell a hint of hickory smoke coming from a barbeque grill as he approached the building.

Before walking inside, Lucas took a moment and sat on one of the few empty benches. The people in front of him were at the ends of their lives. Not one of them knew exactly when their time would come, but based on what history has told them, they knew their time would be soon.

In a way, the people here dealt with death as much as Lucas did, only theirs was at a more personal level. He thought about how unhappy he had been over the last twenty years. Every time he looked in the mirror he was looking into the eyes of death. If he looked hard enough into the eyes of his reaped, those panicked eyes which were filled with horror, he could see his reflection. He is the man they call Death. Though he doesn't wear a cloak or carry a scythe as the one folklore describes, Lucas was just as lethal, if not more lethal. When people saw him, they weren't scared. In fact, his charming looks lured people in. People would not answer the door if they saw a man in a cloak at the doorstep. But when Lucas Braun came to their doorstep, dressed in corduroy pants and a t-shirt and asking about the neighborhood, they invited him in.

The people in front of Lucas didn't look as if they were in the presence of death. They were smiling, laughing and hugging each other. These people were close to being on the receiving end of death, but they weren't letting it distract them. They were doing what Lucas had been hoping to do his entire life. They were living.

On the bench to Lucas's right was a couple sitting hand in hand. They weren't talking, just sitting. The woman rested her head on the man's shoulder, and the man rested his head on the top of her head. He couldn't help but think of his mother and father. If they weren't killed in the car accident, would they have ended up in a place like this? He remembered the way they looked into each other's eyes. It was a look of both appreciation and awe as they reflected on being with the one who they loved the most. Lucas could tell they loved him dearly too. They were always there to support him. His mother was always there to cheer him up after missing the big shot in a soccer game, and his father was always there to pick him up after he received a poor grade on a test. They made Lucas feel as if he could do anything.

*Maybe they were right. If I can act as death for twenty years, then perhaps there isn't anything I can't do.*

He then switched focus to his task, his reason for being at the assisted living center today. His final reap, Bethany Mandel, had also lived too long with missing pieces. Her only daughter ran away right after having Chloe and then passed away a few years later. Her husband, the one true love of her life, died over fifteen years ago. The only source of happiness left in the life of Bethany Mandel was that which came from her granddaughter, Chloe Benedict. It didn't dawn upon Lucas until now that perhaps only so much happiness can come from one person. Chloe had kept her Gammy happy all of these years, and now that Lucas was getting happiness from Chloe, it was time for Gammy to go. The balance of energy.

He rose from the bench with his hands full, carrying in two cups of tea from the Chinese restaurant. Mrs. Chang gave Lucas a curious look when he came in to order two teas to-go. Not only was it during working hours, a time when Lucas had never been known to pop in at the restaurant, but it was also an unusual order for Lucas. Outside of his date last week, he had always ordered for one, and the order always included food.

The inside of the assisted living center was not as populated as the outside. There were a few in the common area watching late afternoon television, but other than that, the place was a ghost town. He turned to his left to walk towards Gammy's room. It still fascinated him that it was this easy to step in and out of the place. No one was there to stop him from

271

entering. The sign in sheet in the front was the only attempt the center made to track its visitors, something Lucas had no intention of signing.

As he walked the last few steps towards Gammy's room he hoped and feared that Gammy would be in the room. Though Lucas didn't see her outside and enjoying the weather, it was entirely possible that she was elsewhere at this time. His hope and fear quickly turned into anxiety when he stood just outside her open door but out of sight. He could hear that her television was at a low volume. He peaked through the corner and saw Gammy in her wheelchair. She wasn't watching the television. Her nose was buried in her copy of The Princess Bride.

*Okay. This is it, Lucas. Your last dance as death. No longer will you have to be the one who people fear. No longer will you have to be the one who tears families apart.*

Lucas gently knocked on the door with the knuckle of his index finger and made himself visible for Gammy to see. She looked up from her book at him with delight and surprise.

"Hello, Gammy. Would you care for some tea?"

# Chapter 24

Chloe sat on the floor of Lucas's kitchen, full of disbelief and confusion. Her legs and shirt were damp from the beer that splattered when it fell from her hand.

"What could this mean?" Chloe shouted to the empty room.

She got up and grabbed the folder, flipping through the names, page after page of impeccable penmanship. She started from the back and didn't recognize any of the names, but she did notice that these papers were different than the one with Bethany Mandel written on it. For one, all of the other papers in the folder had a red border. So far, the one with Bethany's name on it was the only one with a gold bolder. She also noticed the ink was slightly faded on the papers towards the back and some had a yellowish hue to them. Lastly, all of the other names were crossed off. Bethany Mandel was the only name which remained untouched.

*How old are these papers?*

Chloe turned to the front of the envelope and began to flip through the names. She still wasn't recognizing any of the names until she saw one that was very familiar to her.

*Bernie Chapman?*

She thought back to the night of the ball. Lucas was sitting right next to Bernie when she saw him. It was minutes later that Bernie was found, dead in the restroom. She recalled that Lucas suddenly needed to use the bathroom when she first saw him at the ball.

"This can't be!" Chloe shouted.

She rushed up the steps and back into Lucas's office. Her computer was slow to respond to her moving of the mouse, attempting to wake it from sleep mode.

"Come on you piece of shit!"

She anxiously double-clicked into the database and began searching for names. She typed in the first name she saw but didn't recognize and crossed her fingers.

"Please don't return any results. Please don't return any results. This is just a list of people he's met. It's not a list of people he's killed."

As the computer searched through the database, the closet behind Chloe became more apparent than ever. She recalled what her Gammy warned her about.

"Did you check his closet for skeletons?" she asked.

Little did Chloe know how literal that phrase would become for her.

The sound of a ding came from her computer. Tom Dempsy deceased earlier this year, leaving a wife and children behind.

Chloe continued to go through the list. With each name on the list came a hit on the database.

*How quickly things can change. This morning I was in love with the perfect man. Someone who was charming, caring, and the most charitable person I had ever met. Now I'm not sure who this man is.*

After going through twenty names on the list and finding a match for all twenty in the obituary database, Chloe then tried one more name, Bethany Mandel. She hoped that maybe there was another woman with the same name. Chloe hit enter and waited for the sound of the ding. The circle on her screen was spinning, indicating that it was searching. She then heard a ringing tone and jumped from her seat. It was her cell phone. Terry was calling, probably for the obituary write up. She didn't have time to deal with that at the moment, but she needed someone to talk to, even if it was Terry.

"Hello," Chloe said in a shaky voice.

Her computer was still spinning through the database trying to find a match for Bethany Mandel. She didn't time how long each search took, but this search felt to her like it was taking an eternity.

"You have that obituary write up for me?"

"Umm," Chloe replied, distracted by her focus on the spinning circle on her screen.

"Umm? It's due. Do you have it or not."

"Umm, yeah I'll…"

Chloe was interrupted by the ding of the computer. It had finished the search for Bethany Mandel. On the screen read the message, *No Results Found*. Every name on the list returned a hit, except for this one. Chloe began to think about what it could mean and couldn't stop herself from crying out loud. Tears began to pour down her cheeks. Her throat felt tight, her nose was running, and when she tried to speak nothing came out but gasps for air.

"What's going on? Are you having your woman problems today?" Terry asked.

Chloe continued to sob on the phone, not saying a word. Her world was crashing in around her. But then a thought entered her mind. *Lucas's happy hour. Is that a cover-up? Do I still have time?*

How could Lucas, the man who gives so much, the man who she fell in love with within a matter of weeks, be someone who would murder the one rock in her life? But what other conclusions could she draw from this list?

"Chloe?" Terry persisted

Chloe continued to sob over the phone. She opened her mouth to tell Terry that she finished and she'll send it over immediately, but that wasn't what came out.

"I think my boyfriend is planning to murder my grandmother this afternoon."

# Chapter 25

Lucas! What a surprise!" Gammy exclaimed as he entered her room.

The room felt warm to Lucas, but he saw Gammy sitting in her wheelchair in jeans and an old faded blue sweater. He smiled and said, "Chloe told me you were rereading The Princess Bride. That happens to be one of my favorite books. I brought some tea. I thought we could have a book club of our own this afternoon and get to know each other a little better."

Gammy turned off the television and smiled at Lucas. "Of course. That sounds lovely. Please have a seat."

Lucas walked over to Gammy and kissed her on the cheek.

"I was never good at making tea, but the nearby Chinese restaurant makes the best tea. I hope you enjoy it."

"That was very kind of you. Thank you."

Lucas glanced again at the cup before handing it to Gammy, making sure that none of the bubbles on the lid were pushed in.

*This cup of tea will be the death of Gammy. If she drinks the entire cup, she'll be dead within fifteen minutes.*

He then took a glance at his cup before taking a drink. The decaf bubble on the lid was pushed in.

The scene was eerily familiar to his first job. He was just a teenager and was still struggling to believe reaping was a reality in his life. It took Sam nearly a month to convince him that he had to reap. Otherwise, he would be reaped. The first name on his list was an elderly woman in assisted living, similar to Gammy.

Lucas introduced himself as a high school student who needed to write a paper about what it was like to live through World War II and that his teacher recommended he come to the assisted living center to find people to interview. The center was not as lovely as the one that Gammy lived in. It smelled of cigarette smoke, there were leaks in the roof, and the people looked as if they were hoping for death to come soon. At least most people looked like that. The woman on Lucas's list, Marie Bailey, appeared to be full of life when Lucas entered her room with his notepad open.

"Please come in. I was just tidying up a bit."

She was standing in her small kitchen, washing a bowl and some spoons. Her room was just a square. Lucas entered in the middle of the room and to his right was a small kitchen and table. A loveseat and chair sat in the middle of the room, and her bed was to the left. Just past her bed was two doors which Lucas presumed to be a restroom and closet.

The room was brighter than the rest of the building. She had pictures of family and a few paintings hanging from the walls. The aroma of chocolate chip cookies escaped the oven and filled the room.

"Are you making cookies?" Lucas asked.

He had stopped by the day before to do the job. She wasn't expecting him when he knocked on the door.

In a shaky voice, he said, "Hello. My name is Lucas. I was wondering if you could help me with a paper I'm writing for school? It's about the World War II era, and I'm hoping to get testimonials from people who lived during that time."

Marie's smile covered her face. She was delighted to have company and welcomed Lucas into her room. He took a step in and saw the pictures of her family on the walls and felt his anxiety take over. He quickly came up with an excuse to leave.

"Actually, I can't today. Do you have time tomorrow, after school?"

"That will be fine," Marie replied, politely.

Lucas hurried out of the building and ran to the nearby park where Sam was waiting for him.

"That was quick. Nicely done."

Lucas's eyes were red and puffy as he admitted to Sam that he couldn't do it and ran off.

"She has a family. What about her family?"

"They all have families, Lucas. Believe me. I get it. Nothing is easy about being a reaper. But what choice do we have? If you don't do it, they will find someone else to do it, and you'll be next on the list."

"Let them reap me then. I'd rather be gone than live my life reaping people."

"You have a lot to learn my friend. You will never be gone."

Confused, Lucas looked at Sam with his watery eyes.

"What do you mean I'll never be gone? People die. They don't come back."

Sam took a deep breath and gave Lucas a gentle, comforting pat on the back.

"People are nothing more than a collection of energy. Energy is something that can never be destroyed, only transferred. It's best to think about it as being a transporter of energy. The world needs the right balance of energy. It needs us to be there to help transfer that energy to its next phase."

"What are you saying then? My energy will be moved to the next phase? Is that a bad thing?"

"I don't know what happens in the next phase, but I know that there are powers at play, and I don't want to be shed in a bad light for when it is decided where my energy is transferred."

The last words resonated with Lucas. He was quickly learning that there was a lot about the world that he didn't know. The next day he walked into Marie's apartment, ready to execute on his reap. She tried to kill him with kindness, but as soon as she sat down, Lucas made his move.

"So, what would you like to know about the 1940's?" Marie asked.

Lucas, wanting to get it over with as quickly as possible before he changed his mind, watched her eyes filled with horror as he lunged towards her with a syringe in hand, stabbing it into her neck and emptying its contents.

"This tea is delicious," Gammy said, breaking Lucas from his daydream.

Lucas smiled politely. *Just a few more drinks from her tea and his reaping days will be over.*

He was feeling nostalgic. Life was passing before his eyes. His new life, right in front of him, was inviting him to come in and enjoy. The energy from Gammy would soon escape her, and Lucas would be able to move forward with a new energy in his life.

"When did you first read The Princess Bride?" Gammy asked.

Like Gammy and Papi, The Princess Bride had a special place in Lucas's heart.

"My mother read it to me when I was a boy. Every night, she'd tuck me into bed, turn on my lamp, and read me a chapter. At the end of each chapter, I'd always ask for more, and she'd kiss me on the forehead and tell me goodnight."

Lucas paused, reflecting on his mother. She was perfect for him.

"She must have read it to me a few dozen times," Lucas continued. "Whenever we'd finish, she'd ask which book I'd like her to read to me next, and I'd always pick The Princess Bride. She'd never admit it to me, but I believe she enjoyed it just as much. The book had a special place in our hearts."

"That's just lovely, Lucas," Gammy replied, looking at Lucas with sympathy. "Chloe told me about your mother passing away when you were young. I'm very sorry about that. She sounds like she was a wonderful person."

Lucas looked at the floor. He could see a little bit of his mother in Gammy. Her soft, kind eyes made him feel welcome, and her calm temperament made him feel at ease. He wanted to hug her to see if it felt similar to the way his mother used to hug him. But he knew he couldn't. That would just make this harder.

"She was wonderful. I miss her every day."

Lucas took a sip from his cup and Gammy took another long drink, letting the herbal flavors rest in her mouth.

"Don't tell Chloe this, she takes pride in making us tea, but I think that this is the best cup of tea I've ever tasted. I can't stop drinking it. My cup's already nearly empty."

Lucas took a look at his watch. He had only been there for ten minutes. Like his first reap, he was anxious to finish this one as quickly as possible.

"Don't worry. I've taken Chloe out for this tea. She agreed that it's the best. There is something about the way that it warms your whole body and mind. It makes you feel better after each cup. But it's best to drink it while it is still warm. Bottoms up."

Lucas took a few large gulps from his cup as Gammy picked up her cup and drank the remainder of its contents.

"Well, as you requested," Gammy said, shaking the empty cup towards Lucas to indicate she had finished it.

*That's it. I'm free.*

Lucas then stood up and took Gammy's cup and tossed it into her garbage can. While walking back, he said, "Can I ask you something personal, Gammy?"

She shifted in her seat before saying, "Please, go ahead."

284

Lucas sat back down in the armchair next to Gammy and took a deep breath.

"Given your condition, how do you find yourself so happy? Isn't death top of mind for you? How do you get over that?"

She looked at the wrinkled skin on her hands as she rubbed them together.

"My life has been filled with moments of tragedy. I lost my husband too soon. I lost my daughter at a young age, but I feel we even lost her before she was truly gone. Papi and I always wondered what we were doing wrong. We couldn't figure out what we could have done that caused her to resent us so much. We tried everything, from being strict to being the easy-going parents. None of it worked. She didn't want us in her life, and it broke our hearts. I spent many nights wondering what I did to deserve this. I had always tried to be a good person. I showed others respect, I tried to give to charity, and if I didn't have money, I was always there to lend a hand.

My husband was the same way. He was kind, gentle, and caring. He even came up with the idea of raising hens to help out our neighbors when he found out they were struggling through tough financial times. They were good people but were filled with too much pride to accept charity, so my husband came up with the idea of raising the hens. He would collect the eggs and leave them on their doorstep, always saying that they laid too many for us to eat. If we would have had the yard for it,

I'm sure he also would have gotten a milking cow. But in spite of all of this, we were dealt a child who was the opposite of us. I think back to what you said about Romeo and Juliet. All must sum to nothing. My daughter was indeed everything we weren't, and we were everything she wasn't."

Lucas listened intently to every word. *Someone awful must be on someone's list to balance out the loss of this incredible woman.*

Gammy continued, "But then we were blessed with Chloe. She is full of spirit, and she is a wonderfully gifted writer. I hope that one day she realizes her gift. I'm glad she's found you. I've always wanted her to find a good companion. I hope you are up for the job."

Lucas smiled and nodded. "I think I am up for it. I love your Chloe, and I'm thrilled to say that she loves me back. I can't wait to spend more days with her, hand in hand."

"Now back to your question," Gammy said, "You asked how I can be so happy when death is near. All I can say to that is, don't waste your time being sad. There's plenty of time for that when you're dead."

Lucas laughed, "I'll remember that."

Ring. Ring. Ring. The sound of Gammy's phone disrupted their conversation like a television commercial during a plot twist. She picked up the cordless phone from the side table next to her.

"Oh, well speak of the devil. It's Chloe. "

Instinctively, Lucas bolted from his seat. Before Gammy could say hello, Lucas had the phone in his hand and hung up.

*She can't know I'm here.*

Gammy gave Lucas a confused look.

Lucas stared back. His mind was racing with thoughts of what he should tell Gammy in explanation. He considered telling her the truth, but she still had a few minutes left and could call out for help. He had to think of something else.

"Why did you do that?" The joy had left Gammy's voice.

Lucas quickly replied with the only decent lie that came to mind.

"Chloe can't know that I'm here today."

Lucas stood tall, but his voice was shaky. Gammy watched him in anticipation of an explanation.

"I had a motive other than discussing The Princess Bride. This is going to sound cheesy, but I'd like to make your princess my bride. I want to ask Chloe to marry me."

"Oh, my goodness," Gammy said as she covered her mouth with her hand.

"She can't know that I'm here because I want her to be surprised tonight when I ask her."

"That is just lovely. It seems awful fast, but who I am to judge. I knew that I loved my Papi the same day I met him. I would like for nothing more than to see my Chloe marrying a man who she loves."

*The perfect lie.*

Gammy held out her arms to hug Lucas, and he went in and gave her a long hug. Her body felt cold to touch. Almost as if her energy had already been sucked away from her. Then Lucas felt it. Gammy's body went limp in his arms. The serum had done the job.

He held onto her for a bit longer, thinking about what Sam had told him about the transfer of energy. She had been broken, not in full balance for so long after losing Papi. The only thing holding her somewhat stable was Chloe.

*Now Gammy's energy can move on, no longer a mold out of balance. And Chloe has me, and I have Chloe. Our energy will mold together, a perfect balance.*

Lucas stepped back and arranged her in the chair, taking one last look at her. As he did, Gammy's phone began to ring, again. He looked and saw it was Chloe, and his heart felt for her.

*She will be devastated when she finds out.*

Lucas took a moment to reflect on what just happened. This was his final reap. The final chapter of his list of lives. He could now move on to the sequel to his story. His nightmare was over, and, like any nightmare, Lucas can now wake up, drink a glass of water, and do everything he can to forget about it.

# Chapter 26

She answered but hung up immediately! I've tried calling back, but it keeps going to her answering machine! Something is wrong! Something is very wrong!"

Chloe was shouting hysterically into her cell phone. Her editor, Terry, was on the other side of the conversation.

"Chloe I'm sure everything is okay," he replied, but the shutter in his voice wasn't assuring.

"Everything is not okay! My Gammy is not answering her phone. Her name is on a list where everyone else is dead, and she's not answering the phone. I've got to get there now!"

"Chloe, stay where you're at. I'll call my inside contacts to get some people on the scene to check everything out. I'm in a cab and only minutes away. We can go together when I get there."

Chloe sobbed into the phone. Her world was collapsing. In her mind, the two people she cared most about were in a room together while one was in the process of murdering the other. She wondered how something like this could happen to her.

*Why did I allow myself to fall in love so quickly? Why did I trust this man who I just met?*

"Chloe. I need the address of where you are at. Can you give it to me?"

There was a long silence on the other side of the conversation. Terry checked his phone to see if the call had been disconnected but the screen still read that the conversation was still in progress.

"Chloe are you there? What is the address?"

"I don't know! I don't know anything! I just met this guy. I foolishly fell in love with him. And now he's murdering my grandmother. How could I be so stupid?"

"We don't know any of this yet. This could all be some sort of twisted misunderstanding."

Chloe was far too upset to realize how compassionate Terry was towards her. It was unlike him to talk to her for longer than thirty seconds at a time, and a portion of that time was typically dedicated to making an awkward sexual reference towards her.

"He lives by the train station. Just a couple of blocks away from it. There aren't any houses between him and the river. There are two bikes on the front porch."

"I'll be there in twenty minutes. I'll call my private investigator and instruct him to go to the assisted living center and check on your grandmother."

———

Terry hung up the phone. He knew exactly where Lucas's house was, but he didn't want Chloe to know that. He wondered if he had let things go too far.

*Was this all my fault? If I didn't persuade Chloe to take this suspected murderer to the ball, would he had ever come across her grandmother?*

The knots in his stomach began to twist as he dialed Bryce's number.

# Chapter 27

It's go time. Send whoever you have to the assisted living center in St. Charles. Lucas is about to strike again. That is if he hasn't done so already."

"Terry. Always good to hear from you. What can I do for you?"

"Dammit, Bryce! I don't have time for bullshit! Send everyone now! I'm in a cab and am on my way," Terry shouted into his phone.

"How can you be so sure? What led you to believe he'd strike at the assisted living center?"

"Chloe. Like you mentioned this morning, she was at Lucas's house. She stumbled upon a list which had her grandmother's name on it. She said there are pages of lists, and every name she checked was deceased, except for her grandmother's. I believe Lucas is there right now."

"You finally took my advice and deployed your resource. It's about time."

Terry wished he could take credit for it, but it all was due to chance. His obituary guy was out. On a limb, he assigned Chloe to it just for the chance some of the names would ring a bell to something she may have seen in Lucas's house. He had no idea it would work.

"I'll send a team to the assisted living center. What about Chloe? Is she safe?"

That was something Terry was fearful of. He knew she was safe the last moment he spoke with her, but he didn't know for how much longer.

*Would Lucas move to her next? What if he was finished with Chloe's grandmother and was already on his way to finish off Chloe too?*

He already felt ashamed for pushing Chloe towards this criminal. If he murdered her too, he wasn't sure what he'd do.

"I'm on my way to get her now. Make sure your guys move quickly."

———

Bryce hung up from Terry and made a call to send a team to the assisted living center to check things out. Although he was retired, he still carried a lot of respect in the field. The Chicago area had never seen a private investigator as successful as Bryce was. He had instincts which couldn't be replaced. Anytime he called, they answered.

Daniel Margeson

He sat back in his recliner and took a drink of his ice tea.

*This is the last time. After Lucas Braun, my work will be complete.*

# Chapter 28

Lucas walked back to his house. It was still too early to be coming home since he told Chloe he would be at a happy hour, but he didn't care. He was willing to lie about his lie. The weather was immaculate. The sun was shining ahead of him both physically and metaphorically. He could go on to live his life as he dreamed about for so long.

Gammy's last smile was still top of mind for him. He told her he was going to ask Chloe to marry him. At the time, it was a fib to keep her from telling Chloe that he was there. But as he walked towards his home and his new life, he thought of nothing better to do than to ask her for her hand. He still had time before the nurse came in to check on Gammy for her evening pills, time before Chloe's world turns upside down. He could sneak up to his room and take his mother's engagement ring from his dresser drawer and ask Chloe to be his wife.

The adrenaline was rushing through Lucas. Not like the way it did when he was reaping, but instead in anticipation of hope. His fast-paced walk turned into a jog. For the first time in over twenty-years, Lucas felt like a kid again. Pure joy and excitement fueled his run. It was the same way he ran to his father and mother when they came home from work. He turned the block, hopped up his porch steps, and entered the doorway. But when he walked in, he could immediately sense that something was wrong.

Chloe was sitting in his recliner. Her eyes were red and puffy, and her mascara was smeared down her face. She was on the phone.

*I'm too late. She already knows about Gammy.*

"I'll be there as soon as I can," Chloe said as she hung up her phone.

She stared at Lucas standing in the doorway. Her throat ached from crying, and she was unable to will herself to speak.

"What's wrong?" Lucas said, approaching Chloe.

Chloe stood up from the recliner and stepped back, signaling she didn't want to be touched.

"Gammy died," she said, summoning the strength to speak.

"Chloe, I'm so sorry. That's terrible. You were just with her today."

He went to Chloe to hug her, but she took another step back. Lucas realized something was off. This wasn't the same Chloe who he was with this morning. That Chloe wanted him to play hooky and spend the day with him. This Chloe didn't even want to look at him.

"And you were just with her a few minutes ago, weren't you?"

Lucas stopped in his tracks.

*How could she possibly know?*

There was no way. He didn't converse with anyone except for Gammy, and Lucas was the only person Gammy spoke with while he was there. *How could she know I was there?*

"I just got off of the train."

Water filled Chloe's eyes. Her throat ached as she screamed, "Stop it! Stop it! Stop it! Don't you lie to me!"

Her raised voice caught Lucas by surprise. He had known Chloe to have a soft temperament. He didn't think she had it in her to shout. He began to feel panicked.

*She knows. Somehow, someway she knows.*

"I don't know what this is about, but let's talk about it."

"Okay. Let's talk about it. Should we start with this list of names?"

She picked up the folder from the side table next to the recliner and held it up for Lucas to see. His face filled with horror as wondered how she could have possibly stumbled upon the list. Against Sam's advice, he had kept every list stored away in the file cabinet in his office. Sam warned Lucas to burn each list after he finished it, but Lucas didn't want to lose track. He wanted to be able to look back and have perspective on how many reaps he had executed. He thought the file cabinet in his office would be the most secure place to store them.

Lucas tried to think of something to say about the list, but he was speechless. It was all surreal. He managed to reap every name on that list without a lick of suspicion. Now, moments after his final reap, the woman who he loved had found his list.

"I checked the names. All have died. Every single one of them, except for one. Bethany Mandel. She was the only surviving name on the list, until this afternoon, when you were supposed to be at a happy hour."

Lucas stood speechless. There was nothing he could say. There was no way she would believe that he's a reaper.

*How could she possibly believe me now?*

"Are you going to say something?" Chloe asked, authoritatively. She waited for Lucas to respond. After a few silent seconds passed, she broke it and said, "Figures," returning to her seat in the recliner.

"What is wrong with the woman who finds out that her boyfriend is a serial killer who just murdered her grandmother and decides to sit in the murderer's living room to talk it out. When I first found the list, I hoped I could find you and talk to you. Maybe I could get to you before you killed my grandmother. I was prepared to overlook all of these people you murdered and sweep it under the rug. Isn't that crazy? We haven't been together that long, but I fell for you that hard. When I look at you now, I'm so angry. Why did you have to do this to Gammy? Why did you have to do this to me? Why did you have to do this to us?"

Lucas cleared his throat. He could see his dreams slipping through hands. He saw no other options than to try to tell Chloe the truth.

*How can I admit to this? I'm a dead man. I've been caught. It's all over.*

"Say something! Say anything!" Chloe shouted. The tears were pouring faster and faster out of her eyes. She looked at the ground and in a softer voice said, "Please tell me that I'm crazy. Please."

Before Lucas could say anything, the shouts of a man came from outside his door. "Chloe! Are you okay? Stand back! Stay there!" shouted Terry as he forced his way into Lucas's house. He ran towards Chloe and was followed by two officers who approached Lucas.

"Lucas Braun. You are under arrest for the suspicion of murder. Do you know your rights?"

Lucas stood motionless as the officer secured the handcuffs tightly around his wrist. He took one last look at Chloe as the officers led him outside to their car. His dream was over before it began.

# Chapter 29

Death. It's an unfortunate truth which we all must learn to cope with. Some are more successful than others. Some, like Lucas Braun, have more to bear than others. When he looks into the mirror, he sees the face of death. It's not the face you imagined death would look like. There is no cloak, and there isn't a scythe. Instead, there is a pair of red corduroy pants, a t-shirt, and a syringe.

Many of us have wondered why we have to die, what happens to us after we die and why it happens when it does. Today, we will explore those questions with the one who has the answers."

Stan Benson adjusted the jacket of his three-piece suit after addressing the jury as he took his seat next to Lucas. He was in his mid-forties and loved money. It was impossible for someone not to find out from Stan that his shoes cost over six-hundred dollars and that he drove a 140,000-dollar car. In the evenings, he spent his time at an exclusive club, drinking fifteen-dollar cocktails. He was the type of person Lucas hated to be around, but he was just the person Lucas needed.

Stan Benson had a perfect record, which he was putting on the line for Lucas's case. He had won over one-hundred cases and lost zero. Lucas knew it was a long-shot, but he was going to take his best shot with his trial. He knew he didn't have much time left in this life, but he wanted to make sure that people knew who he was when he left it. He hoped Stan Benson would be able to help him do that.

Stan was intrigued when Lucas initially called him but wasn't interested in putting his perfect record on the line.

"Lucas, I'm flattered, and you've been good so far by not saying a word to anyone. But there is a lot of evidence against you. Apparently, you've had the editor of the paper on your trail for a few months, and it is hard to refute the evidence he has," Stan told him.

Lucas was upset with himself for being so careless. *Why wasn't I more careful?* He was even more upset with himself that he allowed himself to be caught by someone as despicable as Terry Horn. In his few interactions with him, and based on the comments he had heard from Chloe, Lucas concluded that Terry was a sick man, always making women feel inferior and uncomfortable around him.

"Think about what it would mean to your name if you won this case," Lucas argued. "You'd forever be known as winning the case which kept Death himself out of prison."

"There's no chance, son. I'm sorry to say it, but even I don't think I can win." Stan replied, his southern accent coming through deeper than Lucas anticipated.

Lucas finally gave in and asked, "How much is your perfect record worth to you? I've got 350,000 dollars set aside that I'm willing to give to you to be my lawyer."

Stan was on a plane the next day to meet Lucas and prepare for the trial.

"The goal here is to keep you out of prison. After hearing your story, I believe we can do that. We can win over the jury and get you into a nice mental rehabilitation institution. You'll have your own room and recreation time. It'll be like living in a retirement community."

Lucas knew his time left was short. Even if he could win the court case and refute the evidence against him, he was sure that he would be first on the list for the next reaper in line. But he had no intention of spending his last days in prison. He had to admit that his story did lend itself to be that of a psychopath. All he had to do was tell the truth. No one would believe that he was sane. But he hoped one person would. He wanted Chloe to know the truth. He wanted her to know that his love for her was real, that she gave life to the one who they called Death.

Over the last few weeks, Lucas felt as lonely as he'd ever felt. He was placed in a temporary holding cell until his case could be sent to trial. He didn't have any social interaction, and the food was terrible. He imagined real prison would only be worse.

His story generated a fair amount of press. It was coined as Death on Trial. Initially, Lucas despised that his case was so publicized, but it did help him secure a quick trial, one which he'd never thought he'd be around to see. He was sure someone would have arrived to reap him before he could talk. Every day he'd listen and look out for two people. A reaper, or Chloe. But no one came.

*She'll never be able to forgive me.*

The courtroom was packed. The wooden pews lining it each had a few too many people squeezed in. The trial came together quickly, only taking a few weeks to put in place.

"Ms. Challens. Who would you like to call to the stand?"

Ms. Challens loved hearing her name being called in a formal manner. Ms. Challens. It sounded so professional to her. It was much better than Pigtail Susie, a nickname which stuck with her throughout her young adult life as a result of her wearing pigtails to school one day when she was in the second grade. She never wore her hair like that again, but the name stuck. She hated it. No one would take someone named Pigtail Susie seriously. She left town for college and came back with a law degree. Her old classmates were tongue-tied when they saw her in her high heels, expensive designer clothes, and a car which cost more than their houses. Pigtail Susie left, and Ms.

Challens came back. Her new-found confidence showed through in the courtrooms when she began to win case, after case, after case.

"I'd like to call Lucas Braun to the stand, your honor."

The judge nodded for Lucas to come to the stand. The judge had seen a lot of cases over the years and had the gray hair to prove it. But in all of his years, he hadn't seen a case quite like this.

Lucas rose and walked towards the officer standing next to the stand. Against the advice of his lawyer, Lucas opted not to wear a suit and instead wore his traditional corduroy pants. He did, however, concede, changing from his t-shirt to a button up shirt at the request of Stan.

"Do you swear to tell the truth?" asked the officer.

"I do," Lucas replied.

He climbed up the stand and took his seat, scanning the courtroom for Chloe as he did. He wasn't sure if she'd come. He missed her dearly. He hoped that she would have come to at least yell at him and tell him off. At least that way he would get to see the woman he loved one last time.

Ms. Challens rose from her seat and handed a stack of papers to Lucas.

"Mr. Lucas Braun. Can you reply with a yes or no as to if you were involved with the deaths of the people on this list?"

Lucas examined the papers. The stack contained a copy of every list he had executed. He looked at Stan and Stan stared back at Lucas, expressionless. The prosecutors had video footage of him walking into a restroom just before Bernie Chapman passed away, and they had video footage of him walking in Tom Dempsy's neighborhood just before he passed. A witness testimonial claimed to have seen Lucas pouring contents into a drink for Scott Banks the morning before he died. They also had record of him buying two teas from the local Chinese restaurant and found two cups in Gammy's trash. None of which was concrete enough to conclusively say he was a murderer, but after Lucas told Stan about the car crash and the last twenty years, they both agreed that the truth would be the path of least resistance.

"Yes. I was involved."

"Who gave you these lists?"

"I don't know. They were delivered through my mail slot."

"Were they delivered with your regular mail?"

"No. Separate," Lucas replied.

Lucas scanned the room again, but this time for Terry Horn and the blue-eyed man who Terry had been working with. While prepping for trial with Stan, Lucas discovered that his suspicions were correct and that Terry was in fact on to him, working with retired detective Bryce Cooper. The two provided evidence which would be tough to overcome. But even if they didn't offer it, Lucas didn't want to lie. He had no intentions of holding back. If he were successful in convincing them that deep down he was a decent man, cursed with a horrible reality, then he at least wouldn't go down in history as a monster. If he failed, his story was likely crazy enough to keep him out of prison.

"In your testimony, you said you would use a serum, and that serum would send people into their next life. Where did you get the serum?" Ms. Challens questioned.

She showed no emotion in her questioning. It was evident to Lucas that she was very confident in herself.

"The same way I received the lists. It came through my mail slot," Lucas answered.

"How would you administer the serum?"

"Through a syringe or by pouring the contents into a drink."

"How did you give it to Bethany Mandel?"

Lucas paused, scanning the room for Chloe. He didn't want to talk about her grandmother's death in front of her.

"Lucas. How did you give the serum to Bethany Mandel?" Mr. Challens asked, forcefully.

"I poured it in her drink," Lucas reluctantly admitted.

Ms. Challens walked back to her desk, the eyes of the male jury members following her every step, admiring her slender frame and tight curves. She retrieved a plastic bag containing the remains of a cup and brought it back to Lucas.

"Was this her drink?"

Lucas took the bag and examined the cup. It was the remains of the to-go cup from the Chinese restaurant.

"It could be. The last I saw, the cup it was still intact."

"I'm sure it was," Ms. Challens said calmly. "This was found in the trash can of Bethany Mandel's room at the assisted living center. The cup was sent to the lab and tested. The results indicated it contained traces of botulinum toxin."

"I was never sure what was in the serum. I was just the administer of it."

The courtroom and judge all sat in silence, watching with great interest as Lucas and Ms. Challens conversed. Everyone in the room could sense she was about to get to something, and they were on the edges of their seats in anticipation.

"You work for Cure-iosity Pharmaceuticals. Is that correct?

"I did," Lucas corrected. "But I haven't been to work in several weeks."

"Right, of course. But it is true that you did work there for several years?"

"Yes."

"Interesting. That company is one of the country's largest sellers of botulinum toxin."

Lucas shrugged. "Yes, that is correct. Pain specialist administer it to patients to help with muscle spasms."

"It's also one of the deadliest chemicals known to man," Susie offered.

Lucas nodded. "Yes, that is true."

"Fascinating that the company you work for is the largest supplier of this chemical and this chemical was detected in the cup of tea you offered to Bethany Mandel, yet you claim to have no idea what the serum is made of."

Lucas didn't respond. He didn't have a response. He agreed it seemed suspicious.

"I saw on your record that you do quite a bit of charity work. Your latest tax filing reported that you made 287,000 dollars last year, and you donated 150,000 of it to charity. That was very generous of you, Lucas."

"Some people would say that. But I still had over 130,000 dollars to myself. The family who makes 50,000 dollars a year and donates 5,000 dollars is worthy of more praise than I am."

Ms. Challens took a drink of water and smiled at Lucas. She was attractive, and her personality was infectious, two qualities she's utilized to win over courtrooms over the years.

"Well, I don't think you have to worry about people praising you any longer, Mr. Braun."

In spite of wearing high heels, she smoothly walked towards the jury to address them.

"Ladies and gentlemen of the jury. What we have here is a man who knows the difference between right and wrong, demonstrated by his charitable contributions, his ability to hold a steady job, and until now, his record was clean. He hasn't even had a traffic violation."

"Objection, your honor. My client doesn't drive a car. Having a traffic violation bears no weight in this testimony," Stan said as if he'd been shaken from a coma.

Lucas forgot Stan was even there. He sat silently as Ms. Challens asked him question after question.

*I hope Stan knows what he's doing.*

"Sustained," replied the judge.

Ms. Challens continued to address the jury. "This man admitted to being involved with the deaths of every person on this list. He admitted to administering a deadly chemical into their bodies. There is no question that he is a murderer. Lucas may claim he doesn't know where the lists came from, or where the serum came from, but we have no evidence to suggest that it came from anyone other than Lucas himself. He worked for a company which produced the chemical agent. It is highly unlikely that a higher order was sending it to his doorstep.

Take a look at that man. The way he carries himself, the way he dresses, and the way he speaks. Think about how much he does for his community and for charity. Do you think of this man as an insane individual? He looks sane to me. He sounds sane to me. Sane people who murder other people belong behind bars."

Ms. Challens walked back to her seat, and before sitting, she looked to the judge and said, "Thank you, your honor."

The judge looked at Stan and said, "Mr. Benson, do you have any questions for Lucas Braun?"

Stan rose from his seat and said, "Yes, your honor."

Stan exuded confidence with each step he took towards the stand. The man was wearing over three-thousand dollars of clothing. His haircut cost north of two-hundred dollars. When he leaves this courtroom, he's going to jump in his 140,000-dollar sports car to drive to his mansion of a home.

"Lucas. Can you tell me when you became the Grim Reaper?" Stan asked, using his hands to make air quotes.

Lucas sighed. He had already been through this with him several times. He could tell that Stan didn't believe him.

"I didn't become The Grim Reaper," Lucas said, also making air quotes with his fingers. "I became a reaper; there are thousands of others like me. But for the sake of answering your question, I became a reaper when I was a teenager."

"You said there are others like you? Why are you the first we have heard of to get caught? It seems unlikely that they would all be getting away with murder if that is truly what these thousands of people were doing."

"Reapers are selected carefully. Only the most detail-oriented are selected."

"Do you know any other reapers?"

Lucas thought of his friend, Sam.

*I wonder how disappointed he is in me?*

"Not any longer. When I first started, I knew one. But he has since moved on," Lucas lied.

"What was his name?"

"Sam."

Lucas figured he would use the name he knew to avoid accidentally saying a different name later in the trial.

"What about his last name?"

"I don't know it," Lucas replied. It was the honest truth. He had never learned Sam's last name.

"Do you know why you were picked to become a reaper and why at such a young age?"

Lucas took a deep breath.

"I was supposed to be dead. My name was on a list. I was supposed to die in the car crash which killed my parents, but the reaper took mercy on me. I never knew who the reaper was, but Sam told me his punishment was taken care of and that I was to take over his role as reaper."

Lucas was proud of himself. His voice didn't shake. He was holding up strong. But Stan didn't let him quit there.

"That must have been very tough. You lost your parents, your only family. You were shipped off to foster care, and on top of that, you had to become a reaper."

"It was tough. It's still tough. When you're the reaper, you spend every day living with death. You're the one who has to send people away. You're the one who has to break up families."

Movement in the courtroom caught Lucas's eye. It was Chloe. She had her head down, and it shot up at the mention of breaking up families. Lucas looked at her and could feel the tears begin to form in his eyes. He missed her face so much. It killed him that he wouldn't get to spend his life trying to bring a smile to those lips.

*Those eyes will never again sparkle for me.*

"Are you okay? Would you like some water?" Stan asked.

Lucas nodded, motioning for a glass of water. After Stan handed Lucas the glass, he drank it all without stopping for breath.

"Better?" Stan asked.

Lucas shrugged his shoulders.

"You mentioned earlier that Sam helped you get started with reaping. Do you know where he lived."

"I do not."

"Did you have his phone number?"

"No"

"How did you go about contacting him?"

"I wish I could have. But I couldn't. He didn't want to leave any trace for me to contact him. He said it was better that way. Sam also had more responsibilities than I did. He oversaw the area's reapers. It would have been too risky for him to give out his information to several reapers."

"Interesting," Stan replied.

He paced the room with his hands folded together behind his back as he talked.

"When you talked with Sam, how would the conversations come about. Were you ever expecting him?"

"Sam would always come unannounced. I never knew when he was planning to show up. Sometimes it would be for reaping, but most of the time it was just to talk."

Stan paused for a moment, looking as if he was working to build suspense before asking his next question.

"There is something which I don't understand. Why would you do it? What would have happened to you if you said no to being a reaper?"

Lucas paused before responding. He looked to Chloe. Her eyes were puffy and red. She looked as if she had been crying for days. He wanted nothing more than to go to her and tell her he loved her. But he didn't think that's what she would want to hear right now. She wanted Gammy back. She wanted her boyfriend to not be on trial for murder.

"Reaping is necessary for the balance of life. If people didn't move on, then there would be an imbalance of energy to sustain the population and the world would crumble."

Stan looked at Lucas with a raised eyebrow. This wasn't something they discussed prior to the trial. Lucas looked to Chloe. She also had a peculiar expression on her face.

Lucas continued, "Energy is something which can't be destroyed or created. It can only be transferred. Reapers are here to help that energy transfer to its next life."

Stan took a drink from his glass of water. He walked back towards the stand shaking his head.

"Lucas, are you saying that when people die, their energy moves on to another life within this earth?"

"Yes. That's exactly what I'm saying."

"How can you believe that? What proof is there?"

"People believe in lots of things for which there is no evidence," Lucas countered.

"My grandfather passed away a few years earlier. I haven't exactly seen him walking around," Stan protested.

Lucas could see what Stan was doing. He was trying to prove further that he was mentally unstable. Lucas didn't care; he wanted to tell his story.

"Take out your cell phone," Lucas asked Stan.

The courtroom was leaning in, observing the conversation between Stan and Lucas with great interest.

Stan slowly pulled his cell phone from his pocket, "Okay, here it is."

"Search for *Blue Dress Gold Dress* and plug your phone into the monitor for the courtroom to see."

Stan did so, hesitantly.

"I'm not allowed to address the courtroom. Can you ask the courtroom to raise their hands if they think the dress is blue?" Lucas asked Stan.

Stan turned to address the courtroom, eying the judge as he did so, waiting for an indication to stop.

"Ladies and gentlemen. We are apparently going to go through with this experiment. Can you please raise your hand if you believe this dress is blue?"

To Stan's surprise, just a little more than half of the courtroom raised their hands. He looked at them and looked back at the dress, then back at the courtroom.

"Okay. Since the keyword search also contained the word gold, I'm going to guess the rest of you see a gold dress. Please raise your hand if you think the dress is gold. Stan said, raising his own hand.

The remainder of the courtroom raised their hands.

Stan turned and looked at Lucas, his eyes appearing as if they were urging Lucas to get to his point.

"Lucas, that was interesting, but I don't know if it was relevant."

"The purpose of that was to illustrate that people don't always see things in the same light. Those who saw a blue dress think those who saw a gold dress must be crazy. And those who saw a gold dress must think those seeing the blue dress must be crazy. If we can't agree on what color a dress is, then maybe we should be more open-minded on other things we can't agree on."

"Do you believe that when we pass on, we take on the lives of others?" Stan asked, circling back to his original question.

"I believe energy cannot be created or destroyed. When new life comes to this earth, its energy must have come from another form which gave up that energy."

"What was your role in all of this? You would administer the serum. Why are you necessary?"

"The serum is needed to release the energy from its existing form. I don't control where it goes from there."

Stan walked the room, scratching his head.

"Lucas, I still don't understand. There are people who died sudden, instant deaths. Look at JFK for example. That was a death which was documented by video. His head was blown off. There wasn't anyone administering a serum."

"It's all in the dosing," Lucas calmly responded.

The rapid-fire questioning surprisingly helped to calm Lucas's nerves, though he had to make a conscious effort to not look in Chloe's direction. Every time he looked at those brown eyes it was a reminder of the life he had lost.

"For those types of cases, there are instructions on the dosing. He was likely given a small dose before the car ride. He could have survived the shooting if it weren't for the serum."

Lucas watched as Stan paced the room. He didn't know what Stan was going to ask next. This line of questioning went nothing like they rehearsed, something which was against Stan's methods. He preached that there should be no surprises once they entered the courtroom. Every detail must be accounted for.

To Lucas's surprise, Stan turned to address the jury. "Ladies and gentlemen of the jury. What we have here is a man. A man whose life altered after a tragic accident when he was a young boy. It is known that people can develop alternative personalities when events like this happen. There isn't anything that can be more tragic for a boy than losing his entire family in one night and then being shipped off to live with strangers. It is evident that this man isn't mentally stable. He believes he is a reaper. He believes his orders come from a higher power and that he controls the fate of human life with a single syringe. What he did is unforgivable. But we cannot deny that this is the type of man who needs to be institutionalized. This is not the type of who goes to prison."

Lucas leaned back in his chair. He'd hoped he would have been successful in getting people to believe his story. It wasn't crazy. It was all real, but none one but him could see it. Lucas took one last look at Chloe. Her brown eyes locked with his for a moment. He hoped that she would send a signal that she understood everything. But instead, she looked back at him with teary eyes, shook her head, rose from her seat, and left the courtroom, taking Lucas's hopes and dreams with her.

# Chapter 30

White is one of the most common colors seen in nature. It can be a thing of beauty to observe in a fresh snowfall. A person can raise a flag of this color to surrender in battle. It can be a part of everything people see while at the same time be nothing at all.

Lucas had been staring at the colorless color for a week. Every wall, ceiling, and floor was painted white. It made him feel cold, alone, and depressed. He wondered why a psychiatric clinic wouldn't try to be more inviting.

*The people here are already unstable, why make them feel more isolated?*

Lucas ended up at the Crawford Psychiatric Clinic after the jury deemed him mentally unstable, and, instead of sentencing him to be behind bars, they sentenced him to spend the remainder of his life behind the color white. The thought of spending an extended amount of time in this place made Lucas's stomach turn. In a way, he was thankful that he was likely on someone's list at this moment. At least this way there would be an end in sight.

Ring! Ring! Ring! The sound of the morning alarm, which Lucas didn't need since he wasn't sleeping, was vibrating through the hallways. It was 7:00 am and time to wake up for the day.

Lucas rose from his bed. The protocol called for patients to make their beds immediately after waking up. But Lucas never got under the sheets, so the bed didn't need to be made. He also didn't need to get dressed since he was already in uniform. The clinic required for every patient to wear the same clothing; which consisted of baggy cotton pants and a cotton t-shirt which was two sizes too big. Like everything else in the building, the clothes were white.

When Lucas stepped out into the hall, he looked in both directions and saw that he was the first one to line into position. The rules called for every patient to stand outside his room while the nurses walked by for a head count. Some patients called for more attention than others. The patient in the room next to Lucas never came out of bed willingly. Every morning, two nurses would enter his room and bargain with him for several minutes, trying to persuade him to come out for breakfast.

"Come on, Jack. It's time for breakfast," the nurse pleaded to the man.

"Go away!" he shouted back.

"They made pancakes today. It's your favorite."

"I hate pancakes!"

The arguing would continue for several minutes before Jack would reluctantly appear from his room, finally being persuaded with an offer to get extra syrup.

Lucas stared straight ahead, not making eye contact with the other patients as they emerged from their rooms. He didn't socialize with the others. He would have made an effort to find someone with similar interests if he planned to stay longer. But he didn't see himself as being similar to the others. It was evident to Lucas that the patients in this clinic needed to be in the clinic. They had mental barriers which prevented them from functioning as independent human beings. Lucas thought of himself as the only sane person in the place.

Lucas sat alone during breakfast. He always opted for a scoop of the flavorless oatmeal over the main entrée. It was easier for him to eat it without having to sit at a table. In the corner of the cafeteria, there was a chair next to the window. He would stare out, waiting for his reaper to come. He had no idea who he would be or what he'd look like, but Lucas had the feeling he'd be able to spot him coming from a mile away.

After breakfast came time for pills. All of the patients would line up, and the nurses would give each patient two small paper cups. One containing their medication, and another containing water. Lucas wasn't sure what his pills were made of or how they were supposed to work. He would empty the cup into his mouth and follow it with the cup of water. He always swallowed the water, but never the pills. They were always hidden in the back of his mouth. He wasn't sure it would work when he tried it the first day, but when he opened his mouth to show the nurse that he took his pills, she replied with a thank you.

Lucas would then return to his room and hide the pills in his small dresser. He wasn't sure who had the room before him, but whoever it was had the same idea for hiding pills. The wood in the top drawer could pry up in the back corner, creating a space to hide the pills from inspecting nurses. Lucas found the previous tenant's medication hidden underneath the wood.

The next two hours after breakfast were designated as personal time. Patients were allowed to read or watch television in their rooms while they waited for their five-minute session with the doctor. Lucas hated the doctor. Her name was Dr. Schultz. Her hair was red, and her eyes were green. She didn't dress like a doctor, always wearing jeans and a blouse. Dr. Schultz was about the same age as Lucas, and she looked at him like he was like just one of the other patients in the building. It infuriated him. Those patients needed to talk to the doctor. Lucas didn't need a doctor. He thought of himself as the most stable person in the building, and that included the staff and the doctors. Lucas hadn't been in his room for more than five minutes before he heard the knock on his door.

"Hello Lucas," said Dr. Schultz as she closed the door behind her.

"Good Morning, Dr. Schultz."

Lucas never made his displeasure for Dr. Schultz known. He feared it would only garner extra attention towards him. He wanted to get through this nightmare with the least bit of notice from others as possible.

"How are you feeling today?"

"I'm fine," Lucas said with an even tone.

Dr. Schultz took a seat in the empty chair in Lucas's room. Lucas sat on the bed.

"When I walked in this morning, I saw you eating breakfast by yourself. I take it that you still aren't interacting with the other patients?"

Dr. Schultz continuously attempted to persuade Lucas to interact and try to make friends. Lucas had no intention of doing this. He knew his time was up. He didn't have time for new interactions or new friends.

"I like to eat breakfast alone. Each morning at home, I would eat breakfast on my deck and watch the sunrise. Sitting by the window is the closest I can get here."

"It's good to try to make this place feel more like home. It will make you more comfortable, helping your mental state to feel stronger and more relaxed. But social interaction is also good for the mind. I encourage you to consider interacting with others when you feel more comfortable."

Lucas bit his tongue. He wanted to point out the problems with what Dr. Schultz just said.

*If they wanted me to feel more at home, then why would they paint everything white? Why do they not allow patients to wear their own clothing, or cook their own meals?*

Instead of verbalizing these concerns, Lucas nodded as if he'd consider her advice.

"Do you think it is possible that the reason you don't try to interact with people is that you think it's a waste of time to get to know people when you believe that you will die at any moment?"

Lucas lifted his gaze from the floor and looked into Dr. Schultz's green eyes. Her observation impressed him. Perhaps she was smarter than he gave her credit for.

"It's only a matter of time. When a name is put on a list, there typically isn't a lot of time left. It can't be more than a day or two before my reaper comes."

Dr. Schultz set her pen down on her paper and scooted her chair closer to Lucas. She reached out and grabbed his hand. It made Lucas uncomfortable to allow this woman to hold his hand but he didn't make an effort to pull it back. Her hands were cold and dry. Most doctors had dry hands from the constant washing before and after each patient visit. Lucas wondered if the same hand washing rules applied to a psychiatrist.

"Lucas," Dr. Schultz began in a low voice, "No one is coming for you. When your parents died in the car accident, your brain wasn't physically harmed, but your mental capabilities took a beating for the worst. The trauma caused your brain to create an alternate reality for yourself to help provide you answers for why your parents had to die. Unfortunately, the reality it created for you was a perilous one. Reapers are not real. The lists are made up in your mind. The man you met, Sam, was not real. You made him up in your mind. You wrote those lists. You killed those people."

Lucas looked away as she spoke. This was the first time she tried to tell Lucas that he had issues. He didn't believe her. He couldn't believe her. That would mean that he was a murderer, that he was in complete control of his misery. There was no way that could be true.

He pulled his hand away from Dr. Schultz. "Are we finished for the day?"

She put her hands on her lap and looked at the floor as she sighed. "Yes. I'll see you tomorrow, Lucas."

She scooted the chair back against the wall opposite of Lucas's bed and left without saying another word. It was the first time she didn't give Lucas a reassuring smile as she exited his room. He questioned if he was perhaps too cold with her.

*But what choice did I have? She was suggesting I made everything up in his mind.*

328

The thought both infuriated and terrified him. The lists, instructions, and serum had always been his assurance of reality.

*How could such detailed lists appear at my doorstep? Surely I couldn't have subconsciously assembled those details on my own?*

The fact that the serum contained traces of botulinum toxin disturbed him. His company produced more of the chemical agent than any other company in the county. But that didn't mean he had access to it.

Lucas thought of Sam.

*Could I have made him up?*

If there was anything that was true about the accusations, making up a person in his mind seemed the most likely. Lucas thought to his interactions with Sam. In all of these years, it never dawned on him that he never interacted with Sam and another person at the same time. Sam for all intents and purposes, did not exist outside of Lucas. He didn't have his phone number, his address, or even his last name. Sam always came to Lucas, never the other way around.

He could feel a lump in his throat forming as the evidence piled up against the idea of Sam being a real person. However, his last interaction with Sam was in a public place, the hospital. Lucas recalled women eyeing Sam up as they walked past him a Sam sitting on the bench in the hallway together.

*And even if they were looking at me and smiling, wouldn't have people thought it was odd to see someone sitting on a bench, alone, and talking to himself?*

His hand reached up and touched his ear, an ear which felt as if it were missing something. His headset.

*I was using my headset that day. People could have thought I was just talking to someone on the other line.*

Lucas let out a sigh and rose from his seat. He wasn't feeling well and rested his hands on the window sill to help keep his balance. When he peered out the window, which had bars on the other side of it, he saw the wind was picking up. The sun, which was shining brightly while he ate breakfast, was now hidden behind the gray clouds in the sky.

*A storm must be coming.*

It was just a month ago that he was riding his bicycle through a storm with the woman he loves. Now he's watching the storm through the bedroom window of a psychiatric clinic. Then he had his whole life ahead of him. Now all that was left for him was death. He wished he could talk to Chloe one last time before he went, though he didn't know what he'd say. It was likely she agreed with the consensus that he was mentally unstable.

To Lucas's surprise and relief, Chloe never spoke at the trial. She provided a written testimony and was never called to the stand. The testimony didn't sound like Chloe. It was fact-driven, no emotion could be traced from it.

Lucas wasn't surprised to see that Terry Horn was called to the stand. He never had a good feeling about the way Terry looked at him. Apparently, his instincts were right. Terry had been investigating Lucas for months. He even summoned the help of a famous retired detective named Bryce Cooper. Lucas had never heard of Bryce Cooper, but he was supposedly the best in the business for twenty years, before retiring at a young age. Like Chloe, Bryce was never called to the stand. Lucas didn't have to see him to know who he was. He was the blue-eyed man with the scar who was with Terry when he bumped into him in Chicago during his date with Chloe.

The jury was able to reach a verdict after just one day of trial. Lucas wasn't able to get any believers in the courtroom after telling his side of the story. He only cemented the thought into their brains that he was a serial killer with serious mental flaws.

The sound of a knock-on Lucas's door rattled him back to reality.

*Was Dr. Schultz back to talk again?*

But when Lucas turned to see who was at his door, he saw that it wasn't Dr. Schultz at all. His stomach turned, making him feel as if his oatmeal was working its way back up. He tried to get out a word, just hello would do. Nothing would come out though. All he could do was gasp as he listened to the sound of the familiar voice say, "Hello Lucas."

# Chapter 31

Lucas had seen Sam more times than he could count but as he entered the room and closed the door behind him, it was like he was seeing Sam for the first time.

"Sam? How did you get in here?" Lucas asked, hesitantly.

Sam paced the square room, ignoring the question. "This place isn't as nice as your other place."

Lucas watched Sam take the seat which Dr. Schultz sat in just moments earlier. He had been hoping to see someone he cared for since he'd been sentenced to this clinic just under a week earlier. But now that Sam, Lucas's lifelong friend and mentor, was here, he didn't feel happy at all. He was scared.

*How could he have gotten into my room? Do they just let visitors come and go?*

Sam, yet to make eye contact with Lucas, was looking at the wall past Lucas. The sound of silence was amplifying inside of Lucas, and he couldn't take it any longer. "It's great to see you, Sam," he said half-heartedly, taking a seat at the edge of his bed.

Sam smiled, looking through Lucas.

"Do you ever wonder about me? My personal life, where I come from, what I do for a living?"

It was as if Sam was inside Lucas's head, verbalizing the questions that were flowing through his mind.

Lucas wanted to play it cool. He knew these details about Sam. He just wasn't sure if he believed them any longer. "What are you talking about. You're a software engineer. You're a bachelor and hook up with a different woman every week."

"What proof do you have that I am these things?" Sam asked.

This wasn't the same person who Lucas had known for the last twenty years. Sam was always there to offer reassurance, a pat on the back. This person in his room would barely look at him. Even the sound of his voice was different. A voice, which generally sounded warm and inviting, was now cold and harsh.

"You. You're the proof. You've told me all of this," Lucas replied.

"Can you search my name on the internet and pull up these facts about me?"

Lucas stiffened.

*Why had I never thought to search for him? I've done this countless times in the past for the people on my list. Why did I never think to do it for the person who I trusted the most?*

In a calm voice, Lucas replied, "Why would I want to do that? Why wouldn't I trust you are telling me the truth?"

Sam shook his head and said, "The answer is no. You can't."

Lucas's heart began to beat faster. His face felt warm. He had never seen this side of Sam, a side he didn't care to be seeing.

"What are you getting at here, Sam?"

"Your list. It was sitting right there on your counter. How could you let that happen?"

Lucas felt as if he was being lectured by a parental figure, similar to how his parents would discipline him when he was young on the few occasions when his actions required discipline. But their tone was never as harsh as Sam's.

That aside, the topic Sam brought up was one which had been troubling Lucas. The list. He never left his list out. He only kept it in his spare bedroom which he made into an office. How his list ended up in the kitchen was a complete mystery to him.

"It's something I've been wondering myself. I can't figure it out. I really have no idea, Sam."

"Stop calling me Sam! My name is not Sam!"

Lucas jolted in his seat. There was so much anger in Sam's voice.

*What on earth is he talking about? Maybe he should be the one sitting on this bed.*

"I don't understand. What are you talking about?"

Sam responded, with his voice now in a lower tone. "I wasn't sure how I'd do it. You had been a good reaper throughout your time, but you were ignorant. You bestowed your trust in me in no time. When you appeared on my list all of those years ago, I had no idea it would take so much time. My final list, twenty years in the making."

Lucas stared back at Sam, or whoever this man was, with a confused expression. His story was full of missing pieces, which Lucas didn't understand.

"I got a call from an old friend. You've met him, Terry Horn. You see, you weren't as careful as you thought you were. You left a trail, and Terry caught on. He called in a favor to a retired detective, the best there was."

"Bryce Cooper. Do you know Bryce?" Lucas asked, anxious to hear where this story was going.

"I know him very well, and so do you."

Lucas sat motionless, unable to fully comprehend everything that was being said to him. It was all happening so quickly.

*Twenty years in the making? Had Sam been setting me up this whole time? And now he claims I know Bryce Cooper very well. Who is Bryce Cooper?*

"I've seen Bryce. I referred to him as the blue-eyed man with the scar near his eye. He had been watching me at the diner when I reaped Scott Banks."

"Is that what Terry told you?"

Lucas shook his head.

"That man you described is Terry's affair. Everyone has secrets, Lucas. I learned Terry's years ago. He's tried to hide it through marrying a woman, but he and his wife lead separate lives. She isn't who he loves. He loves the man you described. The man who lives in St. Charles and eats at the same diner every morning. Or he did until the place closed down after you reaped Scott."

*Terry's affair? That might explain the uncomfortable tension I felt coming from them. He was concerned about being outed. But now I have no idea who Bryce Cooper could be.*

Things were changing in front of Lucas so quickly. He began to doubt everything.

"If he's not Bryce, then who is?"

Sam exhaled, seeming irritated at the question. "Do I have to explain everything to you? I'm Bryce Cooper. I'm the retired detective. I've been playing the role of Sam in your story. The story of Lucas Braun.

*Could Dr. Shultz be right about me? Am I making all of this up in my head? Is there anyone else in the room with me?*

"How can I believe any of this to be true?"

Sam, or Bryce, pulled out his wallet, took his I.D. from it, and handed to Lucas. It had a picture of him with his trademark blonde hair combed over to the side. His name read Bryce L. Cooper.

"Why?" Lucas asked trying to say more but struggling to get the words out. "Why would you lie to me all of these years?"

Sam leaned forward in his chair before speaking. "What advice did I give you when you were young? Do you remember? It was that you should never let anyone get to close to you. There's too much risk. I kept you distant from me. I never gave you my name or phone number. I made up a fake job occupation, and I made sure that I wouldn't get too friendly with you. Sure, I may have acted the part, but that's all it was, an act."

Lucas couldn't believe what he was hearing. *I had been played this whole time, a piece in someone else's puzzle.*

"I thought this day would never come," Sam continued. "But Terry called me a few months back as a favor to an old friend. The pieces were finally coming to place. Then, when the time was right, I walked in through your unlocked patio door and left the list on the counter."

"A needle to the neck would have been a lot easier you know?" Lucas said.

"Wouldn't it have been? Oh, I wish it could have been that easy. But I couldn't. You were on my final list. A list in which I took care of the first two twenty years earlier."

Lucas swallowed the lump in his throat. He wanted to ignore it earlier, but now Sam, or Bryce, whatever his name was, brought it up again. "You were the man on the road?"

Sam nodded his head before speaking. The fierceness in his eyes now exuded confidence. "I was the man. As I said, I received my final list, and you were part of that list, twenty years in the making. I've had a lot of lists, but you were my toughest. The list called for your parents to go in the crash. But you, you were meant for so much more. You hit your head so many times, you had no idea that I pulled you out of the car and brought you to shore."

Lucas felt numb and conflicted. He didn't know if he should be angry. After all, this was the man who reaped his parents. The man who set him up. He ruined everything. But Dr. Shultz's words ran through his mind.

*"The man you met, Sam, was not real. You made him up in your mind. You wrote those lists. You killed those people," she said. Could she be right? Am I again altering my reality?*

This was all too much to take in. The man he thought of as his best friend turned out to be his enemy, at best. At worst he turned out to be someone who didn't even exist. He didn't know if he should continue asking questions or leave the room to get away from the conversation. But he couldn't move his legs. He could barely hold up his head and feared that he might soon pass out if he didn't rest it on his bed.

With his head laying on the pillow and eyes closed, Lucas asked, "What was special about me? Why was I twenty years in the making?"

Lucas opened his eyes and looked towards Sam. He was pulling a piece of paper from his pocket and unfolding it. "Lucas Braun. Reaper. Death by suicide in a psychiatric clinic."

Lucas exhaled, letting out a deep sigh.

"I have to admit this seemed like a stretch. I'd never received a list with such detail. But you know the game. All must sum to nothing. We need a perfect balance of energy, and we needed you to do some work to get the world to a point where you could be reaped. I didn't know if I could pull it off. But after twenty years, here we are."

Lucas rose from his bed. Ready to fight back.

"Let's go. If you really want me, if you want it to be over, then try and get me. Take out your needle. I'll fight you off. The commotion will bring the staff into the room in no-time. You'll never be freed from your list as long as I'm living."

Sam didn't budge. Smiling back at Lucas. "There isn't a needle."

*No needle? What's he thinking?*

"How will you finish your list without the serum?" Lucas asked.

"There is serum. But it isn't in a syringe. It's in the pills in your drawer. All I need is for you to take those pills which I left in your drawer before you moved into this room."

Lucas was puzzled. "How did you get into my room before I moved in?"

"An infamous retired detective still has his connections, my friend. I can come and go as I please, leading the staff to believe I'm visiting old patients who I tracked down and brought to the clinic."

Lucas thought it seemed like a stretch, but if he wasn't willing to believe that, then what business did he have believing that he was a reaper?"

"I won't take those pills. You killed my parents. You ruined my life. Why would I voluntarily help you?"

"Would you prefer the alternative? If you don't take those pills, you're stuck here, in your hell. Chloe is never coming to see you. All that you'll be left with is you and your mind. I can see it in your eyes. They are already changing you. As we speak, you're questioning whether or not I'm real or just in your head. If you aren't reaped, you'll be left to think that over for the rest of your years. Those pills are your only escape."

Lucas sighed. He had been waiting and hoping for his death since he was caught. At that moment, the life he dreamed of was reaped. He had nothing left to hope for or live for. He was thankful for this brief time with Chloe, but at what cost did it come?

*Her heart must be shattered into pieces right now.*

Not only did her boyfriend appear to be a serial killer, but he also appeared to have killed her best friend and last living relative.

Lucas had endured the ache of living alone for the last twenty years. It was hard enough with it just being him, but knowing that he was the cause of that pain for Chloe was too much to bear.

*I don't have any other options. I have to take the pills.*

Without saying a word and without looking at Sam, Lucas rose from his bed to retrieve the pills from the dresser. He grabbed the two which were left for his reap, along with the medication he'd been hiding, and without hesitating, he put them all in his mouth and swallowed. He then returned to his bed and waited for his death. At that moment he wasn't sure if he'd been part of a bigger plan along, part of a world that keeps order and balance, right in plain sight. Or perhaps he was the only person in a world inside his mind. The only thing he knew was that he didn't want to be a part of either world any longer. He took one last look at the white ceiling above him and closed his eyes.

# Chapter 32

Loneliness, one of the many feelings Chloe Benedict had felt for the past month. Her knack for not getting close to anyone backfired on her. The only people who she loved were now gone. She didn't even have work to keep her mind occupied. When she found out that Terry was investigating Lucas behind her back, she quit. Terry tried to apologize and offered her double her salary if she stayed, but Chloe couldn't stand to look at him any longer. She couldn't stand to look at anything. She was reminded of her pain in every direction she looked. She needed a change and decided she was going to move to Petoskey, Michigan. A small town known for cold winters seemed like the perfect escape. Last week, Chloe made the trip up north to find a place. The landlord of the small duplex was surprised to get a call on his empty unit so close to winter.

"Moving up from Chicago, what for?" said the all too nosey, elderly man.

"Just getting away. Trying something different," Chloe replied shortly.

She signed the papers and paid first and last month's rent, nearly emptying the remaining of her savings. She would have to watch her budget very closely until her inheritance was settled. Her Gammy and Papi made a modest income, but they were remarkable with money and left Chloe with a sizeable inheritance, her ticket to a new life. With money and work not being distractions, Chloe could focus on writing her novels. At least she hoped that's what she could focus on. It was all she had left.

There were a few people at the coffee shop across from Chloe's apartment building in Chicago. Everyone was alone and seemed almost as sad as she was. She stopped by for one last cup of coffee before going back up to her lonely and empty apartment to collect the remainder of her things. Though the sky had taken on its winter gray and there was a cool breeze in the air, Chloe opted to sit outside. She needed all the preparation she could get for the brutally cold temperatures she was about to embrace.

She thought back to Gammy's funeral. The turnout was small, mostly people from the assisted living center. She was devastated but had no more tears to bear on that day. She had cried them all out during the week proceeding. Chloe knew when she checked her Gammy into the assisted living center that it was only a matter of time before she would be at a cemetery, burying her last living relative and best friend. But it was too soon. She wasn't prepared for it to end, especially in the manner it ended.

When Chloe left the funeral, she had no idea she would be going through another in less than a month's time. She found out about Lucas's death through the news reports. The headlines all read *Death Found Dead in Room*. She opened the article and learned that the staff had found him dead on his bed. It stated he had been hiding his medication in his room before one day taking all of it at once, stopping his heartbeat. She was surprised to see that funeral arrangements were made, and even more surprised that she went to the funeral.

Chloe had butterflies in her stomach as she walked up to the casket to look at Lucas one last time. When she looked at his pale skin and his lifeless body, she was astonished that she didn't feel any anger towards him. This man lying in the casket wasn't a murderer. He was harmless. He was a charming man. A brilliant man. A charitable man. A poet. He was a man who loved her. A man who she loved. A man who she would one day marry, and who would one day be the father of her children. The man who murdered her grandmother and all of the other people on all of those lists was another man. A man she didn't know.

Chloe took a drink of her coffee. It was lukewarm, a queue she had stalled long enough. She crossed the street and entered her apartment building for the last time. The elevator was stuck on the top floor. Instead of waiting for five minutes for it to return to the bottom, she opted for the steps, enduring the stories of stairs with her head down. As she climbed, she heard another person racing down the steps. Chloe accidentally overstepped the imaginary center line in the narrow stairway, grazing his shoulder as he walked by.

"Oh. I'm sorry," Chloe shouted back.

But the man was gone, already down one more flight of stairs. The brief physical contact sent warming sensation throughout her body. It was a feeling which she hadn't felt since she had been with Lucas. She had forgotten what it felt like to have physical contact with another human being.

*Am I so deprived a human contact that the graze of a stranger's shoulder makes me feel warm inside?*

She continued up the flight of stairs with her legs aching and her vision blurring from her shortness of breath. But Chloe welcomed the struggle. For too long she's felt nothing. The sweat which formed under her arms made her feel real, almost like she was living.

The final flight was the toughest. Each step burned through her thighs and down to her calves. She used the arm rail to help pull herself up the remaining steps. When she got to the top, she leaned over, resting her hands on her knees to hold herself up as she tried to catch her breath. Her head felt light and dizzy while she panted.

Once Chloe was able to hold herself upright, she headed towards her apartment. She began to type the security code into her keypad, but the gentle force she applied to the pad pushed the door open. It was as if it wasn't closed all the way from the last time she was there. Chloe's heart, already racing from her victorious march up the flights of stairs, began to race even faster as she pushed the door open. Her eyes scanned the empty studio apartment, looking to see if whoever left her door open was still in the room.

"Hello."

The echo of her voice bounced off the bare walls of the place she once called home. Though she tried to step quietly, her sneakers may as well have been tap shoes bouncing off of the hardwood floors. If there were an intruder in her apartment, she certainly wouldn't be able to startle him.

The bathroom door was open. Chloe slowly stepped towards the middle of her apartment to gain a vantage point without getting too close. It was empty. The longer she was in the room, the more confident she felt she was alone. Behind her were the only other doors in the apartment a person could use for cover. She turned and saw her closet doors were still open as she left them from when she was packing her clothes.

Chloe thought back to her first night in this apartment. When she signed the lease, she imagined that it was the ticket to her happiness. She could finally live in the city, enjoy the food and nightlife, write, walk to work, and meet new people. Now when she looks at it, she sees an empty space. It was foolish for her to think this place could bring all of those things to her, and she couldn't help but think she might be setting the same expectations for her new home in Petoskey.

The air felt cold as Chloe inhaled it into her lungs. She had turned her heat off, and her exterior walls had no insulation to keep the Chicago cold out. It was time for her to go. Time for her to move on from this life. She didn't know what the next would hold, but she figured it couldn't have a more tragic ending than this one.

But as Chloe headed for the door, something caught her eye and stopped her. She couldn't move. It seemed as if what she was looking at had cast a web and was reeling her back in. While she stared ahead, her legs began to shake so much that she fell to her knees.

*Impossible.*

Chloe's mind was racing. She thought to Lucas, and the settle hints he left for her and everyone to hear.

"All must sum to nothing," he would say. That was his interpretation of Romeo and Juliet. All must sum to nothing. When Romeo and Juliet were together, they balanced each other perfectly, summing to nothing. When Romeo died, Juliet saw no other option but to die too, recreating the balance of nothing they once had.

"When we pass, our energy doesn't go away. Energy cannot be created or destroyed," Lucas said in his trial.

Chloe didn't know what to think of that. It was impossible for her to imagine the energy from the dead being transferred to someone else.

But what else could explain what she was seeing right now?

The couple at the beach entered her mind. The large, unattractive man, sitting with the young, beautiful, and successful widowed doctor.

"When she looks at him she sees something different than what everyone else sees."

Tears began to pour from Chloe's eyes and down her cheeks. Tears which she thought she'd never shed again. She rose to her feet and walked to her countertop. The more she stared at the items on her countertop, the more she believed that what she was seeing was true.

*Who was the man I bumped into in the stairway?*

She didn't get a good look at him, but if she did, would she have seen those big brown eyes which she fell in love with? What would the rest of the world see when they looked at that man?

She arrived at the countertop and touched the vase, bringing the freshly picked purple dahlia to her nose and inhaling the floral scent. Next to it, the cheapest bottle of bourbon money could buy. She picked it up, feeling the weight of it in her hands. Lucas's voice came to her mind.

"If we perceive this to be the reality, then who's to say that it isn't?"

How could this be possible? She went to Lucas's funeral. She watched as he was lowered into the ground. But no one knew about the purple dahlia. No one knew about the cheap bourbon. How else could these things have ended up in her apartment?

She wondered if she was now the one who was crazy.

*Did the deaths of Gammy and Lucas put me over the edge?*

The sound of her apartment door creaking broke Chloe's concentration from the bottle of bourbon. She could hear footsteps coming to a stop at the entrance. When she turned to look at the doorway, she gasped in astonishment, unable to keep the smile from spreading across her face.

# About the Author

Daniel Margeson has spent the majority of his career working as a data analyst, turning lines of code and billions of numbers into the tales of human behavior. With *The Life of Death*, Daniel broke free from the bounds of his cubicle walls to write the thriller he had been crafting in his mind for over a decade. With a strong cup of coffee at his side, Daniel can be found plotting twists and developing characters between the hours of 4:00 am and 5:30 am. He resides in a small town in Illinois with his lovely wife and two beautiful children. Watch for his next thriller by following Daniel on Twitter - @Margeson_Danny and on Facebook - @DanielMargesonBooks.

*Author photo taken by Justin Camerer – JustinCamerer.com*

.